Entwined

A ROMANTIC JOURNEY BACK INTO HEALTH

Holly Fourchalk

PhD., DNM®, RHT, AAP

CHOICES UNLIMITED
for
Health & Wellness

A ROMANTIC JOURNEY BACK INTO HEALTH

Holly Fourchalk

PhD., DNM®, RHT, AAP

Copyright 2015 © Choices Unlimited for Health & Wellness

Dr. Holly Fourchalk, Ph.D., DNM®, RHT, HT

Tel: 604.764.5203

Fax: 604.465.7964

Websites: www.ChoicesUnlimited.ca

www.DrHollyBooks.com

E-mail: holly@choicesunlimited.ca

Editing, Interior Design and Cover Design: Summer Bay Press

ISBN: 978-1-926466-01-9

Digital ISBN: 978-1-926466-02-6

DISCLAIMER

Every effort has been made by the author to ensure that the information in this book is as accurate as possible. However, it is by no means a complete or exhaustive examination of all information.

The author knows what worked for her and what has worked for others but no two people are the same and so the author cannot and does not render judgment or advice regarding a particular individual.

Further, because our bodies are unique any two individuals may experience different results from the same therapy.

The author believes in both prevention and the superiority of a natural non-invasive approach over drugs and surgery.

The information collected within comes from a variety of researchers and sources from around the world. This information has been accumulated in the Western healing arts over the past thirty years.

Research has shown that one of the top three leading causes of death in North America occurs because of the physician/pharmaceutical component of the scenario.

Perhaps the real leading cause of death and disability is a result of the lack of awareness of natural therapies. These therapies are well known to prevent and treat many common degenerative, inflammatory and oxidative diseases.

The author loves to research and loves to teach. This book is another attempt to increase awareness about health and the many options we have to bring the body back into a healthy balance.

Ever-increasing numbers of people are aware of healing foods and herbs, supplements and modalities but there are still far too many who are not. The fact that our physicians are part of this latter group makes healing even more challenging yet we are now seeing more and more laboratories around the world and more universities in and outside of the U.S. studying herbs, nutrition and various healing modalities with phenomenal success.

The unfortunate fact is, those who can profit from sickness and disease promote ignorance and the results are devastating.

It is not the intent of the author that anyone should choose to read this book and make decisions regarding their health or medical care based on ideas contained in this book.

It is the responsibility of the individual to find a health care practitioner to work with to achieve optimal health.

The author and publisher are not responsible for any adverse effects or consequences resulting from the use of any of the suggestions or information contained in the book but offer this material as information that the public has a right to hear and utilize at its own discretion.

CONTENTS

One	Just to BE	1
Two	Papa Johnny	7
Three	The Kids	12
Four	Her Husband	17
Five	Sex, Sensuality, and Making Love	20
Six	Food and My Sex Life	29
Seven	Communication	35
Eight	Are you Depressed or Frustrated?	42
Nine	Was it Her Thyroid or Her Adrenals?	46
Ten	Capturing a Moment in Time	55
Eleven	Expressing and Getting the Love You Need	70
Twelve	Reversing Allergies	75
Thirteen	Grabbing Some Afternoon Delight	81
Fourteen	Hugs Anyone?	89
Fifteen	Choices are the Fundamentals of Life?	100
Sixteen	Prescriptions are Synthetic Toxins!	106
Seventeen	Forgiveness versus Acceptance	120
Eighteen	Family Secrets	126
Nineteen	It's All About Eating	129
Twenty	Let the Games Begin	132
Twenty-one	Loving is About Giving More Than You Take	137
Twenty-two	Kids Can be Awesome	148
Twenty-three	Understanding the Human Condition	152
Twenty-four	Flaky Eastern Stuff or…	159
Twenty-five	Uncle Dan's Experience Making Pancakes	163
Twenty-six	You Never Know Who You are Going to Meet	170
Twenty-seven	When You are Old, Wrinkled and Grey…	174
Twenty-eight	And Another One Makes the Move	177
Twenty-nine	Patient Tactics Work in the Long Haul	183
Thirty	It's All in the Timing	186
Thirty-one	And Then There were Five, and Then There were Six	192
Thirty-two	The Summer Experience	202
Thirty-three	Getting Back into Health-Sex Better than Makeup-Sex	207
Thirty-four	Returning the Favour had Never Been so Much Fun	215
Thirty-five	I'll Love You Until the End of Time	229
Thirty-six	"Everything Happens for a Reason"	235
Thirty-seven	It's a Small World	247
Thirty-eight	Do You Like Salsa Dancing	248
Thirty-nine	There's Nothing Like a Dame	261
Forty	Sufficiently Serviced, My Lady?	264
Forty-one	Stepping Out of the Box	272
Forty-two	The Best Part of Going Away is Coming Home	286
Forty-three	Please Put Me on Your Dance Card	289
Forty-four	Let the Party Begin	298

Forty-five	The Healthy Cover Up	306
Forty-six	How Many Causes are There of Weight Imbalance?	311
Forty-seven	Addictions can be Driven by Pathogens?	313
Forty-eight	And Another One, and Another One...	317
Forty-nine	Meridians, and Teeth, and Cancer?	319
Fifty	Gluta...What?	323
Fifty-one	Being Patient has its Rewards	326
Fifty-two	A Day to Celebrate	329
Fifty-three	Sickness Hides Behind Closed Doors	331
Fifty-four	Tricky Separations. Hidden Challenges	334
Fifty-five	So the Right Food Give the Tools for Good Sex?	337
Fifty-six	It's All about Choices	349
Names and Families		346
About the Author		349

One

Just to Be

"I still find each day too short for all the thoughts I want to think, all the walks I want to take, all the books I want to read, and all the friends I want to see."
John Burroughs

Maria felt the warmth of the sun, high in the bright noonday sky. She squinted up at the few soft, white, fluffy clouds against the brilliant blue background. The warm spring air had a lovely scented breeze in it—maybe lavender with some mint. It was a perfect day to sit out on the deck.

Maria loved to take moments like this out of her busy day to just sit and be. She loved to just let her mind go. At forty-seven, Maria had a large family to look after and spent most of her time taking care of the needs of others. While it used to give her a sense of purpose and value, now it just seemed to wear her out. In fact, she had been diagnosed with adrenal fatigue five months before. She knew she was on the rebound and was beginning to feel like her old self again. She took a deep breath as she appreciated how good it was to feel alive again.

She still had to keep reminding herself to take care and to watch herself. In the past few months she had become aware that she had never learned to stop and look after herself. Like too

1

many women, she took care of everyone else but herself. To stop and take care of her needs was still such a foreign thing to do.

Thankfully, her husband, Duncan, reminded her to do this regularly now. He had been so good about all of the setbacks she had experienced in the last several months. She had explored the inter-dynamic issues several times with Dr. Jim, the psychotherapist from across the street, and the adrenal fatigue issues with his father Pappy, the Medical Herbalist, and his daughter, Dr. Jane, who was a Dr. of Natural Medicine. For all of the Gibson family and for her husband, she sent up prayers of thanks, daily. They were all truly a godsend.

There were always so many things Maria felt she needed to do. It was a challenge to find moments like this, when she could allow herself to just be. She frequently asked herself now, how she was supposed to suddenly start looking after herself, when she had spent a lifetime looking after others? It felt so selfish.

Thanks to their in-depth discussions, she now realized that as a child, she had learned that she didn't really count, in and of herself. She only counted when she put others first, took care of them, and made them feel good about themselves.

For most of her life, Maria had enjoyed living with the program she had unconsciously learned, but now it was wearing thin. Yes, it still felt good to take care of others and make them happy but she now recognized that there was an element of control in it and she didn't like that. It was a heavy responsibility and one of which she was ready to let go since it wasn't hers to take on anymore.

She guided her mind to relax and take in the spring flowers, the scents in the air, and the gentle breeze. She took a swallow of the flavourful Chai tea she had made for herself earlier and lay back in the patio chair. She took in a deep breath and allowed herself to experience the moment with her senses.

Despite all of her intentions to simply let her mind flow free of any worries, it wandered around without her as she reflected on the family she loved so much. Her mother was really a powerhouse of a woman. Few people really understood Grandma Mary, as most people called her. She was brought up in a world where a woman's intellect was scoffed at and men were far more important. Consequently, she didn't really embrace and acknowledge the accomplishments of her granddaughters. Instead, she focused on the often lesser achievements of her grandsons. She had never developed her own mind but instead relied on her husband. It was too bad because she could have really done something with that mind of hers. But such were the beliefs with which she had grown up.

Maria had talked with her mother about how important it was to recognize her granddaughters like she did her grandsons. Fortunately, the discussion had gone well and instead of feeling hurt or criticized, Grandma Mary acknowledged that she had not been aware of what she had done in the past. She was very proud of her granddaughters and now she made a concerted effort to acknowledge them and let them know she thought that were beautiful, intelligent young women. Born in Scotland and brought up on the good ol' "Protestant work ethic", Grandma Mary was a hard-working woman. Despite whatever endeavour that Papa Johnny might have been engaged in, she was always a workhorse.

Grandma Mary was well known as a "tea granny". She always liked her Orange Pekoe in a little "china cup". The thing was, she didn't really drink a lot of tea. She always put three heaping teaspoons of sugar into the little china cup. Consequently, she drank a little tea with her sugar. Everyone smiled but no one ever said anything about the loaded toxins she poured into her tea. They didn't know either. But things were changing, thanks to Maria's growing awareness.

Dr. Jim's family lived across the street and regularly reminded Maria's family about healthy eating and avoiding toxins. Dr. Jim's daughter, Jane, was a Doctor of Natural Medicine and his son, Daniel, had a Doctorate in nutrition. Daniel had created a new integrative model for the biochemistry of cellular healing in his doctorate and they all continued to work with it. Maria loved to just sit and listen to them all discuss all the different issues involved in health and wellness. They were a great group of people.

It also made it more and more obvious to Maria how unhealthy her family was. Which, of course, just added to the list of things for which she felt responsible.

Maria wondered if all of the sugar that Grandma Mary ate and drank had anything to do with her arthritis.

"Come on, Maria. You know better," she interrupted her thoughts out loud. "Relax, concentrate, and meditate. You can do it," she chided herself. Sometimes it was easy to meditate but other times it was such a struggle. Today was one of those days it was a struggle. She just couldn't stay focused.

Her mind was usually as busy as she was. It never stayed in one place too long…maybe she was ADHD…maybe she just wasn't good at focusing…maybe constantly moving was just a habit. Whatever the reason, it was often difficult to slow down her thoughts and focus. Today it was a real challenge.

She started to focus on her breath. *Slow down and concentrate*, she told herself. *You can do this.* She deepened and slowed her breathing…deep and slow, deep and slow. It lasted for a few minutes. Then once again her mind took off on its own, as if without her permission.

She came back to the present with a chuckle. No, the mediation had not occurred. Her mind had its own agenda today. Rather than admonish herself and struggle to keep the discipline, she decided it was better to just let her mind wander. She gave herself permission to work on it again next time and let it go for today. As if her permission really mattered.

Maria's family reflection stopped after a few minutes when her mind jumped to all of things she needed to do. She really *should* get going. On the other hand, there was that 'should' word again. Did she really need to get up and go, right now? She looked at her watch and thought for a moment. It was really nice to just take a break and reflect for a while. She would give herself another ten minutes and then she would get up and do the things that needed to be done. It felt like when she put the alarm on snooze, in the morning. Just a few more minutes....

When the ten minutes were up, Maria stood up, stretched out her limbs, and took a deep breath. "Let's get back to work," she said out loud.

Two

Papa Johnny

"By the time you're eighty years old you've learned everything. You only have to remember it."
George Burns (1896-1996)

Grandma Mary and Papa Johnny lived downstairs from Maria in a beautiful suite that Duncan and Uncle Dan had built for them. It provided Maria the opportunity to keep an eye on them. She hated to intrude on either their privacy or their sense of independence. On the other hand, whether it was considered control or not, she liked to know that everything was okay.

Most days, she found an excuse to take a pot of tea down with some homemade biscuits, scones, or cookies for them. They loved the treats and it gave her a chance to make sure Grandma Mary was warm enough. The Renaud's disorder was apparently why she was always cold. It could be thirty degrees out and she was cold. Well, at least that was easy to manage—it was her arthritis that was difficult for Maria. She hated to see anyone in pain.

Maria was thankful for the fact that Grandma Mary, at least, listened to Dr. Jim's family. Pappy, Jim's father, was a Medical Herbalist, and was a great resource. He could identify which "ol' wives tales" had substance to them and which didn't. He knew his herbs like he knew the back of his hand.

Pappy also had a variety of tricks up his sleeve that sometimes seemed strange, but boy did they work. He had told Maria how to soak a special kind of raisin in gin, let them sit for several days, and then give up to seven a day to Grandma Mary as a pain killer. While Pappy said that in and of themselves, the raisins and gin would not eliminate the arthritis, one could use the technique to manage the pain without harmful painkillers, while they worked to eliminate the underlying issue.

Of course, the family had a number of other tricks up their sleeves and Maria tried to use all of them instead of prescription drugs. She had learned that most prescription drugs are not only synthetic versions of the real thing but that they depleted the body of nutrients.

She took a platter with tea and biscuits, and a bowl of soaked raisins, downstairs and knocked on the door. Grandma Mary opened the door to let her in.

"Hi Mom, how are you doing today?"

"You know, I am doing just fine. But I love you always looking in on me." Grandma Mary was no fool; she knew what was behind the suite in the basement. But the two of them loved it here. They were close to Maria and Duncan and the kids. And secretly, Grandma Mary admitted that she loved to be looked after.

"What have you got there today?"

"I made myself some tea, so I made you a pot as well. And I made some of your favourite biscuits this morning, so I thought I would bring some down for you. Where is Dad?"

"You are a sweetheart, and thank you. Dad is playing solitaire crib out on the patio. Anything else, dear?" she asked with a chuckle.

"Okay, okay," Maria acknowledged. "I have to go shopping and I will get Dad's new prescriptions. Do you need anything?" Grandma Mary shook her head no.

"Then I have a bunch of chores to do, so I will be home later." She gave her mom a quick kiss on the cheek and left.

Papa Johnny, Maria's father, had been the cook in the family. Man, could he cook! Maria had often wished he would take over the cooking in her family. She used to love to cook but lately it was just another huge chore.

Unfortunately, Papa Johnny's cooking days were long over. He wanted to be pampered now. And, he loved to think he was sick with one thing or another. Was it just to get the extra attention he so loved or did he really believe it? Who knew? But he was a hoot.

He loved to make people laugh. In fact, Maria often wondered if Papa Johnny thought making people laugh was his sole purpose in life. She chuckled to herself. He was good at it.

His biggest challenge was not his physical health but rather dementia. The doctors had diagnosed him with Alzheimer's. If they listened to Dr. Jim's family, Alzheimer's was just an easy diagnosis that MDs would drop people into. In fact, issues like Lewy Bodies either in the gut or in the brain were often misdiagnosed as Alzheimer's or Parkinson's. There were various other causes and diagnoses that were actually reversible. Usually, however, it was easier for an MD to dump people into the Alzheimer's group. They claimed they could slow down the progression of the condition with drugs. The drugs, however, could cause more harm than benefit, especially if it was a misdiagnosis. But that was all the allopathic medicine had to offer.

Maria learned so much from Dr. Jim's kids, Dr. Jane and Dr. Daniel. Currently, she was focusing on all the things she could do to help her father. As of yet, the doctors across the street had done nothing, because Papa Johnny wasn't interested in that "flaky stuff". He listened to what his "real doctor" said, and consequently, he was going downhill. The prescriptions never solved any of the problems; they only seemed to manage some of the symptoms while they created other symptoms in the process. And now that she knew that they usually depleted the body's nutrients, she was more concerned than ever. But you couldn't force someone to wake up and look at the alternatives when they were both familiar with the conventional medicine and had been taught to believe that anything else was "flaky" at best.

Maria gave a little chuckle as she remembered Grandma Mary and Papa Johnny back in the old days. Man, could they dance. Not only could they dance up a storm but also Grandma Mary had won various awards for the Charleston. They had looked grand together.

The two of them came from very different backgrounds. Grandma Mary had only one brother, Uncle Dan, and her family background was Scottish and Protestant. Whereas, Papa Johnny was Italian, came from a family of twelve kids, and obviously was Catholic. What a mixture! But they knew how to make it work.

Maria wished that if she could just get her parents to stop smoking, life would be easier. Maria loved them both dearly but it was a big job to take care of Grandma Mary and her arthritis and Papa Johnny and all of his stomach complaints, never mind his dementia—or whatever it was—without adding health issues caused by smoking.

Perhaps it was a big job, Maria thought, because she tried to be so subtle and discrete with them. She didn't want them to think she was nosy or a nuisance and she wanted them to maintain their independence.

Three

The Kids

Maria picked up her purse and car keys, and went over in her mind what she needed to do. First, she needed to pick up Jessie, her eldest, from college and take her to the doctor. Hopefully, they wouldn't have to wait too long this time.

Jessie had been diagnosed with diabetes several months ago and their MD wanted to put her on a medication to manage it. Typical of most physicians, he identified the problem and gave them a prescription to manage the symptoms. Lately, however, he was becoming wise to their family's preferences and asked if they planned to go the Gibson Clinic. He now understood that Maria was working with *real* medicine and using food and herbs to get the body to engage in its own healing processes rather than use drugs to manage symptoms. He hadn't told Maria, but he was starting to do his own research into *real* medicine.

Maria and Duncan had let it be Jessie's decision to take the prescription or go to the Gibsons. She was twenty, after all. Jessie decided she wanted to give the Gibson's program a try first. So she worked with the Gibsons and followed the regime they had put her on. It only took a couple of months to get great success. She was just going into the MD's office to get her blood glucose levels monitored and to get it noted on his charts. The MD acknowledged the progress that Jessie had made, and he was impressed with all the results Maria's family was making which just provoked him to look even more into the alternative options. Maria's family was teaching him to look at the alternative options as opposed to the old routine of writing out prescriptions.

Openly, Maria had been pleased with the MD's transition and secretly applauded herself as the catalyst. Rather than just write out a prescription like he used to do, he now asked more questions, especially of Maria. She liked him; he had an open mind, which of course indicated intelligence—a good trait to have in a physician.

Jessie was waiting for her mom, in their usual pick-up spot. Dressed casually in jeans and a t-shirt, with her packsack full of books on her back, she looked like a typical college student. What made her stand out was her smile. She always had a radiant smile that attracted everyone. Maria was so proud of Jessie on so many levels.

"Hi hon, how was school today?"

"Frustrating, but I got through it. Now I am really anxious to see the doctor. I really want those tests to be good. I've been thinking about it all day!"

Jessie was a smart one. As soon as she was given the diabetic diagnosis, she went over to visit Uncle Jim. She had started to call Dr. Jim, Uncle Jim when she was a small child. She had asked him who she needed to talk with about the diabetes. Both of Dr. Jim's kids had been kind enough to sit down with Jessie and explain how and why people developed diabetes: the sugars, the sodas, the junk food, the fast food, the AGEs, the heavy metals, the environmental toxins, free fatty acids in the blood and other compounds. They also explained how the "diabetic" issues often started long before the insulin receptor and pancreas issues that the MDs focused on. The process could start in the gut, or in the liver or with the adrenals. In addition, even a respiratory virus could cause diabetes. They explained how all of these issues interacted, and at what detriment to the body. Then they explained how taking the drugs usually did not resolve the underlying issues which could continue to cause more problems if not addressed. Finally they explained how when they cleaned up the underlying issues, the diabetes could be eliminated.

They had explained that she had a choice to manage the diabetes, in accordance with Western medicine, in which case she would probably be prescribed a drug like Metformin that could cause lactic acidosis, muscle pain, trouble breathing, stomach issues, vomiting, and kidney issues, or she could eliminate the diabetes with *real* medicine, like herbs and foods.

Jessie had sat and listened patiently; she asked a lot of questions and then she proceeded to follow through with their program. Now she only went to her MD to get tests that monitored her progress from a Western perspective. So far, the MD had to agree; she no longer had diabetes.

Jessie high-fived her Mom and bluntly told the MD he needed to make an appointment with the Gibsons and learn about what they did. When they left his office, Maria gave her daughter a big hug and told her how smart she thought she was in deciding to go to the Gibson's clinic.

On their way to pick up Maria's next eldest, Jasmine, she talked with Jessie about how easy the regime had been to eliminate the diabetes. They talked about all the people who just believed their MD and went on dangerous drugs like Metformin.

When they got to the high school to pick up Jasmine, Jessie called out the window, "Hey Jasmine, over here."

The sisters each had their own group of friends and their own interests, yet they got along great. They had gone through a few years when Jessie didn't want Jasmine around. It wasn't "cool" to have your younger sister tagging along. But they had got through those years and managed to come out of it as good friends.

Maria watched as Jasmine said goodbye to her friends and walked over to the car with a friend.

"Mom, can we take Jean to dance lessons? Her Mom can't make it today."

Maria recognized Jean and agreed. When the two younger girls were settled in the car, Jessie explained that they had just come from the doctor's office and proudly explained that she no longer had diabetes.

They dropped off Jasmine and Jean at dance lessons then Maria had to pick up her youngest, John, named after Papa Johnny, from elementary school and take him to his Martial Arts program.

When they got to John's school, he had already changed into his Martial Arts gear and was ready to go. They talked about his math class and how frustrated he was with it. When they arrived, he jumped out of he jumped out of the car and ran into the dojo with barely a wave goodbye.

Maria called out that she would see him in an hour but didn't think he had bothered to listen.

"Don't worry Mom," Jessie predicted, "he knows the routine."

Four

Her Husband

"Coming together is a beginning;
keeping together is progress;
working together is success."
Henry Ford

Maria still needed to go grocery shopping for a few things she wanted for dinner, and then pick up Jasmine and John before going home to make dinner.

She wasn't sure what time Duncan planned on being home for dinner tonight, so she gave Duncan a quick call to confirm.

"Hi hon, how's your day going?" she asked when he answered.

"Great, now that I am talking with my favourite gal. How about you? How's your energy today?"

"Not bad, thanks for asking. Just wondering when you expect to be home for dinner?"

They continued to talk until she found her parking spot. As she got out of the car, she thought about how she had lucked out with Duncan. He was the best. He had been so supportive while she was working through her adrenal fatigue. He never pushed her, always asked how she was doing, and was good about asking her how he could be supportive. *Not too many guys around like that*, Maria thought.

She adored him and was still very much in love with him after all these years. She always remembered what Dr. Jim had told her years before. "The more you engage in a marriage, the more time and effort you put into the relationship, the more in love you will be down the road."

She had never forgotten their discussion about what makes a good marriage versus a marriage that falls apart. Dr. Jim had explained that it takes two to make a good marriage. If one partner does all the work, then the other partner will naturally "fall out of love". If both partners put all their effort into the children or their careers, then they will both fall out of love. It takes two to make a good marriage and Maria was always so thankful that Duncan put as much time and effort into their relationship as she did. They had a good thing going and she wasn't going to let it fall apart.

They had had many long talks over the years, about what kind of time and effort they put into their kids, their careers and into one another. They both put conscious attention into hearing, understanding and meeting the other's needs. It wasn't always easy, and many times there just hadn't seemed to be enough time to go around but as long as they could sit and discuss issues they seemed to make it through.

Dr. Jim had told them years ago that a healthy marriage developed from a healthy competition. Duncan and Maria had laughed, not understanding why you would want competition in a marriage. Dr. Jim had explained that if you made it a competition to see "who could make the other feel more loved and special more of the time", you could ride through a lot of challenges a lot more easily. That sounded like a good plan and so they had made that a basic vow between them. It had worked for them.

Five

Sex, Sensuality, and Making Love

"Sensuality is the total mobilization of the senses:
an individual observes his partner intently,
straining to catch every sound."
Milan Kundera, The Unbearable Lightness of Being

It was 9:30 and Maria was tired. She hadn't done a lot of activity throughout the evening but she had made a lot of phone calls. She had checked in on a few people and it had exhausted her. Dr. Jim's voice was in her head. "Stop taking care of everyone else and start taking care of yourself." She knew that was why she was so tired. But everybody needed her. "Maybe not as much as I think they do," she muttered out loud to herself. Maybe a good shower would help to wash off the emotional drain.

Her brother, Dave, was a good man but in a bad marriage. He had finally decided he needed to leave the marriage but it seemed to lead only to an even more difficult struggle through the divorce. Dave had fallen madly in love with his wife, Joan, but she was bipolar, if you listened to her psychiatrist. Or, she had a Borderline Personality Disorder if you listened to her psychologist. *Man, couldn't these professionals get it together?* Maria wondered.

Regardless of whom you wanted to believe, the therapies and medications just didn't cut it. Joan still had all her episodes that caused chaos for everyone.

The thing was, when Joan was in a "good place" everything was great. She was a charmer and had lots of fun; she was cooperative and dug in and pulled her weight. But when she was in the middle of an episode, "all hell broke loose". She never seemed to understand how she caused all the chaos. She always thought it was everyone else's fault. But whether it took days, weeks or months for her to come out of it, when she did Dave would fall back in love with the woman he thought he was married to. And of course, he always thought it would get better. It just never did.

The problem was, she repeatedly went on and off her medications, and apparently that was the cause of even more problems. Every time she went off her drugs her psychosis was worse than the time before.

After twenty-five years, Dave had finally given up and said, "Enough is enough". For twenty-five years, he cycled through the chaos and the good times with her but now he was burnt out. Many said he should have left years before but he always wanted to believe that *this* time it would be different. Problem was, it never was. The cycles continued and it just simply wore him out.

Now he was in the middle of this horrible divorce and Maria struggled to be there for him. Her heart ached for both of them because she could understand how scared and devastated Joan must feel. Joan had never been able to hold down a job because of her ups and downs and the chaos she created, yet she always blamed everyone else. Socially, she also thought everyone else was to blame and therefore had few friends. The thing was, when she was stable she was so much fun and loved life. The whole thing was so sad.

Maria didn't want to take sides but how could you not? She loved her brother who was a real gem of a man, always emotionally steady and affectionate. He always gave more than he took.

Maria admired him for how long he had stayed with Joan and put up with her episodes, and at the same time, thought he should have left years ago. And now he had.

The problem was, he had such a good heart. He felt so guilty when he left Joan. He bent over backwards to take care of her and organize things so she wouldn't be without anything. Joan was in the middle of another episode and didn't appreciate anything he did for her. She just demanded more and more. Even the lawyers had told him that he gave her far more than anyone else would have and certainly far more than the law required. If only Joan could appreciate all that he continued to do for her, it would make it easier for everyone.

Maria didn't want to get involved and yet she always seemed to be. She tried hard to just listen and not take sides. *How did those psychologists do it?* She was exhausted.

Dr. Jim had been a psychotherapist for years when Maria asked him how he did it. He explained the challenge therapists had being fully empathetic with the client yet remain objective and how they had to let the client go physically, mentally, and emotionally when they walked out of the office. That was why psychotherapists never worked as therapists for their family or friends.

As Maria stood in the shower allowing the steady flow of warm water to bathe her body and wash away all the hurt and pain she had listened to tonight, Duncan called from the bedroom.

"Hey hon, is there room in there for two?" She smiled. Duncan knew what to say and do to remove all the heavy emotion from the calls tonight.

"You betcha," she replied. "The water is just right and I have lots of soap to play with."

Duncan stood at the entrance to the open shower, tall and broad and wearing nothing but a mischievous smile. Maria loved times like this. Both she and Duncan had always had fun in the water. They both appreciated how water could be soothing, romantic, playful, and healing, and it held a lot of possibilities, whether it was the shower or the tub or the pool or the ocean. They even enjoyed the playful water fights outside in the yard with the kids.

Maria quickly brought her thoughts back to Duncan and the shower. Unlike most men that Maria had heard about, Duncan enjoyed the sensuousness of life as much as the sexuality. It allowed them to have a wonderful sexual life, full of romance and sensuality.

Duncan had often acknowledged how most men really didn't have a clue about sexuality because they didn't "get" the romance and sensuality, only the sex. Right now though, other people were not the focus.

Maria and Duncan lathered each other up. They playfully teased and tickled and enticed one another. Then Duncan started to serenade Maria and she laughingly joined in. The playfulness eventually turned into lovemaking, as it so often did, as they dried each other off and moved to the bed.

Duncan was so grateful that here they were, almost fifty, and they still had a good sex life. He had thought it would never slow down but in this past year it had. Between him not being able to stay hard for very long and Maria's fatigue, their sex life was okay but it was nothing like it used to be.

They used to sneak into the bedroom for some "afternoon delight". Or they would wake up on a Sunday morning and stay in bed and exhaust one another with their lovemaking. But this past year, their sex life had dramatically slowed down and it concerned Duncan, although he never said anything to Maria.

Maria didn't know how much Duncan had relied on his good friend, Dr. Jim, across the road, when they had been a young couple. Dr. Jim, had once told Duncan that truly making love to your wife, as opposed to just having sex, was the foundation of a good marriage and the best anti-depressant one could get. That sounded good to Duncan but he had had to ask Dr. Jim what the difference was.

Dr. Jim had taken out some homemade wine and they sat down and discussed lovemaking for a couple of hours. Dr. Jim explained what foreplay meant to a woman, that it wasn't just what happened in bed before intercourse, but rather how you treated a woman all day, every day. It included your tone and attitude, being loving and affectionate, engaging in the relationship, digging in and doing your part around the house without having to be asked or told.

Then they explored the topic of sensuality—how to entice all the senses when making love, which was why women love scents and candles and music—not to just go for the erogenous zones, but entice the whole body. They explored how to utilize all the emotions when making love—one time, playful, another time passionate and intense. One golden rule, Dr. Jim claimed, was to always make sure she comes first.

According to Dr. Jim, lovemaking is about giving and pleasuring each other. "Too many men focus on themselves or what they think their lady wants rather than actually asking and listening to what she says. Make sure you recognize how her needs and desires change. You wouldn't order the same meal from the menu every time you go out for dinner. Why would anyone want the same thing from the sex menu every time they made love?"

Dr. Jim also explained that how you make love reflects how you do life—how, and how much, you communicate, how trusting you are, and how creative you are. "Do you take the lead or allow her to lead, and do you listen to her needs and make sure you meet them? Or do you simply attend to your needs?" Dr. Jim concluded with the comment that men who only focus on their own needs are selfish and immature. "Remember, the art of loving lies not only in the capacity to give more than you receive, but to meet the other person's needs or desires."

Dr. Jim also explained how healthy women give more than they receive. "You give them a house, they turn it into a home; you give them food, they turn it into a meal; you give love and affection, they turn it into an awesome relationship."

It all sounded good to Duncan. He worked with conscious intent to implement the information into their marriage. His parents had a lousy marriage and he wanted something totally different. So he always kept the advice Dr. Jim had given him active in the back of his mind. After a while, he didn't really have to think much about it because he had created good habits. But he did take time to reflect once in a while to make sure he was still on track.

Dr. Jim was one of Duncan's best friends and provided all kinds of wisdom about effective relationships and tidbits about how to keep a wife happy. "Happy wife, happy life," Dr. Jim always said. And it had sure played out true in Duncan and Maria's relationship.

Years later, Duncan and Maria knew how to move from stroking and kissing and savouring one another to intense passion, thrusting and devouring one another, and back again to stroking and kissing, in order to enhance both their connection and their experience. They explored and embraced each other in a variety of different ways to increase the tension and allow it to dissipate and then increase it again. They would go back and forth until neither of them could stand it anymore and with a look that they both knew so well, the mutual agreement, to allow a full release.

"Wow," Maria purred to Duncan. "How come it just gets better and better? How long have we been married? And you still send me to the moon. Do you know how much I love you?"

Duncan waited a moment before he answered. He wanted to savour the aftermath. He knew that when he made love to Maria at night, it always gave him the best sleep. But he also knew that Maria was a typical female and loved to have that little bit of conversation and a cuddle after making love so that she could have a great sleep, too.

But there was something more. Should he tell her he had talked with Dr. Jane about his performance as well? And that she had told him to start eating watermelon and 100% pure chocolate every day? It had sounded crazy but he himself couldn't believe how long he had held out. Maybe it was just a placebo effect; maybe he should wait awhile and see.

He lay back on the bed and stretched out. "Let's see, twenty-three years coming up. But if you go to the moon then I must go to Mars. And I don't really know how much you love me but it can't possibly be more than how much I love you." He rolled over towards her and gave her a gentle kiss. They always seemed to sleep the same way. Face to face, they often held their hands between them; it gave them lots of space to breathe and stay independent but with their legs entwined. He smiled as she closed her eyes and went right to sleep.

Six

Food and My Sex Life

"Great food is like great sex.
The more you have the more you want."
Gael Greene

Duncan had been very concerned about Maria's lack of energy. Although her extra weight was not an issue for him, he knew it really bothered her. The problem with her mental clarity was a big issue for him. She had said on a number of occasions that it was difficult to think. It was like she was in a brain fog or something. Was it possible to get early Alzheimer's or did she have a brain tumour? He had even had nightmares that he had lost her.

So he had made an appointment for himself at the clinic. He saw Dr. Jane and explained to her all the symptoms Maria had.

Jane asked a number of interesting questions, even about their sex life. He had to admit it had got pretty sluggish in the last few years but owned up that the problem was partly with him. He didn't seem to have much drive and couldn't hold on for very long like he used to. He had put it up to his age.

Dr. Jane said that shouldn't be an issue and that a healthy man of fifty should have about the same testosterone level as a man of twenty. Unfortunately, she claimed, there were not that many healthy men out there in today's world.

She explained that part of the issue might be that he did not have enough nitric oxide in him. She asked him to put some salvia on his finger and she tested it with it a little strip. He was in the low zone. He asked what nitric oxide did and what it had to do with a member.

Dr. Jane explained that nitric oxide, the only gas in the body, was useful for a few things. One, it helped to relax the smooth muscles in the arteries which meant the arteries expanded and allowed more blood flow. This took pressure off of the heart to pump the blood through the arteries.

The expansion and contraction of smooth muscles in the arteries were supposed to be responsible for movement of the blood around the arterial vascular system, not the heart, as most people thought. Nitric oxide also worked in the immune system to kill certain pathogens. But too much, and it could become toxic to the body.

She continued to explain that it had various functions in the brain and nervous system, as a signalling molecule. It helped to maintain neural plasticity and regulated various ion channels. An imbalance in the nitric oxide in the brain could contribute to such issues as neurotoxicity, MS, Parkinson's, and Alzheimer's.

With regard to one's sex life, without sufficient nitric oxide in the blood, men found it difficult to both get and/or maintain an erection if the penile arteries can't expand.

Duncan definitely wanted to know how to get some of this nitric oxide in his body. Dr. Jane explained that it is far better to get the nutrients into your body that help you make nitric oxide. "Nutrients like L-Citrulline, an amino acid. The name is a Latin word that means watermelon, which is where it was initially discovered," she continued. "When you get citrulline in your diet, the body converts it to arginine which is a precursor for nitric oxide. Many men like to take arginine supplements and many find that it works for them initially but then they have even less success. Part of the reason for that is when you take arginine, on its own, the body metabolizes it in such a way that is difficult to convert it to nitric oxide."

"On the other hand, when you eat foods rich in citrulline, the body can easily convert the citrulline into arginine and then make nitric oxide. And, to take it a step further, foods that are high in citrulline and arginine help eliminate ammonia from the body and stimulate the immune system."

Duncan said nothing.

"I saw that raised eyebrow," Dr. Jane, acknowledged. "We constantly produce ammonia in the body. It is a natural by-product when we break down amino acids. Back to watermelon…it is not only rich in citrulline and arginine but it is also rich in another compound called glutathione.

"And why is gluta… whatever, important?" Duncan probed.

"It is called glu-ta-thi-one, and it is a hugely important compound in the body that is involved in all kinds of processes and functions, although typically it is only known as the master-anti-oxidant. But what we want it here for is to regulate the nitric oxide in the body. Again, if we have too little, we have problems. But if we have too much we also have problems. Bottom line, start to eat foods like watermelon. I will get Daniel to give you a list of foods. When your sex drive improves and you start to pay more attention to Maria, it may have an effect on her as well. While watermelon is great, and I do recommend people to eat lots of organic seeded watermelon, another great food that Maria may really appreciate is chocolate. But it has to be good chocolate. Now if you want all the anti-oxidant and Omega 3 benefits of chocolate you need to eat 100% pure chocolate, but if you want it for the arginine and citrulline, you can eat the 80%-90% pure chocolate."

"Chocolate," Duncan said, shaking his head.

"Chocolate is known to be so good for the heart but if you eat poor quality chocolate, you simply end up with another burden on the body. Did you know that chocolate comes from the seeds in the cocoa fruit? That the seeds have over 1200 molecules, over 300 nutrients that are required by the body? It is a pretty good fruit to eat. But like with so many things, you need to focus on the good stuff."

"I'll have to try that," Duncan said, still not entirely convinced.

"Enough about you and your sex drive...you came in here to talk about Maria. I would bet that the challenge with Maria is her adrenals. Certainly, on the surface that sounds like the problem. The issues that you mentioned like fatigue, insomnia, weight gain, and foggy brain syndrome are usually related to the adrenals. Unfortunately, western medicine typically diagnoses the problem as hypothyroid," Dr. Jane explained. "They look at blood hormones like TSH, T4 and T3. And when T3 is low they assume that must mean hypothyroid and typically put women on drugs like Synthroid. The problem is, most of the conversion from T4 to T3 is done in the liver, and so it could be a liver issue and not a thyroid issue."

"If the adrenals are either hyper- or hypo- they interfere with the enzymes that do the conversion. And in middle-aged women that is typically the problem. Adrenal fatigue is also commonly why women have menopausal issues."

By now, Duncan was listening attentively.

"The challenge is," Dr. Jane went on, "that it could also be a number of other things. So why don't we make an appointment for Maria, get her to come in and get assessed, and see what we come up with. In the meantime, you may want to buy watermelon on a regular basis. You might want to buy some good chocolate as well. Nuts, like almonds, also have good levels of arginine in them. Let's see if we can raise that nitric oxide level in you. If not, then I will give you a supplement that will do the job. Just don't go and buy any health food store kind of arginine supplement for nitric oxide. As I said, they often work for you for a couple of weeks and then they work against you."

Duncan stood up with Dr. Jane and shook her hand.

Seven

Communication

"Children who are not spoken to by live and responsive adults will not learn to speak properly. Children who are not answered will stop asking questions. They will become incurious. And children who are not told stories and who are not read to will have few reasons for wanting to learn to read."
Gail Haley, (20th century). Quoted in The New Read-Aloud Handbook, by Jim Trelease (1985)

Duncan woke up, as usual, around 5:30 AM. They rarely ever used an alarm clock and he usually woke up just before Maria. He loved to wake up next to her. She still had a smile on her face, even in her sleep.

It always gave him a chuckle when he thought about how they could stay so connected through the night. He gently removed his legs from their entanglement and let go of her hand. She looked so peaceful and she had been so tired lately. He wanted her to get as much sleep as she could. But no success.

Maria slowly came out of a dreamy cloud. She smiled lovingly at him. "You wouldn't believe the dreams I had last night," she said with a grin.

"Was I in them?"

"Well, there was this really handsome, sexy guy and he was great in the shower and he was even better in bed...but I can't remember his name."

Duncan laughed and climbed out of bed.

A while later, they were all at the breakfast table—Jessie, Jasmine, John, Duncan, and Maria. Duncan always made a point of going around the breakfast table and encouraging each person to share what they were doing that day. It was an easy way to keep track of everybody's activities without all the questions that provoked defenses and resentment in other families. The family had grown up with the daily sharing, so it was just a normal ritual that they went through without question.

Maria had made a ham and cheese omelette and Duncan had made coffee. He gave Maria a squeeze and a kiss on the neck, while she cooked the breakfast.

"Get a hotel room," Jessie laughed while she made lunches for everyone.

"Is that what you and Steve do?" Jasmine asked teasingly while she poured juice for everyone.

John continued to set the table and pretended he hadn't heard anything.

Now they all shared what they wanted to do or had to do that day. John said that he was not impressed with his math teacher. He had done all his homework but still got a lousy mark on his exam. Duncan asked him if he wanted Uncle Dan to help him out. Math was not one of John's strengths, but it wasn't one of Duncan's either.

John didn't want Uncle Dan's help; he just wanted to get good marks. He put in the work and effort and it frustrated him that he just didn't get better marks.

"Hang in there, kiddo, and if you want some extra help, just let us know," Duncan told him.

Jessie had a boyfriend named Steve. They had started to play with a new aspect of their of their relationship. They had been friends for years, but now there was a different kind of sparkle between them, though nothing too serious at this point. They did a lot of activities together with a group of friends. Both of them had been popular in high school, but neither of them had got involved with anyone seriously, despite what the rest of their friends did. Now, apparently, there was a new dimension that was developing between them that Duncan and Maria were observing. They didn't want to be intrusive but they attentively listened for any tidbit that gave them information about how the relationship was developing.

"We are all going out to a movie tonight, now that midterms are over," Jessie volunteered. "We're going out for dinner beforehand, so I won't be home for dinner, okay?"

Maria chuckled. "Make the most of the weekend. Next week you all have to buckle down again for the second half of the semester."

Jasmine had met another teen at her dance class. There were always a lot more girls than guys in the class but there was a "hottie" in the class and they had made a connection. It made Jasmine feel special, that of all the girls, Nick liked her. There was a lot of competition in the class and it wasn't just on the dance front.

"Can Nick come over for dinner tonight so we can study afterwards?" Jasmine asked.

"Is he your boyfriend?" John teased.

"Not just yet," Jessie teased, "but it's getting close."

Jasmine just rolled her eyes and refused to say anything. She and Nick had started to study a lot together. Their passion for dance also gave them the excuse to practice together, which sometimes raised questions for both Maria and Duncan. Was more going on than met the eye? They both listened carefully to the spoken word and the facial expressions to find out more.

When the kids had finished sharing what their plans were for the day Duncan asked Maria if they were having family over this weekend. Potluck suppers were common events that they all enjoyed but he also knew that Maria put a lot of work and effort into these family dinners and wanted to make sure that the whole family would dig in and pull their weight.

Duncan knew of too many families where the children had learned entitlement instead of appreciation. They expected everyone else to do the work while they got to simply enjoy the results. He didn't want his children to grow up that way. He wanted his children to be effective, responsible adults who always gave back more than they took.

"Well, we have invited everyone for a potluck tomorrow night," Maria explained. "We need to all be very supportive of Uncle Dave. This divorce is really tough on him."

The extended family all loved Dave and all supported him whatever they thought about his situation. Maria knew that Joan didn't want a divorce. Despite all the times she had threatened to leave, or told Dave to leave, when she was in one of her episodes, the thought of being on her own terrified her. Maria felt for Joan and hoped her family would be supportive of her but Joan was a difficult one and had burned many bridges, including the ties within her own family. Over the years Joan had created many scars with both her own family and their friends – whether she had made the friends or if Dave had made them. So who knew who would be there for her?

"Is everyone coming?" Jasmine asked

"Yes," Maria responded. "Everyone's coming. I also invited Dr. Jim and Julie to come to lend some extra support. Uncle Dave needs all the emotional support he can get."

"If it's the usual potluck, are you making your lasagna?" Jessie asked. "Can I make one this time?"

"Did you plan what everyone is going to bring, or is it just a surprise potluck?" Jasmine queried before Maria could answer Jessie.

"Well, it is going to be a surprise potluck. It's easier that way. But I think all of the food groups will be covered. And by all means, Jessie, I would love it if you made lasagna tomorrow. I was going to make a couple of lasagnas, one seafood, and one vegetarian, so you choose which you would like to make. I was also going to make a big green salad—if you could do that Jasmine that would be super. I do need everyone to be on top of your chores tomorrow morning. Girls, I want the house spic and span by lunchtime. Duncan, if you and John can take care of the yard and back deck, barbecue, table and chairs, that would be great. If we all dig in and do our thing, then it should roll off without a hitch. Everyone game?"

"Sure Mom. Can I bring Steve?" asked Jessie.

Jasmine, turning a little red, asked if she could invite Nick.

"Oh, we are getting close to boyfriend status, aren't we?" Jessie teased.

"Of course, you can, both of you. And you know, I should ask Dr. Jim and Julie if they want to bring any of the rest of their family. It might take a lot of the focus off of Dave. Good idea." Maria stopped and thought for a minute. Was there anything else she needed to do? "I think that should be good", she concluded more to herself than to anyone else.

Breakfast was done and everyone had put their dishes in the dishwasher; Jessie had made lunches; Duncan had made chai for all of them. He liked his coffee, Jessie and Jasmine liked chai and Maria like Earl Grey, but now because of the Gibsons they all drank homemade Chai. Jasmine and John had their homework; and Jessie had promised to take the two younger ones to school.

That left Maria to go do the grocery shopping for tomorrow night. She looked around the kitchen, and sent a quick prayer of gratitude up.

Eight

Are You Depressed or Frustrated?

*Depression refers to when we feel deep sadness, hopeless, empty, worthless, or agitated – and it may reflect a response to the internal world or the external world
Frustration refers to when we feel blocked, trapped, or in conflict – and it may reflect either an internal situation or an external situation
Whether depression or frustration, whether internally or externally provoked – don't simply assume that it is a psychological condition, it may be a symptom of a variety of physiological conditions.
Observe it, understand it, correctly identify the cause, before you lose control in someone else's diagnosis of it and end up on pills or in psychotherapy – that may never solve the underlying issue.*
Dr. Holly

Maria knew what she wanted to make two lasagnas and a green salad, so what did she need to purchase? Maria wrote herself a list and where she had to go to get what.

She continued to incorporate all the tidbits that Jim's family taught her about healthy eating, not just for the family in general but also for specific issues her family had:

- No microwaved foods

- No fast foods

- No junk foods

- No sugars, processed or artificial

- No simple carbohydrates that turned into sugars

- No genetically modified foods

- No processed foods

She had learned the benefits of good health food stores. She purchased only whole, real foods and foods that were more nutrient dense and less likely to have toxins in them.

Gradually, she had learned to incorporate all of the tidbits, from the Gibsons into her shopping habits and meal planning and preparations. She wasn't perfect at it but she was a lot more aware and paid a lot more attention to what she was feeding her family now. It was no longer just for the pleasure or convenience of it but rather for health as well.

Between Jessie's diabetes, Jasmine's sports-related asthma, and John's allergies, never mind her own adrenal fatigue and Duncan's enlarged left ventricle in the heart, healthy food and a good diet were now an important component of their lifestyle.

They had all thought they were so healthy. They didn't eat a lot of junk food or fast food. They all ate good portions of both fruits and vegetables. They were an active family.

They all enjoyed sports. As a family they hiked and rode their bikes, swam in the summer and skied in the winter. Duncan had always been an avid runner. He knew it was important to keep in shape as a contractor. He had seen a lot of sloppy mistakes made by men who didn't keep fit and ended up hurt in accidents.

Unfortunately, as Dr. Jane had explained, when someone exercised too much they could get an enlarged left ventricle in the heart. Those who were the diligent runners, who thought they were healthy, often ended up with a sudden massive heart attack and dead. When they heard Dr. Jane explain that, Duncan used Maria's favourite line, "Really? I never knew that".

He also immediately made an appointment with the MD to see if he was a candidate for an enlarged left ventricle and found that he did indeed have one. Consequently, he pulled back on all of the running and cross training. And he worked with Maria to make sure that they all ate healthy meals.

When she first had the adrenal fatigue and life had become so such a challenge overnight, it had seemed so weird. She was so tired all day long and would fall into a dead sleep around 10:00 PM. But by 1:30-2:00 AM she was wide-awake and couldn't go back to sleep. Eventually she would go to sleep but when she woke in the morning, she would be dead tired.

On top of that, she felt like her mind was in a brain fog. All her life she had experienced a good quick, clear mind and then it seemed to all disappear. She found that it was a struggle to even make simple decisions. She was so frustrated with it all.

The physician diagnosed depression and suggested that it maybe caused by hypothyroid, then sent her for a blood test.

When the reports came in, the MD claimed that she did in fact have hypothyroid and gave her a prescription for Synthroid. She had told Duncan that night that she had gone to the MD and he said that she had hypothyroid and had given her a prescription. Duncan cautioned her not to buy them and told her he had made an appointment for her at the Gibson Clinic with

Dr. Jane. He explained that he had been worried about her and so talked with Dr. Jim who told him to make her an appointment with Dr. Jane.

Maria appreciated that Duncan was that concerned about her and followed through with the appointment. It was at that appointment that she learned all about adrenal fatigue.

Nine

Was it Her Thyroid or Her Adrenals?

*"It is health that is real wealth
and not pieces of gold and silver."*
Mahatma Gandhi

Maria always enjoyed her conversations with Dr. Jane; she was such an encyclopedia of information. She couldn't wait to hear what Jane had to say.

When she first went into the office, she knew to have copies of her MD's reports on hand. She handed them to Dr. Jane and explained why she had gone to see him.

Dr. Jane looked over the reports and started to explain adrenal fatigue to Maria.

"A huge number of people in North America have hyper-adrenal activity. The adrenals were designed to help through emergency situations. For instance, imagine if you were in the woods hunting or hiking and a bear comes out of the forest. The body needs to shut down all the digestive processes and send all viable energy and resources to the peripheral areas of the body so you can run, fast! Sounds good, except that those adrenals are not meant to be working constantly in that manner. They are expected to get their rest and take a prolonged period of time to rejuvenate so that they are available for the next emergency."

Maria nodded.

"In North America, it seems that everyone runs his or her life on the adrenal rush. People start to rush the moment they wake up in the morning to go to the gym or get the kids ready for school and get themselves ready to go to work. They rush home in the evening and rush to put the dinner on, and then rush to get the kids off to soccer or dance or whatever. They just keep going and going, like the Everready® battery, especially women, which is why adrenal fatigue is much more common in women.

A man typically works from 7:00 to 3:00 or 8:00 to 4:00, or whatever for five days a week, but a woman works, in effect, not 24/7 but 35/11."

"Why do you say that?" Maria wanted to know.

"Well, she goes to work and puts in a full day. She is still predominantly responsible for taking care of the house and the cooking and the children. On top of that, she is usually responsible for organizing their social life or their holidays. If kids are sick, she is typically the one who stays up all night with them or listens through the night for any cries. Consequently, she doesn't get a full night's sleep. She never gets time out to calm down long enough to allow her adrenals to rejuvenate.

Now, those poor little adrenals just keep pumping and pumping until they are exhausted and they fall into adrenal fatigue or hypo-adrenal activity.

When the adrenals are functioning too fast or not fast enough they interfere with an enzyme that converts the thyroid's hormones, T4 to T3. These hormones, and in particular the T3, are responsible for the metabolism of every cell in the body. They also have a number of functions in the brain. In addition, the adrenals secrete hormones like epinephrine and norepinephrine that are hugely important to the brain. So typically, when women are tired and they have brain fog, one of the first things we look for is adrenal fatigue."

"Wow! I've never heard of this before," Maria said.

"In alternative medicine, you would never treat the adrenals without treating the thyroid. They work in tandem and need to be dealt with that way. Let's take a look with the ASYRA and see if you are toxic with anything like heavy metals and whether you are deficient in anything like glutathione or Vitamin C."

Through the initial assessment, they found that Maria was deficient in both, and in some B vitamins. She learned that it was useless to take glutathione orally, that it would basically give her expensive bowel movements and so Dr. Jane put her on a protocol that turned on the DNA to make the tools that made glutathione, two B Vitamins essential for the folate cycle, which supported the methionine cycle which regulated and helped to make the glutathione. Later if necessary, she would follow up with a supplement that provided all the nutrients to make all the different types of glutathione.

In the meantime, she was advised to take high doses of a combination of different types of real Vitamin C, not synthetic ascorbic acid. Dr. Jane explained that the second highest concentration of Vitamin C in the body, was in the adrenals.

Dr. Jane also suggested that she should incorporate some herbs into her cooking, such as ginger, garlic, vanilla, cloves, cardamom, and cinnamon. In addition, she told Maria to avoid coffee, as it was particularly hard on the adrenals and instead make a Chai tea of ginger, cardamom, cloves, nutmeg, cinnamon, and vanilla, and drink a few cups a day.

She was also supposed to take a tablespoon of a herbal tincture two times a day. It had all kinds of herbs in it that Maria couldn't remember. Since the initial appointment with Dr. Jane, she talked with Pappy a couple of times about the tincture they created for her. He said that as her adrenals started to respond the tincture would change.

Dr. Daniel had also come in and told her she should start to eat foods like watermelon, 100% real chocolate, and foods rich in Vitamin C and the B vitamins like nuts, bananas, avocados, legumes, organic meat and turkey, and for the Vitamin C, citrus fruits, peaches, mangoes, broccoli, and other greens.

All in all, she was glad she had come.

Dr. Jim had also put in his two cents worth. "You realize that women who try to do everything and be everything to everyone usually end up with adrenal fatigue, don't you?

You need to learn to set better boundaries. Identify what are your responsibilities and what are other people's responsibilities. For instance, you are not responsible for making everyone happy. Although you do have a responsibility to guide your children to learn how to find their own happiness; they are responsible for their own happiness.

Second, everything is not meant to be perfect. We live in a perfectly imperfect world, so allow it to be that way or the world will have its way with you.

Finally, understand the difference between frustration and depression. Too many physicians and therapists give a diagnosis of depression when, in fact, the real problem is frustration. It may be frustration with your children, your spouse, your health, your career, your colleagues, your finances, or something else. There are all kinds of things one can be frustrated with but frustration is very different from depression. Unfortunately, too many physicians and therapists miss this important differentiation."

"Really? I never knew that!" That fact alone had been a huge eye opener for Maria. She had grown up with the belief that it was her responsibility to make everyone around her happy. She had never thought about it—she simply lived her life that way. And she usually took the responsibility for everything even when it wasn't perfect. She had never actually seen her life that way until Dr. Jim gave her a framework to work with so she could understand it.

She had also thought she was depressed and had agreed with the MD when he gave her the diagnosis. But when Dr. Jim explained the difference between frustration and depression, she could see that she was definitely frustrated with her health, not depressed. She was also frustrated with her lack of sleep and her lack of energy. She was frustrated that she couldn't cope like she used to. She was frustrated that she couldn't think clearly and quickly like she used to. Yes, she was definitely frustrated! And if she didn't know the Gibsons, she would have just accepted what the MD told her and would have just started taking Synthroid.

A few pointers and some clarification was all she had needed. What Dr. Jim said made sense and she started to work with it.

Now she had both the psychological tools and the physiological tools that she needed to bring her adrenals and her psyche back into health. There was an enormous sense of control in all of that. She knew what she had to do and set about to organize her life so she could do it.

Now several months later, she felt like she was on the mend. Her adrenals were obviously better and the fatigue was less. She slept through most nights and when she woke up in the morning, she felt refreshed and alive. Well, most mornings. She still often took naps in the afternoon but not for as long nor as often, and without the intense tiredness. She knew her body had responded well, even if it still had a ways go.

She had even started to miss her work as a realtor. She loved to meet with people and to show homes, and she was good at it. But she had decided to put it on hold, until she totally eliminated the adrenal fatigue. Duncan had been behind her one hundred percent. She knew she was lucky she had the option to do that and wondered how single moms who had no one to fall back on dealt with adrenal fatigue.

Dr. Jim had explained that what she had was, in fact, very common. Unfortunately, most people simply followed doctor's orders and went on anti-depressants and/or drugs for hypothyroid and other drugs. They struggled to manage their symptoms. Too bad the tools they used to manage their symptoms often only made matters worse by creating another problem, rT3 dominance.

On top of it, people who had been brought up with the "stiff upper lip" mentality would even drive themselves to override fatigue. They would work out with the belief that it would benefit them when, in fact, the exercise could make the adrenals even worse. In addition, they would drink coffee to keep themselves going, which was also very hard on the adrenals.

Again the words, "Really? I never knew that," slid out of her mouth.

The three of them had continued to talk and explore a variety of topics that related to health, both psychologically and physiologically. She loved to learn about all the contradictions, myths, and misunderstandings in health and medicine. It both intrigued her and made her angry that the medical profession was so far behind the health sciences; that pharmaceutical companies were required to provide certain components in Europe that they left out in North America and that physicians were trained to simply manage symptoms rather than address and resolve the underlying issues.

She was so grateful for Dr. Jim and his family. They were trained in so many different healing modalities. She had learned how differently various healing traditions viewed the body, from the East Indian Ayurvedic, to the Asian Traditional Chinese Medicine, to the Western perspective on the body. They had various commonalities, but they also had unique individual differences.

This family of health care professionals was just a real treasure for Maria and her family. They provided different perspectives and yet worked effectively, cooperatively, and respectfully with one another. Each practitioner worked effectively in his or her own field but with both grace and respect for the other healing traditions.

Research was also a huge priority for the whole family. Keeping up to date seemed to be almost a competition between them. Maria wished she could believe that about all medical people.

Ten

Capturing a Moment in Time

"Be happy in the moment, that's enough.
Each moment is all we need, not more."
Mother Teresa

Steve came by to pick up Jessie to go to the movies. Like Jessie, he was dressed in jeans and a t-shirt. He looked comfortably dressed but thoroughly drained physically.

"Wow, is university doing a number on you!" Duncan exclaimed as he opened the door to Steve.

"Yeah, am I glad midterms are over, Mr. Smith. You would not believe what I went through. I had three classes in physics that just pushed me to the limits."

"You're a smart young man, Steve. You will work your way through it." Duncan wanted to be supportive and validating as always but he wondered if he should talk to Steve about adrenal fatigue. He sure looked wiped.

"I wished my Dad would say that." He sounded frustrated. "If I don't get top marks then I am a failure as far as he is concerned. I try hard but I know I don't always get the best marks."

Duncan had talked with Steve before and had heard how tough his father was on him. It added a lot of stress that Steve didn't need as he worked his way through the engineering physics program.

"Not to negate your father or the influence he has on you, Steve, but it is up to you to determine whether or not you are a failure or a success. If you think you are a failure, then you are. If you think you are a success, then you are. You decide, don't let anyone decide for you. Part of growing up and truly being you is using the brain that God gave you. Look at all the possibilities, choose which attitude, belief, or philosophy you want to live by and then engage in it and live it to the fullest."

Steve turned around and looked at Duncan. It was as if he had to absorb what Duncan had said. Then he held out his hand. "Thank you Mr. Smith. I know you have told me that before and I try to remember it when I get down, but I needed to hear it again."

Duncan smiled as he shook Steve's outstretched hand. He put an arm around Steve's shoulders with the other. Duncan's heart went out to the kid.

As though on cue, Jessie walked into the kitchen. She was dressed as comfortably as Steve but looked a lot healthier.

"I thought I heard you come in," she said, kissing Steve's cheek. "Are you ready to go?"

Duncan made a mental note that he hadn't had a heart to heart with Jessie lately, and like Steve, she needed it. Both of their programs were tough and they needed all the support he could give them. Jessie wanted to go into the biological sciences but wasn't sure yet what she wanted to focus on. She had always been interested in biology and chemistry. At one point, she had wanted to be an MD, but after all the time she spent with Dr. Jim's extended family and experienced their ability to eliminate her diabetes, she had started to look at other options. She had decided to do her pre-med and choose later how she wanted to apply it.

Maria came in on the heels of Jessie with an armload of laundry.

"Hi Steve, how did your midterms go?"

Steve glanced up at Duncan, smiled and simply said, "I did my best, Mrs. Smith."

"That's all anyone could ever ask of you, hon. Keep up the good work!" Maria had no idea of the brief conversation that Duncan and Steve had exchanged, but her philosophy supported it. Duncan just raised an eyebrow and gave a nod to Steve. *Way to go Maria. Perfect timing*, he thought.

"You know Steve, you are an adult now. You don't need to call us Mr. and Mrs. Smith anymore. Why don't you call us Duncan and Maria?"

"Thank-you for that, Mrs. Smith, I mean, Maria. It may take a while to get out of the habit."

Jessie started to laugh and asked if she should call them Maria and Duncan as well. She was met with a unanimous, "No".

"Oh well, it was worth a try," she laughingly returned.

As Jessie and Steve left for dinner and the movies, Duncan followed Maria to the kitchen table. Duncan was the kind of guy that simply dug in and helped with whatever was at hand. Years before he had decided to do whatever he could to become a good husband. Duncan didn't want to be an alcoholic like his father. He loved his dad but also recognized that he was a useless, irresponsible, ineffective husband and father.

Duncan felt sorry for his mom who had suffered a lot because of his father. But he also recognized that she also had the choice to leave. She chose to stay. She had suffered a massive stroke and had died shortly thereafter.

His father's drinking became even worse after his mom died. His liver could only handle so much and eventually they had to put him in a home. A short time later, he too had died.

When Duncan met Dr. Jim, the psychotherapist across the street, he saw Dr. Jim as the father he never had, even though the doctor wasn't old enough to be his father. Dr. Jim never told Duncan what to do or how to do it, rather he would answer his questions with personal stories providing Duncan with more material, information, or wisdom that he needed to grow and develop as a human being. Dr. Jim inspired, provoked, and supported Duncan to always move towards his greatest potential, something Duncan's alcoholic father had never taught or modeled.

But thanks to Dr. Jim's wisdom, Duncan had learned to appreciate that his father had made his own choices, both conscious and subconscious, to live his life the way he did. Duncan learned not to resent his father for being a useless alcoholic or to be bitter, but rather he could appreciate the lessons his father had provided him with. Dr. Jim abided by the philosophy that "life is 10% what happens to you and 90% what you choose to do with it". Duncan liked that philosophy and had taken it on as his own.

Now, Duncan stood at the table and grinned at Maria as he automatically started folding the laundry with her.

"What are you grinning about?'

"You were perfect," Duncan replied, smiling.

"Well, of course I was, but how exactly was I perfect?" Maria looked up at Duncan, puzzled.

Duncan explained the short conversation he'd had with Steven earlier and how Maria's question and comment played in beautifully with what he had tried to convey to Steve. He gave her a quick kiss and a hug.

"Do you think he might be starting to have adrenal issues, too?" Duncan asked Maria. "He looks like he is just wiped. I didn't know if I should suggest it to him or not."

"Oh, you are funny. Now you are on the bandwagon and want to get everybody back into health. It's contagious, isn't it? But you are right. We should keep an eye on him. It may be just a difficult time he is going through, but if it continues, we can sit down and have a chat."

Maria loved that Duncan was interested in everyone's health and well being as well. The challenge was to provide information without the need to control the person's decision to engage.

"Sounds like a plan. Where are Jasmine and John?"

"Jasmine is eating dinner with Nick's family and they decided that they are all going to a movie tonight. John complained that he was the only one not going to a movie, so Grandma Mary and Papa Johnny decided to take him to one. I am always so glad when they decide to go out and do something that I just smiled and said 'great'."

Duncan responded with a mischievous look. "You mean we have the house to ourselves? On a Friday night? Wow...what could we possibly do? Maybe I should go out and work in the shed?"

"Somehow that look and that suggestion just don't go together. But if you would like I can go and volunteer at the senior's center tonight?" Maria tossed back at him.

"Like hell you will, you brat. Why don't you order in Chinese and we can have a nice relaxing meal on the deck. I'll turn on the hot tub, go downstairs and get a bottle of wine from the cellar, and you can light all your favourite candles. I will put on some romantic music...then we can relax for a while and we will see where it all takes us?" he suggested with a devilish wink.

"Now, that sounds like a plan. I will order the Chinese and put the piles of laundry in each room. Anything in particular you would like me to order?"

"You know my favourites…surprise me," Duncan said over his shoulder as he walked outside to turn on the hot tub.

Maria pulled out the menu to their favourite Chinese Restaurant, took a glance at it, and phoned the number. The restaurant was close by and always pretty quick with deliveries. She looked on the menu for the healthiest choices, none of the deep fried foods, and lots of vegetables. After she had put in her order and put the piles of clothes in each room, she went to collect candles and her favourite romantic CDs.

They moved back and forth from inside to the patio as they created a lovely romantic ambience. Both of them were in a great mood. Evenings like this didn't come along very often and they weren't going to miss out on it. Duncan started to hum a song and Maria joined in, singing the words. They had brought out wine and glasses, dishes, and cutlery.

The music was on and the candles lit. Duncan stepped behind Maria and put an arm around her and gently moved them to the music.

"I love it when you want to dance," Maria crooned to him. They moved from a gentle sway into a waltz and then back to just swaying together as the songs moved from one love song to another.

Maria had bought them dance lessons years ago but they found it hard to find the time to dance with three growing children. But now, the floor, or rather the patio, was theirs. Maria loved to dance with Duncan. Prior to the dance lessons he had been an awkward dancer but he learned quickly and soon became a man of the floor.

The front door bell chimed announcing that the Chinese Food had arrived. Duncan let Maria go as he gave her a quick kiss and went to answer the door.

"That was quick," Duncan smiled at Sam, the deliveryman.

"Yours was the last order to come in before I left but the first delivery."

"That deserves a good tip," Duncan replied, digging into his pockets.

"Thanks, Mr. Smith. Much appreciated."

Duncan danced onto the patio with the goods. Maria wasn't too sure if the movements were an attempt to be goofy or romantic but had to laugh nonetheless. She had set the table and lit some candles. Duncan opened up the Chinese food containers as Maria poured the wine.

The air was warm and full of perfumed scents and now the scent of Chinese food. A gentle breeze floated in and out. The music played softly in the background.

"What more could you ask for?" Maria said as they filled their plates from the boxes of Chinese food.

"Right now, nothing. It feels good to relax my body after a long day's work. It has been a long week."

As a contractor, Duncan sometimes worked long hours; sometimes he worked hard hours. He had a few different crews of men working for him in both residential and commercial projects and always had a few different projects on the go at the same time. Right now, he had one project with a residential developer and they had a subdivision that they were engaged in. In addition, he had a contract with the new stadium in town. He was one of several contractors working together on that project.

"How are you doing—your adrenals, in particular?" Duncan knew she didn't like to talk about her condition in front of the kids.

"So much better," Maria said simply. She would rather think of herself as strong and able to do anything, anywhere, anytime, than weak and needing rest. So she tried to cover it up for everyone else. But with Duncan, it was different. He always made her feel loved and special and so it felt safe to be open with him.

"Are you still working with Pappy on it?"

"Yeah. He says, that I was lucky I caught it in time. If I had ignored it and let it go, it could take upwards of two years to get back on track again. I still have to take that horrible herbal tincture and that special Vitamin C. And I try to work all the foods and spices into our regular meals."

"How long do you have to take that stuff?" Maria had always been so healthy and full of energy but last fall she suddenly became tired all of the time. She complained several times that it felt like her brain was foggy. And then she started to gain weight. He was glad he had talked with Dr. Jim about it and made the appointment for her.

They had both talked about what Dr. Jane had said, regarding the MD diagnosing hypothyroid and the Synthroid prescription he had given her. Dr. Jane had explained that she understood how the MD had been trained, and why he would diagnose it as hypothyroid and want to put her on Synthroid. She then explained why she thought that the symptoms were due to adrenal fatigue. She explained to Maria the role of the adrenals in the body and how the adrenals impacted the thyroid and the conversion of T4 to T3. She also explained that even the World Health Organization claimed that way too many people in North America were prescribed Synthroid when they shouldn't be and how they would end up with rT3 dominance and become dependent on Synthroid for the rest of their lives.

Maria's common response to anyone in Jim's family was, "I never knew." Dr. Jane's presentation of the information made it sound very logical. Duncan was pleased that Maria agreed to do whatever Dr. Jane told her to do.

Now she avoided all white sugars, artificial sugars, anything with high fructose corn syrups and simple carbs that turned into sugar (except for the odd occasion when they ordered in Chinese food) and anything that would stimulate the adrenals, like coffee. She had also agreed to only walk for exercise, so as not to push the adrenals. They had taken a lot of easy walks in the last few months. It gave them a lot of private time to be together and just talk.

She took the special herbal tincture to support and strengthen her adrenals and a special kind of Vitamin C. She explained to Duncan that ascorbic acid is *not* vitamin C but a synthetic replication of the outer ring of Vitamin C and typically made from GMO corn.

"Well, Dr. Jane and Pappy have already changed the tincture twice but said I was supposed to continue with all the other things I am doing. And Dr. Jane also said that I am responding really well. I certainly don't feel like death warmed over all the time now so I must be improving. But let's forget about that stuff for now."

She wanted to focus on them now and their romantic evening. To help change their current conversation topic, Duncan started to feed Maria. She in turn fed him. They used to do a lot of those silly romantic gestures but in the past twenty years, they had to grab special moments like this to be romantic.

As they enjoyed the romantic meal, the topic changed to one of philosophy. They were both philosophers at heart. They enjoyed everything from an exploration of the definition of love or God, to the origins of the universe, to politics, economics, and the human experience.

When they finished dinner, Maria went in to get her bathing suit on. Duncan simply stripped down and got into the water in his briefs. When Maria came back, Duncan had turned on the jets. She joined him and they both floated around in the tub, stretching out their limbs before settling in their favourite seats.

They held hands as they listened to the birds, the crickets, and the gentle breeze as it danced on the leaves.

Duncan could feel his muscles relax in response to the jets, and let out a long sigh. He turned down the jets and reached over for Maria and pulled her to him as they floated on the water. He ran his hands over her curves and under her bathing suit. He could feel her nipples harden as he touched and stroked her body and kissed anything above water.

Maria loved to stroke his strong muscled body. She felt his member get aroused and harden. They wrapped their legs around each other as they continued to move in and out of the water and around each other. It had moved from being romantic to being sensual and they both loved it.

All of a sudden, their lovemaking came to an abrupt halt. Jasmine and John arrived home at the same time. They saw the candles through the sliding glass doors and John ran out to the hot tub.

"Can we come in Mom?"

"Can we, Dad?"

Duncan winked at Maria and told the kids to go get their suits on.

"Can't we just come in, in our underwear?" John begged, pulling off his t-shirt.

"Not tonight. Go get your swimming trunks on." Jasmine caught on and pulled John behind her to go and get bathing suits on and give Mom and Dad a bit more time.

Maria called to them as they ran upstairs, "Where are Grandma Mary and Papa Johnny?"

"They went downstairs," John shouted back.

Duncan had built Grandma Mary and Papa Johnny a beautiful ground level suite in the basement. It was a large 1400 square foot suite with all of the latest appliances and décor. They loved living there with access to the family anytime they wanted and yet they could shut themselves off whenever they had had enough.

As the kids left, Duncan reached for Maria and pulled her to him, "It couldn't last all night when we have three kids." He slid one of his hands between her legs, and stroked her softly while the other hand caressed a breast already full and tight with longing for his touch.

Maria responded in kind, as she stroked his already hard member and reached her hands across his tight behind.

Duncan loved all the sounds Maria made when he delighted her body. Her verbal response always excited him even more and she knew it so she didn't usually hold back. But tonight she had to keep her voice low, as she listened for the kids, while they took advantage of the last few moments of pleasure.

"When the kids return, don't forget where we left off. I want to have my way with you later when we can continue on without interruption." Maria giggled in response.

She pushed him away as John bounded through the sliding glass door. Jasmine took a little longer, either just because she had more to change or because she was sensitive to give her parents more time alone.

John chattered on about the movie and when he finally wound down, Maria asked Jasmine how it went with Nick. Did they enjoy their movie, too? Jasmine had chosen the movie but Nick's parents had wanted to see it too. Nick didn't want to have his parents come along. It was the first time he had taken a girl to a movie so his Dad agreed to take his Mom to a different movie.

Jasmine finished her explanation of the movie just as Jessie and Steve came through the door.

"Are you guys coming in too?" Duncan inquired.

Jessie looked at Steve to see his response and it was unanimous.

"Give him a pair of my trunks," Duncan offered.

The tub was designed for the family when everyone was young, now with an older family and another adult, it was a little crowded. Nobody cared.

Eventually, Duncan winked at Maria to signal it was time to bring it all to an end.

"Come on, John, time for bed," Duncan said. "It's after ten."

Maria was next to excuse herself from the tub. She needed to clean up the Chinese food containers and wine glasses still on the table.

Jasmine didn't want to stay in the hot tub with Jessie and Steve so she excused herself and went up to shower and go to bed. She went to sleep wondering what Nick was thinking about their first date.

Eleven

Expressing and Getting the Love You Need

"Immature love says: 'I love you because I need you.'
Mature love says: 'I need you because I love you."
Erich Fromm

On Saturday mornings the kids and Maria usually slept in until around 8:00 AM. It used to be by this time, Duncan would have run his marathon and had a shower but nowadays, he was kinder to his body. He got up and did his stretches and yoga with Maria. He used to think yoga was a flaky eastern thing for hippies but since Maria had got into it—thanks to Dr. Jim's wife Julie, the physiotherapist—he now appreciated the physiological benefits of it, along with the chocolate, watermelon, and almonds that he ate every day.

He was never one to keep things from Maria but this thing about his sex drive and the nitric oxide and all that Dr. Jane had explained, well, he wanted to see if any of it worked before he shared it with Maria. He didn't want to get her hopes up and then find out he had just engaged in the placebo effect. So he still hadn't told her.

When Dr. Jane had explained to Duncan that most western styles of exercise could be detrimental to someone with adrenal fatigue, she had also explained various types of eastern exercise. They explored Tai Chi, Qi Gong and Yoga. How they differed, how they were similar, what they achieved in the body.

Maria had started explore each of them when she was diagnosed with adrenal fatigue and had decided that yoga fit best into her schedule and personality. So when Duncan discovered he had created an enlarged left ventricle from exercise overkill and that he shouldn't do all the exercise he used to do, he simply fell into routine with Maria.

Personally, he found the Qi Gong more interesting and would have liked to do the Tai Chi but Maria had already settled on yoga and it was easier to simply fall into routine with her. If Jessie joined them, she was interested in the movement from a biological perspective. If Jasmine joined them, she was interested in yoga from a physical movement perspective. If John joined them, he was simply interested in the fun of it. He liked to laugh at how funny the movements looked.

This morning's routine seemed to have just simply extended the fun they had in the hot tub last night. Everyone was in a cheerful mood but appreciated the reverence with which yoga was done. After about thirty minutes, John started to make jokes. Soon everyone was laughing and playing off of each other's jokes. Maria looked over at Duncan and with a shrug they grabbed their mats and moved to the showers.

An hour later, at the breakfast table, Duncan asked everyone what his or her plans were for the morning. Jasmine, always the intuitive one, laughed and asked, "You don't think we know what you do every morning, do you?"

"What does he do?" John chimed in.

"He gets…" Jasmine started but her dad cut her off.

"Let's let John say what he thinks I do."

John looked puzzled. "I don't know what you're doing."

"Come on John, think about it. What do we do every morning when Dad sits down at the table?" Jessie coaxed.

John didn't want to be left out or look stupid. Maria smiled at him and made movements with her hands to indicate someone talking. That's when John caught on.

"He gets us all to talk," he said with pride.

"And what does he get us all to talk about?" Jasmine asked.

John only needed to pause for a bit. "Our chores."

Jessie explained. "He gets us to talk about our chores, our plans for the day, what is going on in school, who we are hanging out with, all that stuff. That way he thinks he is being both subtle and in control. He doesn't have to ask questions, we have all learned to just provide all the information he wants."

"Wow, aren't you the smart one," Duncan observed.

"Oh come on, Dad. You really don't think we are that naïve, do you?" Jessie paused for a moment to reflect. "On the other hand, maybe I didn't really start to recognize it until I had a breakfast with Susan's family. Nobody talks at their breakfast table. With Robin's family, everybody just fights. When I stayed over at Pat's house, everybody made his or her own breakfast and ate somewhere else in the house. Steve says his family just eats in silence, and they hope not to get his Dad angry.

But here, we all sit at the table, and you always get us all to talk. It's like it's a habit. We have always done it, so we just do it without realizing what we are really doing. John just hasn't spent many meals at other people's houses yet to know how many different ways families interact."

"Wow, are you going to be the psychologist in the family?" Maria was aware of how attentive Jasmine was to the conversation and how interested John appeared not to be. He looked like he was more interested in the peanut butter swirls he was making on his toast, but Maria knew better. "So what do you think, John?"

"Well, I know it's really different when I go downstairs and have breakfast with Grandma Mary and Papa Johnny. They eat breakfast together but it is like they both pray when they eat. They don't talk. But because they get this look between them, I thought maybe they just talk to each other in their heads or something, like they do in cartoons."

"You are all growing up to be such wise young people. I am proud of you all," Duncan concluded the conversation. "Now let's get breakfast cleaned out of the way, so we can get our chores under way."

Maria and Duncan also exchanged a look. The kids had often had the skirmishes through the years, but nothing really big. Overall, they respected each other and cooperated well. The older ones always looked out for the ones younger. Maria had often wondered if that was because of the spacing between the children. Or perhaps it was because Maria and Duncan so rarely fought. There never seemed to be power struggles or a need for dominance from anyone. It had certainly not been the case in either of their families when they had grown up.

Dr. Jim offered a different perspective. He suggested that if a person, whether it be a spouse, parent, child or sibling, felt loved enough, enough of the time, there was no need to squabble, bicker, and fight. How each person defined love, received love, or gave love contributed to the overall dynamic.

When Maria and Duncan had discussed this, they concluded that they each focused on the "doing of life" and affection as their primary way of showing, giving, and receiving love. Because they were so similar in how they received and expressed love, it made the relationship easy.

They both agreed that Jasmine showed love by taking time and listening to others. Jessie was much better at validating and acknowledging others. Both Jasmine and Jessie were good at making things to celebrate each person. John needed to be acknowledged and validated, perhaps that was because he was always in a struggle to live up to his older sisters' reputations.

Twelve

Reversing Allergies

*"Are we allergic to food or are we increasingly allergic
to what has been done to it?"*
Robyn O'Brien

The children had finished all their chores by lunch. Jessie had finished her lasagna and Jasmine had cleaned, washed, and cut everything up for the salad for dinner.

John and Jessie had set the tables outside. Jasmine had made up some pretty floral arrangements with flowers from the garden. Duncan had gone into town to get some new light bulbs for the patio lights.

Maria had just started lunch for everyone when she heard John cry out. She called from the kitchen to ask whether he was okay. Jessie replied that he had got a bee sting. Maria ran.

John had allergies to a few foods like corn and apples, some types of breads and dairy foods, and to various insect stings. They kept an EpiPen® always on the ready for him, just in case he had an anaphylactic shock reaction.

Last time he had been stung, John had been at Dr. Jim's playing with his dogs. Dr. Jim's parents had both been there and did something different. Jim's mother, Nanny Sarah, a Chinese

Medicine Doctor, gave John acupuncture. Jim's father, Pappy, the Medical Herbalist, gave Jim an herbal tincture.

Pappy claimed that the herb blocked the receptors on the mast cells in the body so that they would not be stimulated to produce histamine. Histamine is the primary compound released that causes the anaphylactic reaction. Pappy claimed that you could actually reverse the anaphylactic reaction. He suggested that Maria give John some of the tincture at the beginning of each month, for a few days. He also cautioned to always make sure the EpiPen® was still available, just in case.

Now was the test. Maria had grabbed the EpiPen® on the way out the door. John was sitting on the ground, struggling to be brave. Maria looked at the site of the sting and saw that there was no reaction! She told Jessie to go and get the bottle of tincture and some ice cubes while she watched for any reaction. There was none.

"Do I have to go to the hospital?" John whispered.

Jessie came out with the tincture and a spoon and some ice cubes. John knew the tincture tasted awful but took it without complaint.

"No, sweetheart, it doesn't look like it. I don't think we even need the EpiPen®. There is no reaction at all. Pappy knew what he was doing. Let's just sit here for a bit and make sure there isn't some sort of delayed reaction. Does it hurt?"

"Well, just a little."

"Can you imagine, if we hadn't followed Pappy's advice, we'd be giving you the EpiPen® and rushing you to emergency? We are so lucky to have such good friends. It doesn't even look like you need any ice cubes. I can't believe it. No reaction at all!" Maria sent up a silent prayer of gratitude.

"Jessie why don't you get us all some juice and we will just sit here and watch it for a bit to make sure. Thanks, hon."

Dr. Daniel was Dr. Jim and Julie's other child. He had a PhD in Nutrition. It was hard to imagine all those degrees and healing modalities in one family. Dr. Daniel had explained to Maria years ago not to buy store bought juice, as it contained no fibre, precious little nutrition and upwards of 200 times the sugar, in addition to other toxins.

Dr. Daniel showed Maria how to make her own juice—not only was it a lot cheaper but was also full of alkalizing minerals, vitamins, phytonutrients, and fibre.

She made a couple of jugs for the family every few days. She bought organic grapefruit, hard crunchy apples (Dr. Daniel said to use apples that were hard and tart, not the soft sweet ones), lemons and limes, and oranges. She scrubbed the outside of the fruit with a mixture of grapefruit seed extra and water, then cut them up into a blender, filled the blender with water, and turned it on.

Dr. Daniel had explained that juicers took out all the fibre, and the fibre is what regulates the sugar/fructose uptake in the body. Without the fibre, people just set themselves up for diabetes. So they just used a plain blender.

Apparently, if you made juice this way you not only made sure it was fresh and full of phytonutrients but most of the fibre and alkalizing minerals that were in the outer and inner rinds, were now in the juice.

She could make the juice as thick or as thin as she wanted. She simply determined the fruit to water ratio and how long she kept it on the blender.

All they had to do to make different juices was change the amounts of different fruits in the juice. Sometimes she added in banana, mango, raspberries, or other fruit, depending on what was in season.

When they had gone to Mexico a couple of years ago, the family had also learned to appreciate the juice with cilantro, which is used for heavy metal detoxification, or kale and spinach, which is good for the liver. It was simply called the "green juice", a big fad in Mexico. There were several different versions using Napoli cactus, celery, pineapple—every hotel had its own particular recipe. Even the kids thought it was good so that was a good thing.

Maria liked it even more when she combined the green juice with lychee milk but she hadn't been able to find any lychees or lychee milk locally, so they hadn't created that juice at home yet.

As she lay on the lounge chairs with John, she thought of how much she had learned from Dr. Jim's family. She found it sad that the school system didn't teach these fundamentals to children.

They had discussed at one of their philosophical Sunday breakfasts how they would have a much healthier society and healthier children if children learned this basic stuff at school. The conversation revolved around how the current school system was overwhelmed with more and more children diagnosed with ADHD (Attention Deficient Hyperactive Disorder), Diabetes, and the Autistic Spectrum Disorders. Between the nutrient-deficient, toxicity-rich foods found in the grocery store, the junk foods, fast food, and microwaved food, children didn't have a chance. They had discussed how the school systems looked to psychologists, psychiatrists, and MDs to put the kids on medications when what they needed was to get rid of the toxicity in their systems, improve the microbiota in their guts, and get the nutrients they required for healthy bodies.

Jessie came out with drinks for the three of them. She and John had talked back and forth while Maria had reflected on the health of children today.

"Let's make a toast to Pappy," Jessie suggested. Maria and Jessie clinked their glasses with John's.

"To Pappy," they toasted. "Thanks, Pappy, you are the best," pronounced John, full of gumption again.

Jessie asked Maria what herb John took that reversed the anaphylactic reaction but Maria couldn't remember. She was just so glad that it had worked. The three of them sat there for a while. They talked causally about the day and the party but all kept an eye on John, but nothing happened.

"I guess we are just going to have to diagnose you as normal and okay," Jessie laughingly diagnosed her little brother awhile later.

"Sounds like a plan," confirmed Maria, "let's put away the tincture and the EpiPen® and get on with the day."

Thirteen

Grabbing Some Afternoon Delight

"Sex is as important as eating or drinking and we ought to allow the one appetite to be satisfied with as little restraint or false modesty as the other."
Marquis de Sade

Duncan and Maria were in their ensuite, getting ready for the evening. Duncan looked at his watch. "The guests aren't due until six, right? It's only 4:30! That means, we could..."

"Check on the kids," Maria replied with a grin.

Duncan winked at Maria and went to take a look. John was watching a movie. Jessie was reading a book. And Jasmine was working on a homework project.

"They are all occupied but ready for the evening." Duncan came up behind Maria, sliding his hands around her and over her breasts. He ran his fingers up under her top and stroked to entice her nipples, which responded to his evocative touch. Maria reached over her shoulders to put her arms up and around his neck, giving him her lips.

Duncan responded to her invitation, covering her lips with his, opening her mouth and penetrating inside, letting her know that he was really turned on. She got the message and moved her arms down and around behind her so she could gently stroke him.

She turned in his arms, as he pulled her top up over her head. As he guided her back to the bed she spread her hands up under his t-shirt and moved it up over his chest, gently sucking each of his nipples as she removed his t-shirt.

He backed her up to the bed and laid her down, moving one arm under and up behind her back. His other hand pulled her lacy bra down enough that he could slide his tongue in and tease a nipple. In response, she arched up and offered her breasts up to him. The nipple hardened as it pushed out of the bra.

He moved up to capture her mouth and as their lips met he could taste her arousal. As their tongues teased, his hand moved behind her back and he released her girls from their lacy support.

His mouth slowly moved back down her neck, kissing her and teasing her as he moved to draw away the lacy garment and give him full access to the beauties he loved to attend to.

They squirmed up further on the bed, as she undid his belt buckle and his zipper. She gently reached inside for his stiffness and stroked, watching pleasure sweep across his face. He looked her in the eyes as he growled his appreciation of her attentiveness.

Between her legs and his hands they managed to get his jeans and briefs off as she played with his treasures. He took his sweet time removing hers. He caressed and stroked and kissed and sucked his way down her chest and stomach, teasing her with his tongue and his kisses.

She moved with delight, but he only teased. He continued to move down her legs. Kissing and stroking and licking her, first here, then over there, behind her knees, around her ankles, unpredictable and sensual as he slowly removed her panties with his teeth.

She lost her hands in his head of hair as he moved down her providing her with all of the appetizers. Each time she groaned or tugged at his hair, he thought, *Oh, that was a good spot, she liked that.* He had long ago discovered that the spots that were most sensitive for her were never in the same place as the time before, which meant he had a lot of ground to discover each time he made love to her. It only provided him with more excuses to explore her lovely body.

He then came up for the full course. They rolled and stroked and enticed one another. He was aware in the back of his mind of how hard he was and that he was holding on. *I'm getting better,* he thought.

He came back to delight in her now full breasts, stroking their soft curves with his hands. Up and around, he gently massaged them while he teased the beckoning taut nipples with his tongue. She groaned her pleasure, arching her back in delight, as they asked for more.

She stroked his back and moved her hands down to grab his buttocks, pulling him in closer, her legs wrapping around his. Then as she released him, she stroked her hands down his chest, repeatedly she moved closer to his member and then moved away, she teased him just as he teased her. They delighted in one another longer than they had in a long time. It felt good, like they were coming home.

"You witch," he growled into her ear, as he stroked around an ear with his tongue. Then over her breasts, taunting her nipples, before he moved down and around her navel and this time he came down on her. She moaned with pleasure as she writhed and stretched and arched under him.

It always amazed her how powerfully sensual those movements were. He loved that they could provoke such intense responses in each other. She arched again. "Oh yes, yes," she responded achingly to him. She couldn't hold it or wait for him, as she released a flood of tension. And he smiled.

As he came back up, she opened her eyes, her expression telling its own story. He held her eyes while he covered her mouth with his, and she let out a deep moan.

This time he penetrated and they pulsated together until she gave him that look that told him she was ready again and before she had a chance to hold it, she vibrated her release, and then looked up at him communicating her surprise. He had no problem with her coming before him. *Twice now, not bad,* he thought. They danced some more as her body stretched to hold the mounting tension, they reached the summit of their dance, and she released again just moments before he allowed himself to come. They both let go on a sigh of immense pleasure and fulfillment as they relaxed back to the bed.

Their breathing heavy, their bodies satiated, there was a moment of silence.

Finally she caught her breath, "Wow, we've been doing good lately," Maria said. "How many times in how many days?"

"Yeah, now that you are getting your energy back, so is our drive. We are just making up for all that lost time, when you had no energy. And you, my dear, came more than once, I believe."

"Yeah, I can't believe it. Three times. I thought for a moment, after the first time, that was going to be it but then it started to build again so fast. And then, to get a third one thrown in for good measure, man, you were great. And you held on for so long...wow!"

"Yes, I am pretty good," he beamed, "and I would like to take full credit, if you don't mind." He laughed.

"Yes, you can take full responsibility if you can make it happen again," she agreed then they lay there in silence for a few minutes.

She reached out and took his hand. "Have I told you how thankful I am that you were so understanding when I just wasn't available? I know how many times you wanted to do the bed dance when I just had no energy or desire for anything. And you never pressured me. Thank you."

"My heart just went out to you. You were always so full of life, and then overnight, you went from high energy to no energy. I am so happy that Pappy was able to help with all that. Are we going too fast now, too often? Will it impede your recovery?" Duncan suddenly sounded a little worried.

"Actually, I never thought of it. I should ask Pappy. Certainly making love always gets the adrenaline going. By the way, Dr. Jim phoned earlier and asked if Nanny Sarah and Pappy could join us tonight. I said of course, but I will also see if I can corner him and ask what effect sex has on the adrenals. He might say it's the best thing for them, just like they say making love is one of the best anti-depressants. Or maybe it depends on the stage of recovery?"

Duncan had helped the Gibson's design and build their clinic in return for all of the time and wisdom they had provided. When Duncan and Maria felt that they were getting more than they were giving, they gifted the clinic with donations. Over the years, Duncan and Maria had gifted their clinic with thousands of dollars. It was a good way to acknowledge the whole family for all the help, guidance, and instruction the family had so generously shared with them over the years.

Duncan and Maria appreciated the amount of money and time their educations had all cost them. They recognized that the entire Gibson family had dedicated themselves to the health and wellness of others and they each had a unique profession. The

Gibsons had never charged them and so in return for all the advice given they donated money several times a year.

The Gibsons were always grateful and the funds went to research, publishing books, and helping those less fortunate, who could not pay the full price of the services. It was a win-win situation.

"Okay let's move this dance to the shower, shall we?" Duncan suggested and Maria almost flew out of the bed as she raced him to the shower.

They quickly created their own desert in the shower, as they bathed, stroked, and washed one another. He loved to tickle her in the shower…it was both fun and sensual to watch her squirm and in the process her soft wet body moved against him. He could have made love to her all over again. His body was sure ready, but he wanted to be careful of her adrenals, plus they had company coming.

They got out of the shower and he decided he better not dry her off, as he was too ready to make love again. So he simply grabbed a towel and dried himself as he moved into the bedroom to get dressed.

Maria quickly brushed her hair and took a quick glance in the mirror. Everything was in place. She was spraying herself with the perfume Duncan had given her for Valentine's Day when Duncan asked if she was ready.

"Hours ago…oh I guess that was when you were having your way with me, okay so minutes ago," she laughed.

"Be careful, or I will take you again," he threatened as he laughed. Maria had always claimed that she never took as much time to get ready as most females. So she and Duncan had set up a competition between them years ago. Now if one was ready moments before the other, the first would claim that he/she had been ready for hours.

"You wish," Maria responded in fun.

"Actually, yeah, I do wish, but we have company coming." He acknowledged his body's readiness for another round.

Fourteen

Hugs Anyone?

"I have learned that there is more power in a good strong hug than in a thousand meaningful words."
Ann Hood

It was only 5:30, they still had time to go down and relax before people started to arrive. John was still in front of the movie, Jessie reading her book, and Jasmine had started to put her project things away.

"Looks like we have good timing?" Duncan whispered to Maria as they moved into the kitchen, noting where and what the kids were doing.

"I heard that," Jessie raised an eyebrow at them. "Don't think some of us don't know what was going on but your secret is safe with me. Steve phoned a little while ago, and I suggested he wait a bit before coming over, to give you more time."

"You didn't tell him what we were doing," Maria asked, embarrassed.

"Well, not exactly. But he might have figured it out. He is male, and twenty—and he's not stupid. On the other hand, I don't think his parents have done it for years, so I don't know. If he went by his parents, it might not have even occurred to him.

But he knows you guys are very different so who knows?" Jessie wasn't concerned.

Duncan didn't appear to care either but it bothered Maria to have someone know what they were up to privately. But she didn't have time to worry about it now as she needed to be in a good space, so she put it on the back burner. Maybe she would return to it later, or maybe not. After all, there was nothing she could do about it now and the company would arrive soon.

Uncle Dave was the first to show up. He simply knocked at the door and waltzed in, as did most of their extended families and close friends.

"Hi everyone, it's me. Anyone want to come and give me a hug? I am in desperate need lately as I don't get any at home anymore...although I didn't get a lot before either..." Dave struggled to make light humor out of his situation, and Maria admired him for it.

Duncan was the first to greet him and gave him a big hug. "I hope you don't want kisses to go with it," Duncan teased him, "because you're sure not going to get them from me."

"Maybe not from you but he can get a kiss from me." Jessie came out of the kitchen.

Duncan took Uncle Dave's platter of chicken wings and bottle of wine and gave him a nod of thanks.

"Hi, Uncle Dave, how are you doin'?" Jessie gave him a big hug and a kiss on the cheek.

"Hangin' in there. Getting better in the long run, I think, or perhaps I just want to hope."

"Well, you're looking great." Jasmine acknowledged him as she waltzed in and gave him another hug and a kiss on the cheek. "You know we all love you and will support you however we can."

Maria felt like she was going to cry. She was proud of her daughter and made a mental note to thank her for her thoughtfulness, later, in private. It was such an adult and sensitive thing for a 16 year to come out with and you could just tell how it came straight from the heart.

She was proud of her daughter but didn't want to say anything that would embarrass her.

"I must say, she's right, you are still a lady killer after all these years. But first is the time to heal before you go out on the prowl. And in the meantime, we are all here for you." Maria suggested.

The doorbell rang and the Gibsons walked in.

"Hey, everybody. Make way. All of us just arrived. Hi Dave, haven't seen you in a while." Dr. Jim greeted everyone.

Dr. Jim handed Maria a bottle of his homemade organic red wine and a huge jug of homemade Chai tea. His wife Julie brought a special coleslaw salad. Dr. Jim's mother, Nanny Sarah, the TCM doctor, brought a huge watermelon that she had cut in a fancy way, and her husband, Pappy, brought another bottle of herbal tincture for Maria plus a bouquet of flowers.

"Wow, look at all the gifts. I need to put on more of these dinners. Dave, why don't you get divorced more often?" As soon as the words were out of her mouth, Maria could have cut out her tongue. How could she have said such a thing? It was meant to be funny, but it was cruel.

Julie chimed in with, "That sounds awfully brotherly of you, Dave, but I was under the impression, Maria put on these dinners and barbecues and what not, pretty regularly. And in consideration of the fabulous job she does, perhaps once in a lifetime should suffice?" They all started to chuckle and the difficult moment passed.

Dave responded to the humor she had intended. "Well, I could. How often do you think? Every three years or maybe an annual program."

Maria sent an apologetic look Dave's way. He winked at her; he knew she meant no harm.

The doorbell rang and Jessie went to get the door hoping it was Steve, but the door opened by the time she got there and her Auntie Carol and Uncle George walked in with their teens. Tim nineteen, obviously no longer a kid, liked to hang out with Jessie and her crowd, so he still came to family functions. Their daughter Sherry at sixteen got along famously with Jasmine so she too still came to all the family events.

Carol brought a couple of her famous deserts. One was lemon custard with whipping cream folded into it and the other a chocolate mousse. No one ever tired of Carol's desserts.

Uncle George had a favourite bakery that made the most delicious sourdough buns. Uncle George knew the owner who apparently made his own sourdough starters to make different strengths and types of sourdough. George always asked for the extra strength sourdough with the potato starter and would buy several dozen at a time. Maria was pleased to see that he had brought his usual gift of buns. She made a mental note to ask if he could get the potato starter sourdough rather than the flour starter ones.

"And for my second favourite lady, here are your buns. Duncan, I hope, is still taking care of your other buns." And with his usual joke, he gave Maria a big bear hug.

Just as Maria reached to give her sister, Carol, a hug, the doorbell rang again. Jessie knew it had to be Steve and stepped by everyone to go and open the door.

Grandma Mary and Papa Johnny had heard the noise and came up to join the group. Grandma Mary brought a potato salad and Pappy Johnny brought a few bottles of his homemade wine.

The doorbell rang again and Jasmine looked at her watch – that would be Nick. She announced that she would get the door and made her way to let Nick in. Nick and Jessie were still shy in front of each other's families. Last night she had been with Nick's family and now it was her family. But it was her extended family and she was apprehensive as to whether anyone, especially her cousins, would give her a bad time. She wanted them to all like Nick, she just didn't want to get teased.

While the others came in and greeted each other, Jasmine told Sherry about Nick. The two had grown up pretty close, even though Sherry seemed a little obsessive compulsive to everyone else, she got along great with Jasmine. Jasmine asked Sherry to not tease and embarrass her in front of Nick and Sherry promised she wouldn't tease her. Sherry would have loved to have a boyfriend like Jasmine, but she didn't let anyone get to close.

Sherry had been seeing a psychologist for a year now to deal with her obsessive compulsive behaviour and she didn't want people to know. It made her feel inadequate to have to see a psychotherapist. Jasmine had always respected her issue, so she would return the favour to Jasmine.

Right on the heels of Nick, came Uncle Dan. Nick had just closed the door behind him, when Uncle Dan grabbed the door and said, "Hey, Nick. Hold the door for me. How are you doing? Good week at school?" Before he let Nick answer any of his questions, he turned to Jasmine. "How are the dance lessons going, kiddo? Has Nick learned how to fling you around in the air yet?"

Jasmine looked up at Nick. "Well, he hasn't flung me up anywhere yet, but we are working on a new choreographed piece together. It's really difficult but it's fun." Jasmine was usually the only one he let answer a question. They all figured it was because she reminded him so much of his Judy.

Uncle Dan was often at the house working on various projects with Duncan and had met Nick a number of times. Nick had also seen that Uncle Dan only ever let Jasmine answer his flood of questions. Nick had never asked why; he just figured that Jasmine must be his favourite.

Nick also didn't realize, and perhaps no one else did either, that now Nick and Jasmine reminded Dan of the young love that he and Judy had shared. But he would never tell anyone that. He was private with both his hurt and pain, as well as, with his thoughts.

Uncle Dan was always on the lookout for something to do. Uncle Dan, was Grandma Mary's older brother. He was another hard worker, but unlike Grandma Mary who knew how to sit back and let others take care of her in her old age, Uncle Dan just kept on going. He didn't like to just sit and be with his thoughts. He was always out in the garage, or his backyard, looking for something to fix. He was certainly no academic, but man, was he creative with his "handyman" abilities. Those "handyman" abilities were virtually a lost skill and art.

Uncle Dan had lost his wife, Judy, years ago. He seemed to have lost a part of his spirit, his sense of humor and his passion, when he lost her. Maria often wondered if he kept busy with improvement jobs and repair jobs as a way to cope with the loss of the love of his life. He had never dated anyone since he lost his wife.

For years he had lost his sense of humor and his passion for living but in the last little while he had changed. He seemed to enjoy life more again. He just didn't want to look for someone else to share it with. He was happy on his own. Maria thought that was too bad, he was such a good man.

His doctor claimed he had cholesterol issues and hypertension and so he took medications for both. Maria wanted to change that too. She knew how those drugs depleted vital nutrients in the body but she kept her mouth shut.

Maria had suggested that he go and see Dr. Jim's dad, Pappy. Pappy, the Medical Herbalist, who like the others in the family talked about what he called the "cholesterol myth". She knew Pappy could explain how he used herbal tinctures to clean the arteries of all the different kinds of plaque, not just cholesterol. But Maria didn't want to push.

Pappy claimed that inflammation was usually the cause of blocked arteries and high blood pressure, not cholesterol. He explained that only when one type of LDL cholesterol became oxidized that it caused a problem. He loved to explain that the inflammation in the arteries was usually due to a variety of different causes from AGEs to heavy metal toxins to environmental toxins.

It was from Pappy that Maria had learned about all the different kinds of HDL and all the different kinds of LDL. In addition, she had learned that the liver will produce more cholesterol to patch up a bleeding artery or vein so you didn't bleed to death. That cholesterol was an important compound in the body.

They all moved to the patio and Dan left his pot of chili on the stove on his way out.

"Wow, the whole crowd is here." Uncle Dan actually knew a lot about people but he learned about everyone while he listened to their conversations. He just didn't really engage in the conversation himself. Maria had often thought he asked questions to simply let you know he cared and that he did listen but he simply didn't like to converse. Judy had been the conversationalist in their relationship. Since she had died, he had developed this way of communicating.

He knew everyone well, including Jessie's boyfriend, Steve. Steve had been around longer than Nick, and Dan had seen a young clumsy kid grow into a good young man. He was also aware that Steve's dad was an alcoholic who put a lot of pressure on Steve to be perfect, perhaps to make up for himself.

Regardless of the relationship between Steve and his father, Steve was developing into a responsible, hardworking young man. Like Maria and Duncan, Uncle Dan was watching how the relationship between Jessie and Steve was developing. He thought they suited one another and wondered if it would last through university.

Duncan raised his voice to interrupt all the conversations and suggested that they all gather for a moment to give thanks and then they could bring the food and that good wine out and simply dig in.

The years of Sunday morning discussions allowed them to be aware of the vast range of philosophical, spiritual, and religious beliefs, so Duncan had developed a kind of interdenominational approach to giving thanks. Duncan and Maria believed that it didn't matter what your religious or spiritual beliefs might be, everyone should still give thanks for all that they had on a regular basis. Neither of them considered themselves to be religious but they both liked the concept of being spiritual.

"Mother, Father, God, Infinite Universe. Thank you for all that you have given us: family and friends to share our lives with, a shelter over our heads to give us protection, and food on the table to feed and nourish our bodies with. Please support us in all of our endeavours to reach our greater potentials and help others to do the same. At this time we ask that you bless this food to our bodies and help our bodies to use it wisely. So be it."

Maria loved the fact that they could give thanks despite all the different beliefs. She gave her own silent prayer of thanks that she had been so fortunate to have such a good husband, three wonderful children and the Gibson family as friends, never mind all the other good family and friends she was surrounded with.

"Okay, let's eat." The hot food was brought out, plates filled, wine was poured. People found their seats and the feast began.

Conversations flowed around economics and politics, psychology and physiology, and religion and philosophies.

As they continued to eat and drink and talk, some of the gang got up and started to clear the dinner food and empty plates, while others helped Carol bring out her lovely deserts—definitely not health conscious deserts but created for the palate alone. No one turned any of it down.

Fifteen

Choices are the Fundamentals of Life?

*"Life is 10% what happens to you and
90% what you choose to do with it."*
Charles R. Swindoll

Maria noticed that Dave had sat next to Dr. Jim. Dave had respectfully asked Dr. Jim, if he could ask him some questions or whether he needed to make an appointment. Dr. Jim had laughed and said, that it depended on both the question and the answer.

Maria knew she shouldn't eavesdrop but she really wanted to know what the questions were and what kind of perspective Dr. Jim would put on it, so that if she could, she could support her brother in a similar manner.

After all, the primary purpose of this was potluck was to support Dave, she justified. She also knew that Dr. Jim would probably not give him any advice per say but rather offer stories, like he did for her and Duncan, whenever they asked for psychological advice.

Dave explained that he had been married for twenty-five years and that his wife had been diagnosed with both bipolar by the psychiatrist and Borderline Personality Disorder by the psychologist. "I am sure you don't need me to tell you what kind of a roller coaster road that has made my life. I don't know what I would have done without the support of people like Maria and Duncan. The challenge is, the divorce seems even more difficult than the marriage."

Dr. Jim nodded and Dave continued. "I have no idea how to deal with Jean. She's in one of her chaotic places again and nothing seems to make sense. No matter how hard I try to be fair and reasonable, she isn't happy or appreciative or cooperative. My lawyer says I am giving way too much. Her lawyer is even frustrated with her because her story keeps changing. Is there some secret thing I don't know about that I could use to help her, to help me? Anything?"

Dr. Jim asked if she was ever fair, cooperative, and reasonable when she went through a chaotic episode.

"Point taken. So what do I do?"

"Have you ever seen a cornered rat?" Dr. Jim asked and Dave nodded his head. "How do they respond?"

"Viciously, chaotically."

"Have you ever seen a lion hunt its prey, say on TV?" Dr. Jim asked.

"Yeah, strategically." Dave responded cautiously. "Are you suggesting I am a lion and she is a rat?"

"No of course not," Dr. Jim said with a laugh. "What I am suggesting is that someone who knows how to move strategically and effectively operates very differently than someone who feels cornered and doesn't have a clue what to do, especially, if she is going through one of her episodes. You are in a sense "pulling the rug out from under her" and she might feel like a cornered rat. She's not going to take the time or have the presence of mind to be able to look at the situation objectively and see how she has caused the mess that she is in. She is simply going to react."

Dr. Jim paused to give Dave time to process the information. "There is an old saying, 'The road to hell is paved with good intentions.' When you have to deal with someone who functions like Joan, no matter how hard you try to come from a place of fair play, honor, and integrity, it just doesn't work. It won't work in her favour and it won't work in your favour. In fact, usually what you find is everybody loses, except the lawyers. Talk with your lawyer about it, he will know what I am talking about."

"So you are basically saying that it is a loose-loose situation?" Dave asked. Maria's heart sank.

"In the short term, yes. It is a matter of what you both end up doing with the situation that will turn it into a win situation for either of you or both of you. Remember, 'life is 10% what happens to you and 90% what you choose to do with it'."

"So what you are basically telling me is that there is nothing I can do to make this whole divorce process easier?"

"No, not really. What I am saying is there is nothing you can do about how Joan deals with the divorce process. You, on the other hand, can choose how you wish to deal with the divorce and with her. Set your intention. Know what you want to achieve. Don't let yourself get caught up in what she is doing with it because you can't change her."

Maria only needed to get enough of the conversation between Dr. Jim and Dave to know how she could support Dave accordingly. She had got what she needed and was about to remove her attention from their conversation, when Dave turned to her.

"I know you are listening, sis, was there something you wanted to say?"

"Was I that obvious? I just wanted to know Dr. Jim's perspective so I could support you in a similar manner. Sorry. I didn't really mean to be eavesdropping."

"Bull," Dave said with a laugh. "You wanted to know, you chose to listen, and you definitely meant to eavesdrop. But it's okay, I love you anyway and I know you just wanted to help. Now go away and let me ask some other things."

She got up and walked away but Duncan caught up with her and whispered in her ear. "What are you muttering about?"

"I was just eavesdropping on the conversation between Dr. Jim and Dave. Dave caught me on it and then told me to leave. I was just saying that I can't get away with anything." Maria nodded her head and smiled as she got up and went into the kitchen. "Geez, you can't get away with anything around here," she said to herself.

Duncan raised an eyebrow. "I thought the conversation you had with Dr. Jim a while back was about how to let go of trying to "take care of everyone and everything". Maybe this is a case in point? You set up the scenario so everyone could be here to support Dave, and I know he is your brother and you care a lot, but maybe this is where you let go and just allow things to unfold as they are meant to."

Duncan moved around in front of her to give her a quick kiss and a hug. He knew this stuff about boundaries and letting other people be responsible for their own happiness was difficult for Maria. She wanted the best for everyone and had a long history of struggling to make it happen. It was what made her a good real-estate agent and a good mother. But he knew it also drained her.

She returned his hug and kisses then tweaked his nipple with a grimace on her face. "Do you have to be so annoyingly right? Like I was just saying, 'you can't get away with anything around here'."

"Well the flip side of the coin, is…" Duncan paused for effect. "I never want you to stop taking care of me. If you know what I mean…" With a mischievous smile, he moved away from her, winking over his shoulder.

She started to laugh at his antics, "Do you ever quit?"

"Why would I, when I have a witch like you around to give pleasure too?"

Jasmine walked into the kitchen with an armload of dishes. "What are you guys laughing at?"

"Just a private joke," Duncan said and winked at Maria again. Duncan and Maria had always openly expressed their affection in the family with hugs and kisses. They just kept the more sexual aspects of their relationship private. So Jasmine, catching the wink, figured they had just taken a moment for a hug and a kiss and left it at that.

Duncan, on the other hand, wondered to himself if what he was eating could make him think more about sex than he had in forever. It wasn't like it had taken over his life or anything, it was just a lot more frequent and he definitely felt younger. Placebo effect or not, he enjoyed his body's reaction.

Sixteen

Prescriptions are Synthetic Toxins!

"Doctors give drugs of which they know little,
into bodies, of which they know less,
for disease of which they know nothing at all."
Voltaire

Outside, Jessie talked with Pappy about the doctor's report on her diabetes—blood sugar levels normal twice now and with no prescriptions. "What are the different herbs you use for people with Type I versus Type II diabetes?" she asked. When John walked by, she put an arm around him and pulled him into the conversation. "We have not only eliminated my diabetes—and as you know Mom has done great with her adrenals—but this morning we saw great success with John and his allergies. Go ahead John, tell Pappy what happened."

"I got a bee sting this morning and I didn't cry!" He announced. "And I didn't flare up and I didn't have to go to the hospital! Mom didn't even poke that pen into me!"

"Good job. Well done, son! I am proud of you. Now don't forget to keep that EpiPen® on hand, just in case something goes funny in your body but it looks like you have licked it. If you go see Dr. Jane, she might be able to reverse all those other allergies you have as well."

"You mean I'll be able to eat ice cream again?" John's eyes lit up.

"Well, hopefully, you will eat the good kind that Dr. Daniel makes. And if you are good, he might give you one of his recipes for homemade ice cream, which tastes pretty awesome. Then you and your mom can make some for the whole family."

"Are Dr. Jane and Dr. Daniel coming tonight?" John asked.

"No, not tonight. They were both already booked before we knew of the party tonight. But I am sure your Mom will have a conversation with them in the next week or so. She might have to make an appointment for you this time. They are both pretty busy at the clinic."

John raced into the kitchen to ask his mom if they could make an appointment at the clinic and get the recipe for ice cream. Maria and Duncan started to laugh all over again. "How often do children love to see a doctor?" Duncan mused.

Back outside, Jessie exclaimed, "Wow, you guys have the best medicine. I used to want to go into Western Medicine, but all they ever want to do is give you prescriptions that only manage symptoms. Why is it they don't have all the different types of training that your family has?"

"Good question, my dear. As you know there is a lot of greed in the world. And while I would like to think that most physicians entered Med School to learn how to help people, what they probably don't realize is that pharmaceutical companies design most of the medical curricula, or at least they write the protocols and procedures by which physicians have to abide. Even when physicians know that their patients don't get the desired effect or that people end up with worse problems and sometimes even die because of the medications, if they don't abide by the dictates given them they can be fined and or lose their licenses.

I can't imagine the moral dilemma that puts really good, observant, aware physicians in. They have to figure out a way to justify what they are doing or leave the profession, and of course, we find more and more do just that—they turn to other healing modalities or try to integrate different healing modalities.

I even know of physicians who move all the way across the board to the energetic healing modalities. That is really big when you consider the money they are willing to sacrifice, to go into a field that has so little support behind it in North America.

But pharmaceutical companies do not have any legal responsibility for your health. They do have a legal responsibility to their shareholders to make money. Consequently, despite the fact that there are numerous formulations and different healing methods that have been proven effective for most of today's illnesses, including cancer, they are not used, sold, or taught in western medicine. I have a colleague who spent a lot of money on a formula he designed for cancer. After he put the formula through rigorous clinical testing, he sold the formula to a pharmaceutical company. When he asked when they would see it on the shelf, he was basically told, not for years, they had too much stuff on the shelf already to sell.

Think about it—if you were cured, how would those companies make their money?"

"But that is both corrupt and obscene."

"Well, you are right. But that is typically how the world operates at the higher corporate levels."

"So why don't you guys go out and teach the world about *real* medicine?" Jessie pushed.

"Well, honey, these big companies have a lot of money. They make more money when you have to stay on drugs for years and years. If you have to add one prescription after another to manage symptoms caused by the prior drugs, they make even more money. As the drugs continue to deplete your body of vital nutrients, they then prescribe synthetic versions of the real compounds and guess what? They make even more money. Your health? Well, it continues to deteriorate and you end up with more and more symptoms. But because people don't like to take responsibility for their health, they are willing to foot the prescription bill. They have been taught that the MDs know everything and will take care of them, so they hand over billions of dollars a day to pharmacies to manage symptoms.

There is a famous quote by Voltaire that describes the situation well: 'Doctors give drugs of which they know little, into bodies, of which they know less, for disease of which they know nothing at all.'

In today's world, that is more apparent than ever, because physicians are not taught anything about the nutrients the body requires and what happens when the body doesn't get enough. Or how all the different types of metal, environmental, air, water, food, or hygiene and cleaning product toxicities affect the body, or what their compound effects are. They don't even know how their own synthetic medications deplete the body of nutrients, and if they do, they prescribe artificial synthetic supplements. It's crazy.

Think about it. Your body is already compromised for whatever reason, you go and take synthetic compounds that further deplete your body of nutrients it requires, and if all that weren't bad enough, you have to use the body's precious fuel, ATP, to convert the synthetic compound into something it may or may not be able to use.

Why not just give the body the *real* food, the *real* herbs, the combination formulas that supports the nutrients the body requires so the body can do what it needs to do. So much more logical.

Pharmaceutical companies have the money to market their drugs to the physicians and on television and unfortunately people, including MDs, are naïve enough to think that that is *real* medicine.

They prevent articles about *real* medicine being published in the major medical journals and then turn around and say that there is no clinical evidence. In fact, there is an overwhelming amount of evidence."

Jessie shook her head.

"We don't have that kind of money. And when you help people to eliminate the underlying cause of their problems, they don't have to come to see you for very long and then their money is spent on good food and herbs and natural things like good exercise, none of which we make money from. So *real* medicine practitioners don't make the money that physicians and pharmaceuticals do. But we continue to work at it. Each of us make our own contributions to society in the best way we can."

Jessie reflected for a minute. "If I didn't go into western medicine and I really don't want to just prescribe prescriptions that manage symptoms, deplete the body, and make money for pharmaceutical companies, like you said, what would you suggest I do? Everyone in your family has degrees and designations in so many different healing modalities. Which is the best one?"

"Well, my dear that is a whole different discussion. I don't believe that any one healing modality is better than another. Even western medicine has its place. If you broke your ankle, for instance, you would be wise to go to the hospital and have it set correctly. It's in all the chronic disorders that western medicine fails so miserably. And unfortunately, that is what most people go to the MD for.

Think about it. People have survived in India for thousands of years with Ayurvedic medicine, the oldest healing modality known to mankind, and a beautiful one at that. Personally, it is my favourite. But they interpret the body and foods and herbs in an entirely different way than Traditional Chinese medicine or western medicine does. In fact, we may find ourselves coming back to it in a big way. It is all based on the energetic sciences and so now that we are in the world of quantum physics, and as we struggle to understand energy, we may come back around to Ayurvedic medicine in our near future.

Then there is Traditional Chinese medicine, believed by many to have evolved from Ayurvedic medicine. Ayurvedic had all the acupuncture meridians and points long before the Buddhist monks brought it into China. In India, they were called Marma points rather than acupuncture points. They used Marma points for both local and generalized anesthesia, without the harm that modern chemical anesthesia causes.

Chinese Medicine is based on the Qi, Yin, and Yang, which parallel the Ayurvedic Vata, Pitta, and Kapha. While they do have their differences, there are more similarities than differences.

And both nations had a long history of herbal medicines, as did the Egyptians and the Africans and various other groups. Some were much more effective than others but that was probably more a function of how effective the individual practitioner was rather than the understanding behind the herbs and foods, just like today.

Whether you believe in one creation belief or another, and there are many around the world, or in one of the many evolutionary theories, or if you believe in a multitude of pre-civilizations prior to ours; it really doesn't matter when it comes to healing, ultimately man and nature are hugely interlinked. We should live with respect of the environment that supports our bodies with phytonutrients, minerals, vitamins, fibre, etc. What many people don't know is that western pharmaceutical medicine tries to replicate the medicinal compounds found in these herbs and in foods from around the world. They can't use the real thing, because they are not allowed to patent the real thing and consequently, can't make their money on it. But ultimately, they use what they find in medicinal herbs and foods as the basis for the synthetic compounds they make.

The biological science departments take a plant or food and profile it for all the compounds it has to protect itself, provide its own nutrients, and do all the functioning it needs to do to grow and thrive. Once they have identified one compound as the "active compound", meaning that they think it is the one that is most medicinal, then pharmaceutical companies come along and take over the research. They isolate that one compound, attempt to synthesize it, patent it and mix it with stabilizers that are usually toxic, and give it to the body claiming that the prescription pill helps the body better than anything natural.

Now, you are a smart gal so tell me, wherever in the biological field or the chemistry field does one compound act in isolation? You know that we are a dynamic complex of molecules, compounds, cellular structures, tissues, organs, and systems, and nothing works in isolation. Why would any intelligent mind think that you could take one natural compound, isolate it from everything it normally interacts with, and then do further damage by synthesizing it, and expect that it would have the same impact or better impact that the natural compound when it is operating in its natural environment, working in conjunction with all of the compounds that it is used to interacting with? And what is worse? Everyone, including the physicians, has bought into this bizarre reasoning. It is like no one even bothers to think it through.

I use a couple of good analogies with my clients. One of them is the government. There are three levels: The national level, the provincial or state level, and the municipal level. In each level we have the leader and a governing council like the senate, then we have all the leaders of the different departments whether they be judicial, health, educational, military, intelligence, financial, etc. at higher levels or whether in parks, sewage maintenance, roads, development, licencing, at lower levels. Then there are various kinds of employees doing the front-end work. There are literally millions of people working for the government and all supposedly communicating to some degree with each other. We will leave the validity or effectiveness of that communication alone for the minute. If you had to choose just one person to be the "active participant" whom would you choose?

It would be ridiculous to think that you could do that and yet, that is what they are, in effect, doing when they decide that just one compound is the active ingredient. That one compound interacts within a huge complex of other compounds. But that isn't taken into consideration. And then of course, they further abuse the whole process by trying to synthesize the compound. It takes real narcissistic thinking to think that man can do better than nature. What a joke!"

Jessie couldn't argue with him. He had good logic.

"Can you tell that I am passionate about this topic?" Pappy asked, as he paused to take a breath.

"Pappy, can you give some examples of how pharmaceutical companies took a single compound from a plant and synthesized it into a drug?"

"Sure. Commonly known ones are aspirin, which came from willow bark; digoxin, which came from foxglove, and morphine came from poppies."

"But those drugs work, don't they?"

"Sure, sometimes and for some things. But let's take a closer look. Let's take aspirin versus white willow bark as an example. Aspirin works faster; willow bark works longer. Willow bark doesn't cause stomach bleeding; aspirin does. Willow bark can be taken over the long term; aspirin cannot. Aspirin depletes Vitamins B9 & C, minerals like magnesium, potassium, sodium and iron, plus important healing compounds like glutathione, whereas willow bark provides you with Vitamin C, flavones and glycosides, which are all terrifically beneficial."

"Wow. I wish I knew all this stuff."

Pappy had provided her with a lot to think about but still hadn't answered her question. Which was the best healing modality to study?

"Are there any other healing modalities I should consider?"

"Well, we haven't even got into the more psychological therapies or the more energetic modalities like Reiki and Theta and a number of others. Each one has its own place. Different people will respond differently to different modalities. Their response will depend on a combination of things such as their psyche and their body functions, their level of awareness, and their spiritual development. I always suggest to my students, when I teach, that they should study a given field and then go into something completely different and study another modality. When you choose to learn this way, it teaches an individual to develop his or her capacity to see things from more than one perspective. For example, you might want to start with acupuncture, then go into psychology then go into herbal medicine.

Personally, I prefer modalities that are more adept at integrating the psyche and the physiology. Western medicine is bad for that. They separate out the mind and body and then they take reductionist thinking even further when they study physiological functioning.

Think about psychologists. They take ten years of psychology but nowhere in those ten years do they study what nutrients the brain requires to function effectively. They believe that the brain is the number one organ in the body, that it controls all other functions. But do they study the gut and how powerful the gut is and that the microbiota in the gut can alter thoughts, emotions, and behaviour? There is actually a two way communication process between the gut and the brain.

Or do they study the liver and how the liver is required to make all kinds of compounds that the brain requires? I could go on and on with this but you get the idea.

They take their training and then say, if the MD has not identified a physiological cause than it has to be a psychological issue. But the MD doesn't have any training on the nutrients the brain requires or the nutrients that other systems require to support the brain, nor does he or she have a clue about nutrient deficiencies, or toxins, or heavy metals, so how would he know?"

Jessie smiled and nodded in agreement.

"Even the physicians' primary journal has articles about physicians being decades behind the actual science. And yet, psychologists are dependent on these physicians who don't have the proper training. Where does that leave the psychologist?

Psychiatrists are even worse. They take their med school and then a couple years of psychiatric residency to prescribe drugs like anti-depressants, which are based on the theory that low levels of serotonin cause depression. How many of them actually look at the clinical studies, the design and the analysis, and question why there is no test that they can give to their clients to determine if serotonin levels are low? Or conversely, really understand the design and analysis of the studies and realize that low serotonin levels have never actually been proven to cause depression, neither has the regulation of serotonin ever been proven to eliminate depression. They don't do their research to recognize that serotonin-based anti-depressants work for about 12-18% of the population and yet the placebo effect is between 32-38%. They don't seem to realize that the anti-anxiety drugs they are prescribing are actually anti-psychotic drugs. The whole thing is very questionable, to put it politely.

Now, let's take it a step further. They haven't even figured out if the mind is the same as or part of the brain, or in the energetic field around the brain, or whether it is a matter of the "sum is greater than the whole". They really haven't a clue what they are talking about, which is why Ayurvedic medical practitioners in India think that western psychology is in

118

kindergarten. The whole thing is a hoot, or just really sad. It all depends on how you look at it.

Ultimately, you have to go with your heart. What modality touches you? Start there, and just keep going."

"Thank you, Pappy. I must admit you always give me so much to think about. The only thing I know for sure right now is that I still don't know where I want to start and or where I want to end but I have a lot more to play with." With that she got up and gave him a hug. "I need to give my mind a rest. I think I will go find Steve."

Seventeen

Forgiveness versus Acceptance

"Acceptance and tolerance and forgiveness,
those are life-altering lessons."
Jessica Lange

"I feel so guilty leaving her," Dave said to Dr. Jim. "I know lots of people think I was crazy to stay so long but when she is in a good place she is so loving and affectionate and can be so much fun. But when she goes off her meds, whether it's because she hates being on them or whether it's because she has already gone into one of her episodes, or whatever, all hell breaks loose. It is like having a lifetime pass for tours through hell. I just can't do it anymore."

"What made you decide you couldn't do it anymore?"

"I don't know…maybe it was because this last time I almost lost my best friend because of her nonsense. Or maybe it's because I am so tired of making excuses for her. I could come up with all kinds of different explanations like that, but I think the real reason is the last time I told her if she chose to go off her drugs again without bothering to tell me and getting a health practitioner of some sort to monitor her, it was over. I asked her if she understood that I meant it. No matter how much I loved her, I would leave. She said she understood but she went and did

120

it again. So to be honourable to myself, to respect me, I had to walk away."

"So in other words, you gave her a choice, she made a decision, and now you have to honour that decision?" Dr. Jim asked.

"Well, yeah," Dave agreed and then paused. "I never looked at it that way but I like the sound of that logic. It makes it easier for me to stand by what I said and did. But the phone calls and the emails and the letters just keep coming. She constantly shows up wherever I am and begs me or threatens me to come back. Or she challenges me by saying, 'if you were really a spiritual person, you should be able to forgive me and come back'. I never know what to do with that."

"OK, Dave, we could do some therapy at this point or I could tell you one of my stories or we could philosophize and try to understand forgiveness.

From my perspective, forgiveness is a vertical thing—yeah, I see your expression. Just follow me here. You can't really forgive another person, unless you think you are God or some other entity that has the right to sit in judgement over them. You are one soul, if you will; you are on your journey alongside of all kinds of other souls. All the souls make choices and decisions about how to live, learn, and reach their highest potential.

Consequently, rather than sit in judgement of your wife, you need to accept her as having the right to make the choices she chooses, whether consciously or unconsciously. That is a horizontal process, between you and Joan. That is about acceptance.

But forgiveness, that is between you and God, or you and your higher self, or you and your soul; whatever it is you believe in. That is different from acceptance.

You chose to get involved with Joan; you chose to marry Joan; you chose to continue to live with Joan; you chose to leave Joan. Those are your choices. Along with your choices comes responsibility for those choices. Likewise, Joan has her responsibilities. Now, there are three things you can do with your choices: You can choose to forgive yourself for your choices; you can choose to learn from your choices, or you can choose to let your choices bury you. It is up to you what you choose to do with your choices. Does that make sense?"

"When you put it like that, it does."

"And now for the story...I don't know if you are a Christian or not and it really doesn't matter but you might remember hearing this story from the New Testament. A group of men brought a woman to Christ, ready to stone her because she had been caught in an affair. According to the Old Testament, they should stone her—we won't get into why they would stone her versus the man she had an affair with. We'll leave that for another time. But the point is they challenged Christ as to what they should do with her. The short version is that he told them, "He who is without sin among you, let him cast the first stone at her."

One by one, the men left because none of them was without sin. Okay, good story so far. But the best part is what Christ told the woman. "Go and sin no more." I wish that he had said something slightly different but suffice to say, she needed to take responsibility for what she had done; learn from what she had done, and not do it anymore. That is part of self-forgiveness. It is about the self, within the self.

So what is self-forgiveness? It is about accepting that you have made choices and you are responsible for those choices, understanding why you made those choices; correcting them if need be; maybe compensating for the harm you may have caused others; resolving them if need be, and changing how you interpret and respond to the world so you don't continue to make the same mistakes. It's about understanding the need you had to draw that mistake into your life because of the lesson it held within it and making sure you learn the lesson.

You could say all of this is between you and God or the universe, or between you and your higher self, or your soul, or your subconscious, or whatever it is that you chose to believe in. But this is what I mean about the vertical process. Forgiveness is between you and something higher that allows you to develop, grow, and reach your greater potential. Because I believe there are higher aspects to us, I see that as vertical."

"Wow, I've never heard that before. Do you about talk about this stuff at the Sunday morning breakfast sessions at Duncan and Maria's?"

"Yes, we have. But there is a huge broad range of topics that get discussed there. You would do well to come more often. They can sure get a good group going."

"I hear you, and I might just do that. But you said that you wished Christ had something different. What would you have had him say?"

"Simply, 'Forgive thyself and go sin no more'."

"Thank you so much for that. I really appreciate it. As always, you give me lots to think about. I recently found out that I have Hep C and I had thought that maybe it was my karma because I had divorced Joan. Now I have to let Joan go and figure out why I got the Hep C."

"How did you get Hep C?"

"I probably got it years ago when I went in for an operation on my knee, a football accident. But I only found out recently."

"My pleasure for the talk, but go and make an appointment with my daughter, Jane, she will be able to help you with the Hep C.

And remember, Karma doesn't mean an eye for an eye; or a tooth for a tooth; or what goes around comes around. That is all very Old Testament, linear thinking. Karma simply means that for every action there is a reaction. Anyone one event can have a multitude of reactions. Which is why good things can happen to bad people and bad things can happen to good people."

Eighteen

Family Secrets

"All families have their secrets, most people would never know them, but they know there are spaces, gaps where the answers should be, where someone should have sat, where someone used to be. A name that is never uttered, or uttered just once and never again. We all have our secrets."
Cecelia Ahern, The Book of Tomorrow

"Hi Nick, can I steal your girlfriend away for a moment?" Jasmine was talking with Nick when Julie came over to talk with her.

"Sure Mrs. Gibson. I was just going to go and get us something to drink. Can I get anything for you?"

"That sounds great, Nick. How about a cup of green tea? Thanks." She winked at Jasmine. "That might hold him off while I talk with you. How is your asthma doing?"

"Thank you for asking. I have been doing the different exercises you taught me to do and I still take the tincture that Pappy gave me, but he said I needed it for only one more month. Dr. Jane said I didn't have to take her pills anymore because I am now making lots of that glutathione stuff.

I haven't had an attack in ages. But I still do all my dance routine, yoga with Mom and Dad, and other sports at school. Most times I forget to even be afraid of an attack any more. When I first got diagnosed with the sports-induced asthma, I was afraid I wouldn't be able to continue dancing and the doctor wanted to put me on various short-term and long-term meds. I am so glad Mom let me come to you guys instead. Please don't tell Nick. I don't want him to know or worry, or anything, especially now that it seems to have gone away."

"Don't worry, Jasmine, your secret is safe with me. Keep up the good work. I loved your last dance performance and can't wait to see the next one."

"Yeah, I'm really excited about it. Nick and I are practicing a new routine, and it is pretty awesome."

As if on cue, Nick came out with three cups of tea. "This is the green tea, Mrs. Gibson. Here is your chai, Jasmine and I get the mint."

"Thanks, Nick. I want to go over and talk with Carol so I will leave you two alone," Julie said. She got up and gave Jasmine a quick hug and turned to Nick. "Looking forward to your next performance with Jasmine, Nick."

Nick just smiled then turned to Jasmine. "Your neighbours go and watch your dance performances?" Only his parents ever came to his.

"Oh yeah," Jasmine said. "Everybody comes. My family, my grandparents, Auntie Carol's family, Uncle Dan and Uncle Dave, and the Gibsons. Just a little pressure."

Nick just shook his head. This family really was different from his. His parents came to see his performances and that was it.

Nineteen

It's All About Eating

"To eat is a necessity,
but to eat intelligently is an art!"
François de la Rochefoucauld (1613 – 1680, writer)

Carol was talking with Nanny Sarah about using acupuncture to help her weight issue when Julie approached them.

"I never knew that you could use acupuncture to help you lose weight." Carol looked up at Julie and invited her to sit with her and Nanny Sarah.

"Yes, you can. In fact, there are all kinds of things you can do to help yourself manage your weight effectively because there are so many causes of weight imbalance in the body," Julie explained.

Julie raised an eyebrow at Nanny Sarah for confirmation, which she got. Nanny Sarah went on, "If you talk with my husband, you would learn about the underlying psychological beliefs, value systems, and coping mechanisms that play into weight issues, and how the different types of psychological, cognitive, and emotional stressors are huge because of what they do to the adrenals.

If you talk with my daughter, Jane, she would work with things like glutathione, toxicities, nutrient deficiencies, the gut microbiota, and a host of other things that effect metabolism and weight.

If you talk with my son, Daniel, he would focus more on your diet and again how to eliminate the toxins and improve the nutrient balance. He would work with different metabolisms and what kind of food your body needs and or should avoid. Let's see," she paused for a moment. "If you talk with Pappy, he would provide you with herbal concoctions that would support your adrenals, help break down fat cells, increase your metabolism, and more. If you went to someone who worked with Ayurvedic medicine, they would focus on what you needed to build up your nutrient profile, then detox you, then rebuild you again.

Julie would help you with movement. Movement allows the body to bring in more oxygen, release more carbon dioxide, move nutrients through the body to where they need to be, and move toxins out of the body. It helps with elimination, muscle and bone metabolism, and a host of other things. Movement is so important, and becoming more and more important in today's world as more and more people work sitting at a desk or a computer all day.

I, as you probably already heard, would help increase the flow of energy in your acupuncture meridians so that they move energy faster to support all the different aspects and functions in the body. There are so many components that can play into weight issues but many people still focus on ridiculous things like counting calories. You might want to consider an appointment with Jane, as she can give your body an overhaul using the ASYRA. With that piece of equipment, she can assess thousands of variables in the body in just minutes. I looked into the science behind that device and was pretty impressed. I now send most of my clients to her to get an overview. She can even assess for vertical alignment. Many of my clients who come in because of accidents and what not, end up becoming her clients as well."

"Your family is such a treasure," Carol said finally. "I don't know what we all would have done without you. Thank you for the summary, I guess I will make that appointment, first thing Monday morning."

"How are you doing, Nanny Sarah. Still going strong?" Julie asked Jim's mother.

"Absolutely, and having a great time talking with everybody tonight. Thanks for including us."

And with that, Julie moved on.

Twenty

Let the Games Begin

"Sometimes fun is just being together."
Wes Fessler

The desserts had been put out and everyone commented on the watermelon. It was a work of art. Nanny Sarah, came over and whispered in Maria's ear. "Make sure you eat watermelon every day. It will be good for both you and Duncan."

"Thanks for that Nanny Sarah, but how?"

"Don't worry about that just now, just do it." She walked away. Maria made a mental note and continued to put out coffee and tea. Jasmine and Carol sliced and scooped up dessert for everyone.

Duncan pulled out the game of Rumoli and three decks of cards. The boys pulled the tables together and set up the game.

They bet with pennies, and the Smiths had jars full of pennies. Maria had always thought that it was a great way to show the children how to have fun without intense competition. There was plenty of space for competition in other arenas of life. But she believed that people should be able to have arenas in their life where fun was more important than competition. Pennies really didn't carry any weight, so whether you lost or won didn't matter, and people could focus on the fun.

Jessie brought out bowls for everyone to keep their pennies in; Jasmine and Nick and John went and brought out the jars of pennies. Everyone found a seat around the table. Uncle Dan started to shuffle the cards and announced, "Let the games begin."

Steve had always loved to play games with Jessie's family. There was usually a little bit of alcohol around but nothing like his family saw, and no one ever got drunk.

Nick had also learned to enjoy these family games with Jasmine's family. His family didn't have the issues with alcohol, like Steve's family, but his parents argued a lot. They never played games together. He had seen Jasmine's parents argue once, and it was quiet and logical, they didn't shout or threaten or call each other names. In fact, the only reason he knew it was an argument was because he heard Mrs. Smith say that she was glad they had resolved the argument. He wished his parents knew how to argue that way. His parents grew loud and swore and threatened things. His mom usually ended up in tears and his Dad often stomped out the door, without bothering to say where he was going or when, or if, he was coming back. It had recently become a habit for Nick to leave home and go see Jasmine every time his parents started to argue.

Nick had thought all families operated the way his family did, until he started to spend time with Jasmine's family. He hoped if he ever got married that he would know how to create a relationship like her parents had. He watched how the parents interacted and how the siblings rarely argued and bickered and thought how nice it was that Jasmine rarely had issues with her brother or sister. He guessed they learned from their parents how to get along.

Tim and Sherry had learned how to play the game when they were about John's age and had always had a lot of fun with it. It was part of why they continued to come to the family dues even though they were older and usually wanted to go out with their own friends.

All serious talk of health issues went out the window, once the game began. Instead, the patio was filled with laughter and teasing. Around the Rumoli table, everyone could make jokes about everyone else, their health, their relationships, their problems, and everyone knew it was all done with love. Nobody ever got hurt. It was a great way to learn how not to take yourself so seriously, how to laugh at yourself and be more authentic than ever.

It was 2:30 in the morning before people started to leave. Nick had phoned home and asked if he could stay overnight and sleep over in John's room and after talking with Maria, his parents agreed.

Steve didn't need to phone home for permission but he phoned home to make sure his Mom was okay and to see how drunk his father was. His Mom claimed that his Dad had passed out on the couch a few hours before and she was ready for bed. Steve told her he would be home much later. She was secretly very appreciative of the Smith family. They were there for her son and provided him with the family life she wished she could have provided for him.

Pappy was the first to give in to yawns, which was not bad for an old man, he claimed. He put his arm around Nanny Sarah and asked if she had won enough to take him home.

Once again, hugs and kisses were exchanged. Tim and Sherry, Jessie and Steve, Jasmine and Nick had decided they would all go play miniature golf the following day. Jasmine had seen an expression cross John's face and she knew that he felt left out so she pulled him into a hug and told him that he could come, too.

After everyone was gone, John said his goodnights and the girls asked whether the clean-up was tonight or tomorrow. Duncan told them and Maria to leave the mess for morning. They could all dig in and help when they were awake. Right now, he just wanted to go to bed.

Nobody argued. The girls went off to their rooms and Maria followed Duncan up to their room where they let their clothes fall on the floor and fell into bed naked.

"That was a good night," Duncan murmured. "Thank you for pulling it all together. And if you want to talk about it and what everyone said and did and was or whatever, it is going to have to wait until morning because I will be out in a minute or two."

Maria had no intention of talking about anything. She slid between the sheets, rolled into his arms, rested her head on his chest, and bet him that she would fall asleep first.

Twenty-one

Loving is About Giving More Than You Take

"You can give without loving,
but you cannot love without giving."
Amy Carmichael

At 7:30 Duncan awoke. He lay still and watched Maria sleep. They were in their usual positions with their legs entwined. She had one hand under her pillow and the other hand lay on the bed between them. He loved how peaceful she looked. He was so thankful that he had such a great wife.

They had met in university through mutual friends. He was in an engineering program and she was in an architectural program. Before either of them finished their respective programs, they both realized that they didn't want to spend the rest of their lives doing what they were studying to do. Maria had decided she would rather sell houses than create their architecture. She was too much a people person to sit behind a desk and draw floor plans.

Duncan decided he wanted to build houses for families to live in, not bridges.

Their relationship grew strong over time. Perhaps because they felt like it was them against the world, or maybe it was just them against their parents. Both of their parents were adamant that they had to finish university. But, they both left university to look for careers for which they each had a passion.

That was some twenty-five years ago, maybe even more. They still had a keen relationship and were still in love with one another. They enjoyed one another rather than suffered one another, as they knew many couples did. They had three great children and a good network of family and friends as last night revealed.

And here he was, on a beautiful Sunday morning, with his dream gal slowly waking up in his arms. He knew he had been blessed and he sent up a prayer of gratitude to the universe.

"Good morning, sweetheart. How are you doing this morning?" Maria asked him as she stretched and then snuggled back into his arms.

"Feeling warm and cosy and lazy this morning. Just want to lie here for a bit and snuggle with my best gal."

"Oooohhhh, that sounds so good." Maria rearranged herself, so as not to breathe on him with her morning breath. She entwined her legs with his and gently stroked his chest.

"I know what you are doing," Duncan said. "Why don't we jump up and brush our teeth and then snuggle back in again?" Before he could finish, Maria jumped out of bed to race him to the bathroom.

"Great idea," she threw over her shoulder, only to find him right behind her. He kissed her on top of her head, swatted her behind and moved ahead of her. Laughingly he claimed first place in the race to the ensuite.

After they brushed their teeth she reached up for a kiss with a nice minty mouth, he returned a quick kiss but broke it off so he could race her back to bed.

"I won again," he declared. "You are just tooooo slow, my love. What's my prize for winning, not once, but twice, on this fine morning?"

"I will have to think about that. But this is unusual, usually you are up and exercising with the daylight. Not that I am complaining. But I am curious," Maria questioned as she snuggled in.

"Last night I had a dream that I couldn't find you. It had something to do with those adrenals of yours and I realized how much I needed you and loved you and how we spend so much of our lives looking after everyone else—our kids, our families, our friends. How often do we take the time to just be? In the last few days, we have taken lots of time to make love, which is great." He paused and winked before carrying on. "But how often do we get to just be together without needing to do anything else?"

"I love how you think. I was thinking along the same lines when we were all sitting around the table playing Rumoli last night. I loved how everyone was having so much fun, not really caring who won, laughing and teasing each other, and it occurred to me that as much as I need to take time for myself to just be, I also wanted us to take more time together and here my wish is already granted."

Duncan waited for a moment and then asked, "Do you have any plans for the day? Anything in particular you would like to do?"

"What would I like to do? Just us for the day?"

"We already cancelled our community breakfast this morning because of last night. The kids can help clean everything up and then they are basically organized for the day." He wanted time for just the two of them, not the whole family. "They are taking John with them, so the day is free for us to plan something just for us."

"Hmmm, I can't think of anything off the top, but give me the morning and I will let you know. Unless you have already thought this through and have some ideas of your own. What you would like to do?"

Duncan turned on his side again so he could look at Maria as their legs just naturally found their places again. "What about a trip up into the mountains, like we used to do? It is a glorious day, and the weather is good. The snow will be gone. We can take a picnic and find a spot to just enjoy the open air and the quiet freedom of being in the mountains."

"Well, well, aren't you becoming the romantic one? I love it." She paused going through the organization of it in her head. "If you want, I can help the kids arrange leftovers for lunch, make us a picnic, take a bottle of wine and leave around 10:30. That way we almost do get a day of it."

"Perfect. Do you know where the picnic backpack is stored?" Duncan asked.

She told him then added, "When you bring it up, bring up a bottle of wine and put the ice packs in the fridge freezer. I will take some of the left over sourdough buns and make some deli sandwiches, pack in some oysters and cheeses and maybe some of the pickles we did last summer. How does that sound?"

Duncan started to laugh. "Sure doesn't take us long to whip up a romantic interlude. I guess we're not so old after all."

"And who suggested that we were old?" she bantered.

He slid a hand under the sheets and searched for a breast to caress. He stroked a finger around the curve he found.

"Hey mister, those are my girls." She looked at him from beneath lowered eyelids. "I think if you get to play with my girls, I should be able to play with the boys." She reached under the sheets to return the favours. She raised her eyebrows and smiled, as she reached up for a kiss. As they locked together, he wrapped an arm around her and pulled her to him and then stopped.

"Hold on a minute." He slowed down the dance. "Last night you came three times, right?"

She smiled. "Why?"

"I want you to lie back and simply enjoy. Let's see how many times we can get your body to respond. You said last night that Pappy said sex wasn't a problem, so let's try a little experiment."

Her eyes twinkled. "You really think I can just lie here and let you have your way with me? I thought you asked for the prize for beating me in the bathroom race?"

"We will find another time for me. This time let's just see how a fine dude like myself can service his favourite lady?"

"I think I would really enjoy seeing how a fine dude like yourself, could service his favourite lady...I just don't know if the lady could keep her wandering hands away from the dude's sexy body."

"Try," was all he said.

He rolled Maria over onto her front as she wondered what he was about to do. He gently massaged her shoulders and neck.

"Oh, that feels good. Don't stop."

After a bit, he traced his fingers down her back, and wrote, "I love you" across her back with his fingertip. "I got that," she smiled. "And I do love the treatment so far, and I think I am in love with the dude giving me the treatment."

"You better be, you witch." And he bent down to give her a kiss on the neck.

When his hands got to her waist, he moved them under her belly and stroked gently down to see how wet and responsive she was.

"Ohhhhh, umhum," came the groan he was anticipating.

"You only *think* you love this dude? I am going to have to prove to you how much you love the dude." He continued to trail his fingers back around her sides and down her back to massage her buttocks.

"Yup, that feels so good," she acknowledged.

He stroked, massaged and moved his lips along the backs of her legs, provoking sighs and groans along the way. He rolled her over and stretched back up to her belly again, just to tease her insides and found what he was looking for. He sought her mouth with his and as much as he commanded her not to reach out to him with her hands, she sure knew how to compensate with her tongue.

He found her breasts and traced their curves. He rubbed a thumb against one of her erect nipples that begged for his attention. He mouth eventually left her mouth and followed the trail his hands had taken. He kissed and sucked his way down to a breast, took a nipple in his mouth and gently stroked it with his tongue.

He repositioned himself so that he could continue to taunt one nipple with his wet tongue while he stroked the curves of her other breast and allowed his other hand to follow the curves of her side and her belly down further until he found her wetness again.

His mouth returned to explore hers, as he stroked her with his fingers, felt her body raise and arch against his. He moved back down to taste and tease the other nipple, and then slowly, ever so slowly, he came down on her.

When she started to arch and stretch with the tension he knew she was about to come and he came back up to take her groans into his mouth and let his fingers continue to bring her to the edge. As she released, she looked up at him with all that she felt. And her eyes told him all he wanted to know.

"Let's see how many times you can come," he whispered. He was so hard, yet felt like he could hold on, and he wanted her to be able to come and come.

She stretched her arms down to return some of the favour but he caught what she was doing and took her arms, spreading them out on either side of her as he continued to taunt and tease her breasts. Her nipples stood up for him, begging for his attention.

"This is your time, just lie back and receive," he guided her.

This time when he moved down her body, he moved right down to her feet. He slid his tongue between her toes, looking up to see what kind of a response he would get. She squirmed and laughed.

"Don't you like your toes being massaged?" he asked innocently.

"Well yes, but that just tickles. A good way to destroy all of your other wanton efforts."

"That may be so, but I love the way your body moves when I tickle you. Such a sexy picture."

"Okay, you devil, you may enjoy watching my naked body squirm but now you are going to have to start all over again." She tried to sound like she was complaining but it was difficult when he serviced her so well and her body ached with the tension of it all.

"Well, okay then, I am just going to have to come up and have my way with you."

"You can do whatever you want with my body. I am all yours."

He was on a mission. He wanted to see how much pleasure he could give her. He could feel the tension build as he enticed every inch of her body. She stretched and braced herself and then spread her legs farther apart to invite him in.

And there it was again, another wave. *This is good*, he thought, *but how long can I go without coming myself.*

He stretched out over her and drew his hands up behind her. "Am I allowed to respond now?" she asked breathlessly. She wanted to touch and stroke and grab him, and he nodded as he touched her lips with his.

She wrapped her arms and legs around him and reached up to respond to his passionate kiss. "I love you so much," she groaned.

"I love you even more," he growled back. And they both came with a huge release.

Then they collapsed and lay there breathing. They could feel each other's heart beat next to their own. It was great. In fact, it was more than great. They continued to gaze into one another's eyes. They communicated their love, their trust, their oneness, until their breathing slowed to a gentle rhythm.

"What made you decide to do that?" Maria asked.

"I don't know. Between seeing you lying here so innocently this morning and having that dream last night and knowing how much you give to me and everyone else, it just seemed as though you deserved some extra special attention."

"Well, I think you just totally wore me out. Wow! I feel alive and exhausted at the same time. That was a pretty awesome performance but I don't know if I have any energy left to do anything."

"Let's just lie here and enjoy the moment." They lay spread out on the bed, just breathing. Her body had never felt so satiated. She turned her head to look up at him. He had the most loving look in his eyes as he gazed down at her. She was too spent to even reach up for a kiss. So the two of them just continued to lie there.

Sometime later, "Want to have a shower?" they asked in unison. "I guess so," they both responded. With a laugh they got up and moved to the shower.

"Geez, what a mess we left last night," Maria observed. "Clothes are everywhere."

"Yeah and we have an even bigger mess downstairs waiting for us." Duncan laughed. "Maybe if we take our time in the shower, the kids will have cleaned it up by the time we get down there."

"That's a thought, not likely but always possible. But it does give us an excuse to spend more time in the shower," Maria connived.

After they spent a luscious amount of time in the shower, they finally decided they should get out and get dressed before they became prunes.

Maria gave him a kiss just before they left the shower. "That was just too awesome for words."

"Anything for my lady."

Twenty-Two

Kids Can be Awesome

"No kid is unsmart. Every kid's a genius at something. Our job is to find it. And then encourage it."
Robin Sharma

Duncan and Maria walked into the kitchen and came to an abrupt halt. The dishes had all been done and put away, the table set and fresh pancakes and juice sat on the table.

"Surprise!" all the kids shouted.

"What took you so long? We heard you get into the shower and then had to wait and wait," John said.

Maria avoided the question. "This is fantastic. Who thought up this bright idea?"

The kids all started to explain at once.

Duncan interrupted all the excited chatter. "Look guys, we just have to say how much we appreciate all of you and what you have accomplished this morning. You have done a great job. So why don't we all sit up to this great breakfast you have made and everyone can have their turn explaining what or why you contributed to this wonderful surprise."

They sat down quickly. Duncan said the same prayer he had said the night before and they all filled their plates with breakfast.

Jessie decided that she got to start the story first, because she had come into the kitchen first and started to clean up the dishes.

Shortly after Jasmine came in and dug in to help. Followed by Nick and John. John said he was hungry and Nick said they usually had pancakes for breakfast Sunday mornings. Jessie phoned Steve to see if he wanted to come and join them. Steve was more than happy to come over because his dad had woken with a hangover and was miserable. Steve promised to do all the dishes just to have an excuse to leave the house.

Most of the dishes had been done by the time he got there, so he just dug in and helped organize the special pancake breakfast. They made pancakes with almond milk, fresh farm free-run chicken eggs, ground flax seed, frozen blueberries, baking powder, and a mix of different flours.

John washed and cut up the oranges, grapefruit, lemons and apples to make juice. They had obviously all been listening and were starting to learn about good healthy eating.

"Well, that was quite the story." Maria applauded them all. "You are the best kids ever and one day you will all make healthy moms and dads. I think we should introduce a new holiday. What do you think, Dad? How about Parents' Day? We already have Mother's Day and Father's Day, and a day like this should be acknowledged as Parents' Day."

"What about Kid's Day?" John spoke up. "How come we have a Mother's Day and a Father's Day but we don't have a Kid's Day?

"Good question," Maria said with a laugh. "But I thought kid's day happened when we took you to Florida, or when your grandparents took you to the movies. What about when we take you bowling, or when we pack a lunch and take you for a hike, or we go bicycling? In fact, I would think most weeks have a Kid's Day in them."

"Do you guys really do all of those things?" Nick asked. "My family doesn't do any of those things."

"No one taught your family about Kid's Day?" Duncan asked. "Then you will just have to come on ours."

"Don't feel bad, Nick. My family never has outings like that either," Steve said. "In fact, I bet most families don't. But the Smiths are always great at bringing along all the friends. I have been on lots of those days with them. They are fun. Mrs. Smith is always organizing something for everyone."

The rest of the breakfast conversation revolved around all the different fun days and outings they had spent. Lots of good memories and lots of laughter and teasing.

When they finished their breakfast, Duncan and Marie cleaned up the second batch of dishes. Maria said that that was only fair. Duncan then explained that they would organize the leftovers for the kids' lunch. Then they would take off and have some quiet time to themselves while the kids went to play Miniature Golf.

Maria didn't mention how she had already been serviced and tantalized to the end of her being. She couldn't believe what an incredible Sunday it had turned out to be. And it wasn't even her birthday, or anniversary, or anything.

Twenty-Three

Understanding the Human Condition

"I am strong because I am weak. I am beautiful because I know my flaws. I am a lover because I am a fighter. I am fearless because I have been afraid. I am wise because I have been foolish. & I can laugh because I've known sadness."
Anonymous

Years ago, Maria had bought a packsack to use for picnics. One part of it opened up to reveal two each of plates, knives, forks spoons, and glasses, plus a tablecloth and cloth napkins. There was a pouch for a bottle of wine and a corkscrew. The largest part was an insulated pouch for foods. She put in deli meats and buns, salads and pickles, into the large insulated food component.

They had used it often, for romantic getaways before the kids were born. They used it less seldom but did use it, none the less, when they just had Jessie. But the pack really didn't work when there was a whole family to take along. Then for many years, they had only used it when the kids were all away at camp or something. In the last few years, when Jasmine and Jessie could take care of themselves, and Maria's parents would take John for the day, they had started to use it again.

To celebrate the day, Maria put in all kinds of fun foods along with the sourdough buns that Carol's husband George had left for them. Duncan added a bottle of wine. They were set for their romantic little picnic.

The weather forecast promised a great spring day, sunny and warm, so they dressed in hiking boots, shorts, and t-shirts. Maria had packed another backpack with jeans and long sleeve sweat shirts, just in case the weather changed.

They reached the turnoff up to the mountain parking lot after about an hour's drive. They followed the road up to the parking lot for about thirty minutes. They got out of the car and stretched, noting that they were the only ones there. They had the whole mountain to themselves. The weather forecast had proven accurate; it was about 18° Celsius or 76° Fahrenheit. Just right for a bit of a hike and a lovely picnic.

They were going to hike up to a large meadow on top of the mountain. On one side there was a great open view of the valley before them and on the other side the taller mountains stretched up towards the sky. A river flowed down the mountain, reflecting the time of year. Sometimes it crawled, sometimes it danced, and sometimes it raced down the mountain.

The hike took about an hour. Just after one o'clock, they arrived at the meadow. Maria always thought of the movie *The Sound of Music* when they came here. She loved it. Usually there was no one else around. Duncan came up behind her and wrapped his arms around Maria as they absorbed the quiet majestic beauty.

"Why are we so lucky?" Maria asked.

"Because our souls decided this was the kind of life we wanted, before we came in?" Duncan suggested.

"Well, let's give thanks to our souls then," Maria responded, taking a deep breath.

"How about we sit over there," she suggested, pointing to an area not far from the river but close to a beautiful tree in case they needed shade later on.

When they got to their spot, Duncan took off the pack sack and helped Maria lay out the tablecloth and all of their goodies. He poured the wine as she unwrapped the sandwiches and opened containers of smoked oysters, salmon cream cheese, pickled cucumbers, asparagus, carrots, and beets.

"As usual, you always put together a great picnic," Duncan said as he sat down beside the picnic spread. "Did you buy any of this or did you make it all?"

"I bought the oysters and cheese but all this pickling is from the recipes that Dr. Daniel gave me. He explained how good pickled and fermented foods are for the body and which foods benefitted the body in which ways. I don't remember all of the details now. I just remember that it helps the microbiota in your gut, which in turn helps the whole rest of your body."

They each took a plate and filled it with some of everything. Duncan then proposed a toast. "To us, our lives together, our children, our health, and our ability to delight in one another until the end of our days."

"I like that. To us," Maria agreed.

As they started to indulge the different picnic delights, Maria returned to their prior conversation. "I was serious, Duncan. Why do you think we are so lucky? There are so many people around the world who live in misery or poverty, or in war torn countries, or are beaten or sexually abused. With all the horror around the world, why do you think we got so lucky?"

Duncan paused to think for a minute. "An age old question with how many different answers? Did we just luck out? What is predestined? Did we decide at a soul level? Is it because of past life choices? Did we even know each other in past lives or in other realms? What if there are parallel universes? The possibilities are endless. I guess it comes back to what we are always saying. What belief system do you want to work with?

Even though everyone in the family seems to have some sort of physiological disorder, we have a family that works pretty well together. So far, no one has gone through any rebellion or deviation, touch wood." They both leaned over and touched the root of the tree.

Maria continued the line of thinking. "And with your heart issue, my adrenal issue, Jessie's diabetes, Jasmine's asthma, and John's allergies, never mind the extended family, we lucked out with great friends and neighbours like the Gibsons. They seem to embrace all the different healing modalities and are always so generous with their knowledge, wisdom, and ideas.

Actually did you know they don't have all of them? I listened to part of the conversation that Jessie had with Pappy. He talked about psychological and energetic healing modalities. Of course, Dr. Jim has the psychology but I would love to talk with him about the energetic ones. I wanted to interrupt and ask him more but I am so pleased that Jessie wants to learn about all the different healing modalities, I thought I had better put it on hold.

I recognized some of the terms he used but have no idea what they refer to. If everything is basically energy anyhow, then the energetic modalities would operate at that basic level."

Duncan reached over for another sandwich before he responded. "I don't know about all this energetic stuff. I can accept that we are all just energy at a fundamental level, that all compounds, and chemicals are different patterns of energy. No problem with all of that.

But, if we look at history, every time we think we know something, it only turns out to open another door to a lot more that we had no idea of previously. Think about it. At one point, Europeans thought the world was flat. You got your head chopped off if you suggested otherwise. Then when they found out it wasn't flat, it opened up numerous other doors, whole continents they had no idea about.

Or think about the discovery that things we could not see actually abound in rock, air, water, food. When that Dutch guy, what was his name?"

"van Leeuwenhoek?" Maria offered.

"Yeah, him. When he created the microscope and they started to discover microorganisms, that opened the door to all kinds of bacteria, viruses, fungi, and all the rest of those things that we can't even see.

What happens when they start to understand energy, quantum energy, kinesthetic energy, and so on? It's possible that once they understand energy, it will open another door to a world more subtle than the energy one, that we have no idea about now."

"Now that's a thought," Maria replied. "I like this. So if we live on a very concrete level of chemical interactions, but below the concrete world of Newtonian sciences is where the more subtle Einstein sciences operate. Now perhaps we will move into a world where the Einstein quantum physics is considered the more concrete and there is a whole other level below that energetic level. Perhaps it is on that more subtle level that people can move in and out of time and across dimensions?"

Duncan laughed. "Oh boy, we could just keep going and going, couldn't we? How do parallel universes and string theory and all of those theories fit into this paradigm?"

"I don't know yet," Maria answered. "I'm still working on it. Give me a minute."

"And we will solve the human experience in the next minute when you solve the question, right?"

"Well, I wouldn't go that far," she returned. "You might have to give me a week to figure that out."

Duncan leaned over and gave Maria a kiss. "Well, being the generous kind of guy that I am, I will give you until the end of our days. How about that?"

"Oh, you are generous, aren't you? Let's make a toast. To spending the rest of our days exploring and understanding the human condition."

Twenty-Four

Flaky Eastern Stuff or...

"Many of those in the medical fraternity instantly label treatments in the traditional, natural or holistic health fields as quackery. This word is even used to describe Traditional Chinese Medicine and the Indian Ayurveda, two medical systems which are far older than Western medicine and globally just as popular."
James Morcan, The Orphan Conspiracies: 29 Conspiracy Theories from The Orphan Trilogy

On Monday night, Jessie decided that the dinner theme would be Thai. Maria, Jessie, and Jasmine all looked up different recipes on their computers.

The phone rang and Jasmine answered. Uncle Dan wanted to speak with Maria.

"Hi there, Uncle Dan. What's up?" Maria queried.

"That was some party you threw Saturday night. I had lots of fun, as usual. Thanks for the invitation."

"You're welcome."

"I got to talk with Dr. Jim for a bit and my cholesterol and hypertension came up. He said that I could either continue to manage it with the medications I was on or, and this was the interesting part, I could see his daughter and actually eliminate it. I know you guys work with the Gibsons all the time, so I wanted to ask you. Do you think I should see Dr. Jane? It seems a little risky to me. After all, I have been on meds for a long time and the doctors know what they are doing. I don't want to risk my health with some flaky quaky stuff."

"You are hoot, Mr. Dan. But I understand your concerns. The thing is, you could set up an appointment with Dr. Jane and see what she has to say. If she makes sense and you connect with her then you follow her advice. If it doesn't make sense and you don't connect, then you either follow your MD's advice or try someone else. Remember, it's your body. They are your health servants, not your health dictators. The way I now look at it is that MDs manage your symptoms with synthetic drugs. *Real,* or natural, medicine works to eliminate the underlying problems. They use foods and herbs and all the things that were given to us to use. The body is designed to heal, it's just that sometimes it goes off track, and we have to help it get back on track again. But you are in charge; it's your decision. It's your body."

"Do they do anything weird to your body?"

"No. Dr. Jane has this really cool instrument that sends patterns of homeopathic sine waves into the body and it can provide all kinds of information. There are a variety of different types of instruments out there that do similar things but she explained why this one is unique and basically the mother ship of them all."

"Okay. I will make an appointment but you realize this is all your fault," Uncle Dan teased.

"I will take full responsibility if I can help you step back into health," she threw back at him. Maria gave him the phone number and sent him off to make his first appointment.

Maria got off the phone laughing and singing, "Another one makes the move, and another one, and another one, and another makes the move." She was singing the words to the tune of a popular '80's song. Both girls started to laugh.

"What was that all about?" Jessie asked.

"Well, our Uncle Dan is about to see Dr. Jane about his hypertension. Jessie, why don't you go bring up Grandma Mary? She will be thrilled."

Maria turned on the kettle to make tea, and took out some special 100% pure chocolate to snack on. Jasmine took out the container with a 101 different varieties of tea, along with almond milk and jaggery sugar. Grandma Mary didn't want to give up sugar in her tea but at least she had changed over to a healthier sugar.

"I hear that there is some big news, what's going on," Grandma Mary said as she sat down at the table to decide which tea she wanted.

Jessie was excited. "Uncle Dan phoned Mom and he's going to make an appointment at the Gibson's clinic."

Grandma Mary looked up at Maria with raised eyebrows.

"He just did, Mom. He had questions about whether what they were doing was flaky and what they were going to do to him and such, but he took their number and said he'd call and make an appointment," Maria explained.

"Wow, if he goes and has success with his hypertension and his cholesterol, then this might be enough to get Papa Johnny to go. He has always looked up to Uncle Dan so who knows? We might get two more who actually want to eliminate their health issues rather than buying synthetic prescription drugs to manage their symptoms."

Jasmine accused Maria of being an evangelist for the Gibsons.

"Excuse me, my dear. And how is your asthma doing?" Maria quizzed her daughter.

"Yeah I know. If it wasn't for them, I probably wouldn't even be able to do my dance, never mind eliminate my asthma. I am appreciative and all of that, but you are actually starting to sound like Pappy. It's funny."

"When you start to learn all of that stuff, it's hard not to get on the band wagon," Jessie commented. "I've been thinking about the conversation I had with Pappy on Saturday night. I love my pre-med program but I don't think I want to go into allopathic medicine. I am just not sure what I want to do, except that I want to be more engaged with actual healing."

Maria beamed as she bent over the dish she was preparing. She was thrilled that her daughter was thinking along those lines.

Twenty-Five

Uncle Dan's Experience Making Pancakes

"I'm a breakfast type of guy. Don't get me wrong. I can cook, I'm kinda nice on the burner, but I enjoy making breakfast. I do it all... Scrambled eggs... French toast... Pancakes... Breakfast is my thing."
Ja Rule

Dan went to the Gibson's clinic feeling more than a little apprehensive. They welcomed him into the clinic and offered him a cup of tea. *So far so good*, he told himself.

Dr. Jane called him into a room and motioned him to sit in a chair. It was a comfortable room with lots of books. She asked him to fill out a short form and then she explained what they would do with the intake and all of her questions and with the ASYRA and the information they would be able to get. They would do a urine analysis, a nitric oxide analysis, an oxygen analysis and a few more evaluations.

All that might take about an hour. Then she asked him what he knew about cholesterol. He simply responded that he knew there was the good stuff, HDL, and the bad stuff, LDL, and then there were TGs or something. He knew that the ratio between the good stuff and the bad stuff was not good and so he was took Statin drugs to drop his cholesterol down and he took blood pressure pills to bring his blood pressure down. He looked at her for confirmation that what he had said was right.

"Good," Dr. Jane said, "We both now know where you are coming from. Let me give you some additional information. You don't have remember all that I will tell you and you won't have to write an exam on it but I want to explain some things to you, so we can get on the same page. Sound good?"

Dan nodded and wondered what more she needed to tell him.

"Let's start with cholesterol. Did you know that your liver is supposed to make over 80% of the body's cholesterol? Now why would it do that unless your body needed it? You need cholesterol to make the bile, which breaks down the fats in your diet. You need the cholesterol for the membrane or outer skin of every cell in your body. Cholesterol is the basis for making all your steroid hormones, like testosterone. In fact, cholesterol is used for all kinds of things in your body. With me so far?"

Dan nodded.

"Good. Did you know that you can get a break in your smallest arteries, called arterioles, just by lying in your bed and breathing?"

Uncle Dan raised an eyebrow and shook his head.

"So you are breaking all the different sizes of arteries all the time. The body has to keep rebuilding them. Just like when you exercise, your muscles break down and your body has to rebuild them. Right?"

Dan nodded his understanding.

"Well, if you get a bleed in one of those arteries and your body can't fix it, what would happen?"

"I guess you would bleed to death?"

"Good answer. Now the body doesn't want that to happen, so it makes cholesterol and sends it up the broken blood vessel and patches it up. Smart, don't you think?"

"Then why do they want us to stop making it?" Dan was clearly confused.

"Back in the fifties, a poorly designed study was done and while I won't go into all the details, they ended up making the assumption that plaque in the arteries was always cholesterol based and that we had to stop the body from making cholesterol.

Let's go through some basic issues here. I am going to explain it in real simple terms. Number 1: Inflammation causes high blood pressure. It makes the arteries smaller and makes the heart have to pump harder to get the blood through. Number 2: Inflammation and plaque can be caused by all kinds of issues from free radicals, to AGEs, to heavy metal toxins and environmental toxins and a host of other things including cholesterol patches. Number 3: There are all kinds of different HDLs and different kinds of LDLs. In fact some of the HDLs are bad for you and some of the LDLs are shown to be even more important than the HDLs. With me so far?"

Uncle Dan nodded.

"Number 4: Statin drugs not only stop the body from producing the very cholesterol it requires but in doing so it prevents the body from making a compound that is required by every cell in the body to make the very fuel the cells require to do anything at all! When the cells can't function properly, because they don't have sufficient fuel, all kinds of things can go wrong."

"Is that why Maria has me taking CoQ10?" Dan asked.

"Precisely. That CoQ10 is the limiting factor in making the fuel in the cell. Do you know what a limiting factor is?"

Uncle Dan shook his head.

"Imagine that I asked Maria to make pancakes for 100 people and gave her an unlimited supply of flour, milk, and baking powder, and only one egg. What would be the limiting factor?"

"Obviously, the egg."

"Good answer. The egg in the pancake analogy is like the CoQ10 in your cells. Your cells have all these little guys called mitochondria trying to make enough fuel, or ATP, in each cell. In fact, just a regular cell has about 500 mitochondria so that it has enough fuel to function. A heart cell, on the other hand, has upwards of 2500 mitochondria so that it has enough fuel to run constantly without stopping. Yet, when you take Statin drugs, your body stops making CoQ10 and consequently, your cells can't make sufficient fuel to function properly. Everything starts to break down. Still with me?"

"I think so," Uncle Dan said slowly. "So, the doctors got the cholesterol picture wrong; they don't know about all the different kinds of cholesterol and when I take the pills to stop making the cholesterol that my body needs, I end up preventing my cells from making the fuel they need. Everything starts to go haywire, right?" He looked to Dr. Jane to make sure he got the concepts right.

"Good man. There is actually a lot more to the story than that, but 'by George, I think we got it'," she said with an accent. "Or at least enough to get the big picture."

"So what do I do?" Uncle Dan sounded worried.

"That's where your choices come in. First, we can look at what you are doing with your MD and simply try to supplement what the drugs are depleting but continue to just manage your health and symptoms.

Second, we can take you off the meds and provide you with diet, tinctures, et cetera, to compensate. But I never recommend this route. It can actually be dangerous.

Third, we can look at what the body needs to function properly. We need to make some changes in your diet to provide the nutrients the body requires to function more effectively. Ultimately, we want your body to do the work but it needs nutrients to do so. Then, we need to get rid of some heavy metal toxicity that is coming up on the scan. We will take a tincture for that. Do you like chocolate, I mean *real* chocolate, not the junk candy stuff you buy in the store?"

"Yeah, if you mean that stuff that Maria buys. It's actually good."

"Good, I would want you to start eating that. Why? Well, your nitric oxide levels are down. We need nitric oxide for a number of different things in the body and the brain, but what we are focused on here is that your body uses nitric oxide to relax the smooth muscles in your arteries so that they widen and allow more blood flow to go through." She diagrammed the explanation with her fingers. "When the arteries relax and widen, more blood flow gets through and takes the pressure off of the heart to have to push the blood.

I want you eat some other things for that as well. But don't worry; I will make you a list of everything you need to do. Your CoQ10 levels are too low, despite what you are taking, so I am going to give you a different type that your body will have an easier time absorbing and using and we will see if we can get those levels up. When your body is strong, we would then start to talk with your MD and see if we can work out a plan to get you off of these drugs. But we need to go slowly. This is my favourite plan, but ultimately it is your body and you have a responsibility to make decisions for it. So, which option do you feel most comfortable with?"

"The last one sounds like a plan, Doc. Maybe I should have done this years ago but let's get on track now. Where do I get my tincture stuff and pills and whatever?" he asked.

"If you just go and wait for a few minutes in the waiting room we will put it all together for you. But before we go any further, I want you to start exercising. Nothing strenuous—you can start by walking around the block. I want you to get up to at least a mile a day but we will do that slowly. We need those fluids in your body to keep moving.

And I know you lost Judy a long time ago but there are a few Bach flowers that are coming up for you, so I would like to suggest we put a formula together for you to resolve some of those old emotional issues that got buried. You can choose to start them now or wait until next time, if you are feeling overwhelmed. The choice is yours. Also, if you want to down the road, you have the options of developing a program with Julie or getting an acupuncture assessment with Nanny Sarah. You always have options. For now, I want you to make another appointment in about three weeks so we can see how you are responding."

"You got it, Doc. I think I will wait on the flower stuff until next time. This is a lot to absorb for an old guy."

Uncle Dan reached out to shake Dr. Jane's hand and walked into the waiting room. *Maria will be thrilled,* he thought. He sat down in the waiting room, and attempted to go over all that Dr. Jane had told him so that he could remember to tell Maria.

Twenty-Six

You Never Know Who You are Going to Meet

"Meeting a stranger can be totally fleeting and meaningless, for example, unless you enter the individual's world by finding out at least one thing that is meaningful to his or her life and exchange at lest one genuine feeling. Tuning in to others is a circular flow: you send yourself out toward people; you receive them as they respond to you."
Deepak Chopra, The Book of Secrets: Unlocking the Hidden Dimensions of Your Life

"Well, imagine meeting you here," Duncan exclaimed, meeting Uncle Dan at the clinic door as he was leaving. "Maria said you were going to make an appointment."

"Don't tell Maria you saw me, okay?" Uncle Dan asked. "I want to surprise her myself."

"It's a deal," Duncan promised. "She's going to love it."

"Why are you here?"

"Oh, it's nothing. Just want to make sure everything is in good order, so I can keep pleasing Maria—if you know what I mean?" he said with a wink.

Dan laughed. "Gotcha. Got make sure we can service the ladies."

As Uncle Dan walked away, Duncan looked back at him. Was he with a lady and not telling anyone? He made a mental note to investigate a little more.

Duncan followed Pappy through to his office and sat down in the chair offered.

"So what's on your mind today?"

"Well, this is kind of private stuff but I was wondering if you could help me out."

"I'll do my best, but let me in on the secret first."

"I wanted to see you about it because you are older. Dr. Jim has always been a big help but he is my age."

"Go on."

"Well, in the last year, I haven't quite had my mojo as much as I used to, if you know what I mean. So Dr. Jane said I was supposed to eat more real chocolate, lots of watermelon, and nuts like almonds. She also tested my nitric oxide and explained what it did. I took it for a couple of weeks and my levels went right back up. So everything's good on that front. I want to know if I am getting some sort of placebo effect. I mean, I can get up more frequently, get harder, and I keep it longer. Is that normal? I mean, don't get me wrong. I love it but it just doesn't seem normal for a guy my age. I want to make sure it's not something that just starts up and then disappears." Duncan paused and collected his thoughts. "Can I ask you if someone your age is still functioning regularly, in that department?" He knew it was a personal question to ask of Pappy but he really wanted to know.

"Yes, Duncan, it is a good question, and we still have a very active, fun bedroom life, if you will. There is no reason why a good healthy sex life should die, although I would surmise it does for most people," Pappy explained. "For instance, most men don't realize that their marriage and their sex life requires attention and nurturing. Like anything, if you don't put energy into it, it will eventually die. They also don't realize that a marriage commitment is like a commitment to court and romance your wife for the rest of your life. If they only knew how well that pays off.

Another reason is that women also can leave their sex life unattended. Often after childbirth, for instance, a woman's hormones are depleted and they don't know how to restore them. And then they think they are depressed and go on anti-depressants, which really doesn't solve the hormone issue.

People don't fall out of love. They fail to put effort and energy into their relationships and, like anything else, without the effort and energy, it will wither and die. A man who puts all his time and effort into his career or a hobby and not into his marriage is going to lose the love he felt. Likewise, a woman who puts all her time and effort into her career or her children is going to lose the love she felt.

Another reason can be physiological health. If the nitric oxide goes down and he can't get it up or hold onto it, he might start avoiding bedroom activities. She starts to think that he doesn't love her anymore and things can go downhill from there.

Another reason might involve the psychodynamics in the relationship. As you know, our Dr. Jim deals with all kinds of couples having relationship issues that are played out in the bedroom. If there is stress in the relationship due to children, or finances, or toxic work places, or needs not getting met, or whatever, sex is often the first thing that falls off the list.

But if you attend to your physiological health, and have a healthy relationship, you can actually get a new lease on life. Couples experience it in different ways, by engaging in activities, in or out of the bedroom, that they haven't for years. Or they start getting creative with their bedroom activities. Compassion develops between them that was never there before. There are all kinds of ways to revitalize and enhance a marriage at any time.

The challenge is that both parties need to play the game. If one party struggles to get their marriage back on track and the other party isn't interested or has already started looking sideways, that's typically when someone starts looking at divorce."

Pappy continued to share different aspects of a good healthy relationship, while Duncan took mental notes, until Pappy's next client came in. Now, Duncan decided, he wanted to share all of this with Maria. He was confident about what they were doing and where they were going and about what his body could do.

Twenty-Seven

When You are Old, Wrinkled, and Grey...

*"To be someone's first love maybe great.
But to be their last love is beyond Perfect."*
Anonymous

Thursday evening Maria got another call from Uncle Dan. Although Dr. Jane had booked him for a couple of weeks down the road, a cancellation had come up and she had fit him in yesterday. He wanted to thank Maria and she invited him for dinner to tell the whole family how his appointment went. They decided to make him a special Greek meal with lots of garlic, a Greek salad, and lots of vegetables, according to the Mediterranean diet.

Maria and Duncan went upstairs to change for dinner. "Are you going to join me for a shower Maria?" Duncan asked hopefully.

"Man, you would think we were newlyweds with all this extracurricular activity going on," she admonished him as she happily stepped into the shower. It felt like they were getting a new lease on life while they still had all their kids at home. It was like they had fallen in love all over again and it was fun to be romantic and silly and playful. Maria loved it.

"Well, I don't know if I want you to be doing any extracurricular activities," he said as he washed her back, "I want them all to be with me. So what does that make it? Intracurricular?" He modified, as he soaped her up her front, taking full advantage of her up stretched arms as she reached up to give him a hug and a soapy kiss.

He slid his arms around her and under her buttocks, pulling her up onto him. She wrapped her wet soapy legs around him and slid easily down onto his member. He groaned deeply.

"That worked well," Maria whispered as he sat down on the edge of the shower seat. She braced her feet against the front of the tiled seat as he helped her to move up and down. They quickly established a rhythm and then continued to lather and stroke one another with soap. Each knew the other's body well and how to get the most reaction.

She wiped the soapsuds away from their faces so they could continue to explore the inner treasures of their mouths. Then she swiped the soapy mixture from his ear and moved to trace his ear with her tongue when an electric shock seemed to go right through her. Her breasts and nipples moved against his chest and seemed to be even more aware and responsive in the shower than they were in bed. The sensuous delight was so erotic she came without even being ready for it. And then again and again.

Duncan started to chuckle. "I love it when you just keep coming and coming. You have no idea how erotic that is for me." Then it was his turn.

"Oooo, that was just sooo good." She let out on a long sigh.

"Life just keeps getting better and better. I love you so much." Duncan kissed her again as he helped her to get back on her feet. They continued to soap and wash each other down, being both playful and sensual.

"We do have company coming, sweetheart, as much as I would enjoy playing with you for the next hour, or even all night, I think we need to get ready and go downstairs."

"I was thinking the same. I just didn't want to stop." They stepped out of the shower and picked up their bath sheets.

"But now I can have fun drying that sexy body of yours." She started to laugh again, as he kissed and nipped her wherever he dried her.

"I am glad you are going blind, and can only remember that I used to look sexy. But thanks, anyways."

"You will always be sexy to me. It's who you are. Even when you are ninety years old and all wrinkled and grey, you will still be sexy to me," Duncan promised.

"No wonder I love you so much. Can't beat that," Maria said, laughing.

Twenty-Eight

And Another One Makes the Move

"The secret of change is to focus all of your energy, not on fighting the old, but rather on building the new."
Socrates

They did manage to get downstairs before Uncle Dan arrived. Maria checked on the dishes in the oven and Duncan went downstairs to get a bottle of wine. Then John came in to see if dinner was ready and Maria asked him to go get Grandma Mary and Papa Johnny for dinner. She had invited them because she wanted them to hear what Uncle Dan had to say. *This should be interesting with Uncle Dan providing all the conversation,* she thought, considering that he usually got information from listening to other peoples' conversations.

"Hi Everybody, I'm home," Uncle Dan announced as he opened the front door and waltzed in and walked to the kitchen. His announcement brought both Jasmine and Jessie down from their rooms.

"Hi there, girls. How are you both doing? How is Nick? Are you still practicing through the summer? How is Steve? Are you guys getting more serious? Hi Maria. How are the adrenals doing?" As usual, he acknowledged everybody with questions pertaining to each individually, but never waited to hear anyone answer.

"I've been waiting all this time to hear what happened. This is killing me," Maria told Uncle Dan as she kissed his cheek.

John bounded into the kitchen with Grandma Mary and Papa Johnny not far behind.

"Hi Uncle Dan," John said reaching for a big bear hug.

Uncle Dan hugged his sister and asked how her arthritis was doing. Grandma Mary didn't bother answering.

"How is your memory doing, there ol' Pal," Uncle Dan asked Papa Johnny. "Still remember who your best friend is?" Uncle Dan and Papa Johnny had always had a good camaraderie between them and a question like that from anyone else would have got Papa Johnny's gears going, but he didn't blink an eye when it came from Uncle Dan. He also knew not to bother answering either. With a smile they all sat down at the table. Duncan was about to say his usual grace, but asked Uncle Dan if he wanted to say grace instead.

Uncle Dan chuckled and said, "I don't normally do that kind of thing, but today, I think I need to give thanks."

Maria, Duncan and Grandma Mary all exchanged looks. "Mother, Father, God, Infinite Universe, Resources Unlimited. How can I say thanks? Thank you for this wonderful family and for their friends next door. Thank you that I might get off of all these drugs. Thank you for all that you have given us. Please bless this food to our bodies. Amen. "Did I do a good job?" he asked Duncan.

"Like an old pro," Duncan returned.

"I am so excited to hear what all happened. Start from the beginning," Maria pushed.

They filled their plates as Uncle Dan told them how he met with Dr. Jane, about the ASYRA diagnostic assessment that she used and the other tests. He said he couldn't remember half of all that she explained, but told them what he remembered she had said about his medications, why his MD would have put him on them; what nutrients they depleted in the body, and what options she provided him with. He told them about the tinctures, the Bach flowers she recommended, the exercise program, and his other options down the road.

"Geez, I can't remember the last time I took that long with a physician. Man, was she thorough. I was really impressed."

"So what are you going to do now?" Maria pushed. She watched Papa Johnny throughout Uncle Dan's story to see if it had any impact on him. A couple of times she motioned to Duncan to be aware of Papa Johnny's expressions. She was hopeful. It looked like it might have the affect she intended.

"Well, I am going to start with changing some things in my diet. I am going to work with some basic kitchen herbs like garlic. And she told me to eat watermelon every day, but didn't explain why."

Duncan choked but covered up with a cough.

"Anyway, then I will add in a tincture with Hawthorne and some other herbs in it. She will monitor my progress. She says I might benefit from taking a homeopathic but she would wait and see how I responded. When my body is stronger and we have things under control then she will work with my other doctor to get me off of the drugs I am taking. Man, I should have done this years ago! I just never knew." Maria couldn't contain a smile.

"Do you really think that flaky stuff will help you?" Papa Johnny asked. "Isn't it just all old wives tales, not real medicine?"

"Oh, you…" Jessie started.

Maria cut her off. "Let Uncle Dan explain."

Jessie picked up the cue, and let Uncle Dan continue.

Uncle Dan explained how the medications he was now taking would never solve the underlying problem. Instead they would just try to manage the symptoms, deplete his body of important nutrients, so he would have to take more medications and/or higher doses.

The alternative was to use *real* medications. Real foods and herbs to solve the underlying issues so that the body could engage in its natural healing processes again, like it used to.

Duncan started to congratulate Uncle Dan, but Maria kicked him under the table. She wanted to get the elders to engage in a dialogue and convince one another. Duncan nodded his understanding and didn't continue.

Grandma Mary threw in her two cents worth. "I am proud of you, Dan. I know when I started to go to the Gibson's Clinic, they sure helped me and my arthritis. They provided me with some natural remedies that managed my pain, and now I am working to eliminate the arthritis. I just told Johnny the other day that I can't believe how much better I am. And no more of that medication!"

John chimed in from the far end of the table. "And my allergies are gone. I had a bee sting the other day and I didn't have to go to the hospital or anything. Nothing happened!"

"Wow, that's fantastic!" Grandma Mary exclaimed.

Jasmine added, "And my sports asthma is all gone. I haven't had an attack for ages. And I am not taking any medications. I thought I might have to quit dancing and now I am doing better than ever."

Maria kept an eye on Papa Johnny, she so wanted him to make an appointment. His dementia hadn't gone too far, but if they could work with it now, he obviously would have a better chance to eliminate it than if he waited.

Uncle Dan pushed the topic. "Look Johnny, why don't you make an appointment with Dr. Jane and I will take you down? We can then go out for lunch or something afterwards."

"I think all of you are conniving against me, Papa Johnny growled. "I feel like I have been cornered and I don't like it."

Duncan stepped in and saved the day. "Look Dad, we did want you to hear what Uncle Dan had to say. And we would like to help you with your health. Why don't you just think about it and when you are ready to make a decision, we will support you whichever way you decide to go?"

"That sounds like a plan. You are in charge," Grandma Mary agreed.

With the pressure off, Papa Johnny decided to make the move. "Okay, Maria, you make me an appointment and I will go down with Dan. You guys win."

"Actually, Papa Johnny," Jessie said, "you are the one who is winning. We just helped you to win the race. We all love you and want the best for you."

Maria had tears in her eyes. Duncan saw her reaction and squeezed her hand under the table. The dinner had been a success.

Maria got up and went to the fridge to bring out the watermelon she had carved. It wasn't as good a job as Nanny Sarah had done, but she was definitely good.

"Geez Mom, you really have a thing for watermelon lately. We seem to have it every day," Jessie observed.

"Yeah, Nanny Sarah told me that we should eat it every day. I looked it up and found that it was good for the adrenals and the immune system and for the heart. So I figured, we should do what she tells us."

Twenty-Nine

Patient Tactics Work in the Long Haul

"Knowing trees, I understand the meaning of patience. Knowing grass, I can appreciate persistence."
Hal Borland

Unfortunately, Dr. Jane couldn't fit Papa Johnny in for three weeks. Maria was afraid he might change his mind, or forget all the stories that he had heard around the table but Uncle Dan was well aware of where Papa Johnny was coming from, as he had come from the same place. So he regularly reinforced the stories that everyone had shared. He also repeated how proud everyone was of him for going to see Dr. Jane.

Eventually, the day came. Grandma Mary came upstairs to be with Maria when Uncle Dan came over. The two women agree that it would be best for the two men to do this together. Maria knew how difficult it would be for her mom to just sit and wait.

Maria made her Mom's favourite asparagus soup and George's sourdough buns for lunch. She had made some healthy chocolate Gibsons-style treats using 100% pure chocolate, which she now knew was a lot different than the 70%, 80% or 90% chocolate. The real 100% chocolate had all of the omega 3 fatty acids that were good for inflammation and helped her mother's body manage its own inflammatory responses.

When she started to learn about real 100% chocolate, she couldn't believe that not only was it a fruit, but also it was loaded with over 300 nutrients that the body requires. Too bad the western world had destroyed its nutrient value with all of the junk chocolate sold today.

She saw her Mom glance at the clock. It was now 2:30. "Remember, Mom, Uncle Dan said that if Dad wanted, he would take him out for lunch or coffee or something. Don't worry, they will be fine."

A few minutes later, the two men walked in the front door. Maria, took her mother's hand and squeezed it. "So how did it go, Dad?"

"He's converted," Uncle Dan announced. "She did the same with Johnny that she did with me. She explained everything and gave him options, right Johnny?" He turned to Papa Johnny for confirmation.

"Yeah, she's a pretty smart cookie, that one. She knows my doctor's stuff and all her other stuff. But now Mom is going to have to prepare a whole bunch of stuff for me."

"Why don't you both sit at the table?" Maria suggested. "I will make us all a pot of tea and you can tell us what happened."

Papa Johnny explained what happened in the appointment and Uncle Dan helped to fill in from his own experience a few weeks before. Rather than just asking questions, Uncle Dan was now carrying the conversation.

It appeared that the first appointment had made a huge change in Uncle Dan. Maria wondered if he had started to take the Bach flower remedy or a homeopathic; if the change was permanent or if he would reverse to the way he had been for years.

Papa Johnny pulled out the sheets that Dr. Jane had given him. He showed Grandma Mary what he needed to do. There were six columns of foods and he had to take so much of each food group, and eat it all within 15 minutes, sometime between 6:00 and 8:00PM. The rest of the time, he had to increase certain foods high in certain nutrients like Omega 3s and minerals like magnesium. Dr. Jane had laid everything out for him. And he was supposed to eat lots of watermelon this summer.

There's the watermelon, again, Maria thought.

Dr. Jane would see him again in five weeks' time. He seemed pleased and was ready to try her protocol to see if it worked.

Maria gave him a big hug. "I am proud of you, Dad. Now I don't have to worry anymore. Thank you."

She then gave her Mom a hug. "And now you don't have to worry anymore either."

A final hug went to Uncle Dan. "Thanks for all of your help. We all love you for it." And she gave him a kiss on the cheek.

Thirty

It's All in the Timing

"Patience is power. Patience is not an absence of action;
rather it is "timing" it waits on the right time to act, for the right principles
and in the right way."
Fulton J. Sheen

A month had passed since Papa Johnny had gone to see Dr. Jane and even longer since Uncle Dan had seen her. They had both been back for second visits to see how well they responded.

Duncan suggested another patio potluck was on order so they could share stories of their progress. "Let's do it the same way that you did with Papa Johnny. We get one person going and just let everyone start sharing their stories." We won't ask the Gibsons this time, because we simply want the family to support the family."

Maria had agreed and sent out an invitation to Carol's family and their parents. They decided that Duncan would do a barbecue for everyone and Maria would make a green salad. Jessie wanted to make coleslaw with Julie's recipe.

Grandma Mary thought it was a great idea and she was going to bring her potato salad. Carol would bring her deserts and George his sourdough buns. Jessie and Jasmine both invited their boyfriends.

This Saturday didn't go quite as well as the last, Jasmine and Jessie got into a bit of spit. Maria, as usual, did not get involved. She thought it was important that they learn how to work things out themselves and they did but not until after a bout of tears. However, after that, it was clear sailing.

Everyone did his or her chores.

Jessie was in the midst of another semester, so she studied for most of the day. She had suggested that Steve come over around 4:30. That gave them both the day to study on their own, but some private time together before everyone else showed up.

Jasmine was involved in another school project and this one was with Nick. So she had invited Nick to come over for the afternoon so they could both work on it.

Maria and Duncan had gone for coffee and dessert a couple of times with Nick's parents. They didn't want to control the young relationship but Jasmine and Nick were only sixteen so the parents wanted to make sure that they had a handle on things.

Nick was a good kid. He was polite and considerate. He dug in and helped clear the table and do dishes along with the other kids without having to be asked.

Steve was an old friend of the family. The kids had grown up together, and as he was older, there was a different connection between him and the family. Duncan had been like a father to him for years, because of his own father's alcoholic issues. Now that he had grown into a young man, Duncan attempted to create a different kind of relationship with him, more of a mentor than a father. It worked well.

Steve was always appreciative of the help Duncan provided, perhaps more because Duncan invited him in to conversations. Duncan didn't dictate or demand anything of him, like his father did. Duncan did let him know that he expected his best but he didn't expect perfection, like his father did. Whatever the reason, it worked well.

Maria and Duncan had discussed how the relationship might be affected if Steve and Jessie decided to break up. Steve would probably suffer the most, but Duncan said he would try to be there for him and not betray his daughter, which could be a challenge.

They had attempted to talk about it with Jessie once but she didn't want to go there.

Maria was concerned that John didn't have anyone to be his pal at the last dinner. Everyone was partnered up except him and Uncle Dan. Maria asked if wanted to have one of his friends join them for dinner. "I could ask Jeff," he replied, "but I think I should be here for Uncle Dan."

"That's very considerate of you, hon. I am sure he will appreciate your loyalty."

Nick arrived around 1:30 and he and Jasmine worked at the dining room table all afternoon. She had made them carrot muffins to eat and she kept their teacups full.

Steve arrived before five and he and Jessie went out for a walk to the park, where they could get some smooching in, Duncan guessed.

John was downstairs playing checkers with Papa Johnny, which left Duncan and Maria with nothing to do.

Maria had put on some lively music while they were put on the finishing touches for dinner. Duncan came up and bowed before her, asked for her hand in a dance. "You are my favourite charmer," she said as he danced her around the kitchen.

"I remember what we did last time we had the dinner to convert your Dad. Want to see if we can do that again?" Duncan suggested with a wink.

"Oh, you are a sly one, but I love the way you think." They proceeded out of the kitchen and up the stairs to their bedroom. Once the doors were behind them, Duncan pulled her into his arms and kissed her thoroughly, as he struggled to undo her top and then her bra. This time he was clumsy and between the hugs and the clothing removal, it wasn't quite as smooth as it could have been, which had the two of them in stitches. But they made it to the shower laughing.

They began to soap one another up with a playful but sensual interaction. They could hear the music downstairs and allowed their wet soapy bodies to move erotically against one another in time with the music. "Hey, we should remember this routine, I like it even better with the music, you wanton thing," Duncan murmured to her as he gently stroked between her legs. Maria spread her legs apart to accommodate him and she gently massaged his already hard member. Duncan nipped at her ear and then down her neck and further down her soapy chest until he found a nipple, pleased that it was already hard and erect for him.

They stroked and caressed and lathered each other until she could feel his readiness. She reached her arms up around his neck and he grabbed her buttocks as he had done last time, and moved her up to slide her down on top of him. Just like last time, she slid into place as if they had done it every day of their lives.

"Oh, God, we're good. I don't think I can hold it anymore," she groaned as they released their energies and came with a powerful rush.

"Oh, God," he responded. "We're more than good. You are so awesome." His breath came in heaves. He gently pulled her up and off of him as his member receded. He just stood there and held her under the warm waterfall from the showerhead.

"Can you imagine doing this out under a real waterfall? With water pounding on top of us. And just being able to stay as long as we wanted and to do whatever we wanted?" Maria created the image beautifully. "The sun high in the sky; erotic scents of the jungle all around us, and tropical birds singing in the trees. And the waterfall keeping our bodies soft and wet."

"Now you are making me horny all over again, my love. That sounds deliciously like an invitation to a tropical holiday? We will have to give it some consideration."

"Well, I was just thinking…" Maria let it trail off as she stretched her arms up to wrap around his neck and allowed her soapy breasts to caress his chest.

He bent over to capture her mouth in a delicious wet kiss. He stroked her back and followed her curves down her sides to her hips and across her buttocks.

John called as he came upstairs from her parent's suite.

"Oh we better get going." Maria grabbed her bath sheet as she moved out of the shower, wrapped up and moved to the bedroom door. She called down to John to tell him they would be there once they changed for dinner.

By the time they made their way downstairs. Jessie had returned with Steve, Jasmine and Nick had put their project away, and they could hear Carol's family in the driveway.

"Damn, we have good timing," Duncan whispered in her ear as he went to make sure the front door was open.

Thirty-One

And Then There were Five, and Then There were Six

"We should be more concerned with reaching the lost than pampering the saved."
David McGee

Carol's family came in and as they were greeted everyone, Uncle Dan came through the door. Moments later, Uncle Dave, drove in the driveway.

As they all moved out to the patio, Maria asked John to go down and get Grandma Mary and Papa Johnny.

Duncan had already put a few bottles of wine in the fridge to cool and turned on the barbecue before the shower. As people were moving out to the barbecue he was tending to the marinated chicken and steaks.

Maria's parents came out, with a salad, and greeted everyone.

"Jasmine, can you and Nick take out the juice and sprite, and make sure there are enough glasses for everyone?" Maria requested. "John, can you get the big green salad out of the fridge and put it on the table outside? Jessie and Steve, can you take the salad dressings out and make sure there are enough serving spoons on the table and start to pour the wine for the adults?"

Maria changed the CD and smiled as she thought about the quickie they had grabbed in the shower. She loved to move to the music in the shower. *Enough*, she admonished herself silently as she went out to join the rest.

"Almost ready," Duncan announced. "Does everyone have a drink?"

"I would like to give a toast," Uncle Dan stated. "I would like to toast my extended family and all of your help getting me to see Dr. Jane. I can't believe the change already. Thank you."

"I want to make one too," Papa Johnny said. "I want to thank you all for that great Greek dinner last month when you all connived to get me in to see Dr. Jane as well. I'm not stupid; I know what you were all doing. But like Dan, I can't believe the difference. I feel like a new man." Again they all took a drink. Maria glanced over to Duncan who gave her a wink. Things had started out as planned. They might have another convert tonight. Only time would tell.

George's interest had been piqued. "Sounds good, but what are you guys talking about?"

Maria suggested that they fill their plates and sit down at the table before they shared stories. Duncan was pulling the meat off of the barbecue so the timing was perfect.

Duncan asked if anyone would like to say grace.

"I don't have the flare that Dan has," Papa Johnny said, "so I will just say, Thank you Lord, for family and friends, good health and good food. Let's eat. Amen."

"Okay, so I want to know what's going on," Carol demanded with a smile.

"Why don't you tell everyone your story, Uncle Dan?" Jessie suggested and Uncle Dan started to relay his experience with Dr. Jane.

"And let the stories begin." Maria whispered to Duncan. "Keep your fingers crossed."

"What are you two are whispering about over there?" Carol asked, catching Duncan and Maria whispering.

"Oh nothing." Duncan answered, not quite so innocently but diverted the attention effectively.

And so the evening began. Uncle Dan continued to explain how he had talked with Dr. Jim at the last potluck. How it had got his curiosity going. He explained his phone call to Maria; the appointment; what Dr. Jane had explained to him; and the big news; he was considerably better. His cholesterol was great. His hypertension was gone *and* he was coming off all of his meds. He felt great, was sleeping better, no more cramps in his legs, had more energy and was enjoying life again.

"Wow, that's quite the story" Carol said, not sure what to make of it.

"You don't miss a thing, do you sweetheart? And you are right.

"Way to go Uncle Dan. We're happy for you." Carol was really intrigued now. "And what about you, Dad? Sounds like you must have done something similar?"

"You are right. When I found out that Dan and everyone else seemed to have benefitted from going to the Gibson's Clinic, I figured I had better try it as well," Papa Johnny explained.

"So what did they do for you?" George inquired.

"Well, I had to eat certain foods between six and eight at night, within a fifteen minute period. Mary took care of all that for me. But all the forgetfulness seems to have gone away. After twenty-one days I can't believe the difference. I no longer feel like I keep getting lost in a fog. And my health is better overall. I learned all kinds of stuff about my body, from my eyes and my tongue down to my poop and all the way down to my feet! It's amazing, but I am sure better for it!"

"Way to go to both of you," Carol said.

John then piped up. "But it's not just them, Auntie Carol, it's all of us."

"Does that include you, John?"

"Yeah, I used to have to go to the hospital when I got bee stings. Now I don't have any reaction at all!" he proudly informed everyone.

"Okay, so who else is in on this program?" Carol wanted to know.

"Well, Auntie Carol, I don't have my sports asthma anymore. I haven't had an attack in months and I am doing more than I ever did before," Jasmine said.

"My readings for my diabetes have been normal for several months and I'm not taking any drugs," Jessie contributed.

"What about your adrenal fatigue, Maria?"

"No more foggy brain routines and my energy is way better. Not as much as I hope it will be but doing great. I don't wake up in the middle of night and lie there anymore. I feel better when I wake up in the morning. I've started to lose weight. I am sure happy with my program," Maria replied.

"And what about you Duncan, what has happened with you?" Carol continued around the table.

"Well, I never really had any symptoms before. They just suggested that I needed to check my heart for an enlarged left ventricle and they were right. So they altered my running and exercise routine. I can't really give you any symptom improvement because I never had any symptoms."

"And what about you Mom, are you going to them as well?"

"Yes. I went for my arthritis. And as you can see, all the swelling is gone now." She held up her hands. "There is still some achiness there, so it hasn't cleared up completely yet, but I am betting that given a little more time, that will go away as well."

"And what about you Dave, are you on this boat ride as well?" Carol wanted to know.

"No, I am not, but I am wondering if they can help me with my Hep C. If they can help all these issues, may be they can help me. I am sure willing to give it try," Uncle Dave reasoned.

"That's a pretty impressive tale," George concluded. "But my depression isn't physiological, so I guess I am left out in the cold."

Maria started out to clarify, "Actually, George," but Jessie cut her off.

"Can I do this one Mom? I just finished a paper on it." Maria motioned for her to carry on. "Actually there are all kinds of physiological conditions in the body that have depression as a primary symptom, from imbalances in the microbiota in your gut, to mineral deficiencies, to vitamin deficiencies, to heavy metal toxicity to environmental toxicity. In fact, many things can cause depression and weight issues and a whole bunch of other things. In fact, the microbiota in your gut can affect how you think, how you feel and how you behave. It's amazing."

"Wow," said Jasmine. "Now you are sounding like Pappy. Pretty soon we're all going to start sounding like Pappy."

"So how come, it's taken you all so long to tell us. Maybe we could use their help as well?" Carol said.

"We invited you to dinner with the Gibsons and I know you were talking with them. We didn't want to push anything onto you. We hoped that you would take an interest and maybe go see them yourselves. It was great the way that Papa Johnny and Uncle Dan opened it all up tonight and now you are interested. We are thrilled."

George wanted to know more. "So you are saying that an imbalance in your gut's bacteria can cause psychological issues like depression?"

"Yeah, and even other kinds of issues from Alzheimer's to Parkinson's to bipolar, to allergies, liver problems, weight issues, and diabetes. It's amazing what they are finding out now," Jessie explained.

Jasmine grinned at her and thought, *yup sounding more like Pappy all the time.*

"That's amazing. I would sure like to give it a go because all these anti-depressants don't work. They leave you feeling flat, you put on weight, you lose your sex drive...sorry kids...you lose all your excitement and life just becomes blah. You have to put on an act for everyone, everywhere. It's certainly worth the risk to get my life back. Although having said that, I am not sure what the risk would be."

"Wouldn't it be something if everyone's issues in our family were because of the gut bacteria? That overwhelms the brain to even think of it." Carol paused for a moment then turned to Maria. "On the one hand, I'm ticked off with you that you didn't push us. On the other hand, I sure appreciate that you kept trying to get our attention. Just thinking that I might be able to get my family off meds and out of therapists' offices is bringing tears to my eyes. I can't wait to start. Give me Dr. Jane's number before I leave and I will make appointments for all of us first thing Monday morning!" George nodded, but Sherry looked apprehensive.

"What do they do to you?" she asked.

"You don't have to worry," Jasmine answered. "They don't poke needles or anything in you, well, unless you go in for acupuncture. But I even did that a couple of times and it doesn't hurt. You give urine samples or salvia or hair or you hold onto rods while she watches a screen. You do have to answer a whole bunch of questions though."

"Well, if Jasmine did it, I guess I can try it too," Sherry conceded.

"Well, I am supposed to be the paranoid one here, but I am certainly willing to try it to get rid of this ridiculous paranoia." Tim, more confident than his sister, was sick of being paranoid all the time. And his therapist certainly wasn't helping him at all.

"I guess that means we are all on board then," Carol concluded. "Thanks, Sis. I sure hope we have the same success all you guys seemed to have had."

Maria glanced at Duncan. They had achieved what they had set out to do. Now the conversation could move on to other things. "Anyone want anything else put on the barbecue?"

"Hey, you have to leave room for my desserts," Carol declared. "We may not be having these desserts for some time if we have to stick to just healthy foods. This may be your last chance for a while." She was met with groans.

"How about, we clear the table, put away the food, do the dishes, and get out the Rumoli board? Then when we have had some time to digest our meals, we will be able to enjoy your desserts?" Maria offered.

"Sounds like a plan," Duncan confirmed. "Last person to take things to the kitchen washes the dishes!"

Grandma Mary pulled Maria aside. "Great job, you sneaky little thing. One by one, you are helping us all to get healthy again. I want to give my special thanks to you for that."

"Thanks Mom, but you know, I find it amazing how resistant some people are to *real* medicine, and how ignorant most of are about it. This stuff should be taught in school, for crying out loud. How we allowed our whole nation to become so dependent on synthetic drugs is beyond me, especially when they don't cure anything. But as Duncan said, enough of all this health talk, let's get cleaned up and play Rumoli."

They gave each other a hug and moved into the kitchen to help clean up.

When they got to the kitchen, Jessie and Jasmine were teaching everyone the victory dance and the song…"Another one makes the move, and another one and another one and another makes the move." And everyone was laughing and joining in.

They put out the coffee and tea, set out Carol's deserts, and the now ever-appearing watermelon. By now both Maria and Jessie had both become good watermelon carvers and their designs were a piece of art. The watermelon had become a real showpiece. Everyone made a comment on the food artwork.

Thirty-Two

The Summer Experience

*"It was a splendid summer morning
and it seemed as if nothing could go wrong."*
John Cheever

The school year had ended well. Everyone passed, not all with flying colours, but well enough. Jessie had got a part-time job in a lab for the summer, which allowed her to make enough spending money for the next school year, pay for her books, and for half of her tuition. That was the agreement Duncan and Maria had made with each of their kids.

Duncan and Maria would pay half of their tuition and their room and board. They wanted their children to learn the concept of earning and appreciate the opportunity to go to university. They had decided that if the children were to pay half of their tuition, it would both create a healthy respect for money and they wouldn't just party through university.

The university offered a program whereby if a student's grades were above the 4.0 GPA, then the government paid their tuition, so if they wanted more money, they had to get the grades and then they wouldn't have to pay their own tuition.

Jessie didn't quite make it the first semester but she had made 4.1 the second semester. She was pleased with herself and had more money for herself. Although, she worked even harder to keep her grades up, so didn't have the time to spend as much.

Jasmine and Nick performed their dance routine at the beginning of July, after school had ended. They had done well and come in second. It was their first performance together and the whole family had attended their recital. Grandma Mary swore her family took up almost half of the theatre. She led the standing ovation for Nick and Jasmine.

Both Duncan and Uncle Dan had bought Jasmine a bouquet of roses to present to her when it was finished. She was so moved she started to cry. Nick put an arm around her and asked her what she would do when they came in first? She laughed and admitted she didn't know. Duncan and Maria then took everyone out for dinner to celebrate. Even Nick's parents came along.

Papa Johnny declared that Duncan could pay for the rest of the family, but Papa Johnny and Grandma Mary were going to pay for themselves and Jasmine and Nick. His turning argument was that Duncan and Maria had the rest of their lives to celebrate their kids. As grandparents, they were just two old farts who didn't know how much longer they would be around and wanted be able to celebrate their grandchildren while they still could. Nick's parents thought they should be paying for Nick, but finally they agreed as well.

John had taken to drawing and was showing real talent. He could be a good artist one day. He seemed to have a natural flare for reproducing people's faces. They had found him a summer camp for artists and he had gone for a week and thoroughly enjoyed himself. Maria and Duncan wondered if it would carry through his teens into his young adulthood. They would support him regardless of which path he chose.

The summer had been a great time for everyone, not just John. The relationship between Jessie and Steve was a lot more serious, although they had both agreed that they wouldn't make any life changing decisions, until they finished university, which Duncan and Maria were pleased to hear. Privately, they laughed about the fact that they had both quit university and gone a different route. And, both acknowledged, had done very well for themselves.

The weather was better than usual. Maria felt brand new. It had taken some time, but her adrenals were healthy again. She had not wakened during the night for some time now. She felt better in the morning when she did wake up—better in general. She rarely took an afternoon nap anymore. The brain fog was definitely gone. She woke up every morning with a prayer of thanks, for her health, her family, and for the Gibsons and their clinic.

With the whole family healthy again they had all gone to Florida on vacation for ten days and managed to get through all seven of the theme parks and most of the rides. Everyone had got along.

When they returned home after the holiday, they all agreed that the best part of any trip was coming home.

Duncan and Maria felt like they had a new lease on life. Their family was so much healthier, her energy was back, their sex life was more than it had ever been, and both of them had become more romantic, more sensual, and more creative than they had ever been before. They even discussed how sexy it was to just discuss their sex life.

Jessie and Jasmine now regularly joined in on the morning yoga routine. John wasn't interested but that was okay. The four of them were able to have better focus on their stretches and stances without all of John's laughter and comments.

Marie was back to her real-estate business and loving it; Duncan's business was thriving. She and Duncan had decided to take a trip to Hawaii in the fall and see if they could find that waterfall that she had envisioned.

They had also decided it was time for another potluck. This time, they would invite the Gibsons again and maybe some other friends who had health issues.

They made the phone calls. There would be the five of them with the two boyfriends who were still in tow, the parents, Carol's four (Tim was now engaged in a romance, so his new girlfriend was invited), and both Uncle Dan and Uncle Dave. The whole Gibson family would be there this time—Dr. Jim and Julie, Dr. Jane, and Dr. Daniel, along with Nanny Sarah and Pappy.

In addition, Maria had invited Jean, one of her best friends from the real-estate office. Jean had lost her husband years before in a car accident and she had no children. Maria had also invited another friend, who had gone through a divorce a few years prior. Her children were all grown up, so it would just be Diane.

Duncan had invited two colleagues, Scott who was married to Bev but didn't have any children and Harry, who was divorced. They had chosen all the people because they had health issues of one kind or another and because most had met each other before at other events the Smiths had put on. That made twenty-seven people in all.

They would borrow two more tables in addition to the three they already had, in order for all to sit down. Because it was a potluck, Maria didn't have to worry about all the food. And she had the family to help clean up the house and yard.

It was John's birthday, so they wanted to decorate everything for John as a surprise. Maria and Carol arranged for him to stay overnight with them. Carol and George and planned to take him out for dinner and a movie for his birthday so he wouldn't get suspicious.

Maria and Duncan also wanted to throw him a birthday party with his friends on Monday night, so there was no reason for him to think there would be another birthday party.

All the details were set in place; it just had to happen now.

Thirty-Three

Getting Back into Health-Sex Better than Makeup-Sex

"Sex is as important as eating or drinking and we ought to allow the one appetite to be satisfied with as little restraint or false modesty as the other."
Marquis de Sade

Duncan decided he wanted to take Maria away on a surprise weekend and the last chance they had this summer would be the weekend before the big potluck.

She had been so sick, and he hadn't been able to do anything to help her. He still remembered how back in the late winter, he had caught her crying twice, when she thought she was alone. She had kept most of her frustrations to herself except for when he asked.

He had been so upset when he had found her crying, he had gone across and talked with Dr. Jim. When he explained the little he knew, like how tired she was and how she had started to gain weight and didn't understand why; how she felt frustrated and irritated all the time when she had always been so upbeat, Dr. Jim suggested he make an appointment for her with Dr. Jane. It was the one thing he had been able to do for her.

Maria went to the appointment and had followed everything Dr. Jane had said. Dr. Jane had explained that adrenal fatigue

207

usually took a couple of years to recover from but they caught it early and so she had the potential of recovering faster.

She finally understood what was going on in her body. She and Duncan had sat down and gone over everything that Dr. Jane had provided Maria with. They both agreed to commit to the program. They agreed that she needed to take time off work and just focus on her healing. "Forget about the money," Duncan had said, when she was concerned about not bringing in an income. "Your health is far more important than our wealth. I'd rather be poor and have us happy and healthy, than rich and you dragging yourself through the day and crying because you can't think straight."

Throughout all of it, Jane never complained. She just did what she needed to do. She took a leave from her job, started to read about health, and how to incorporate different foods into their diet. Her increased awareness about physical health appeared to be addictive with the entire family. Now, some eight months later, she was full of energy, could think clearly again and there was a new vigor, depth, and compassion in her relationships.

Duncan talked with Grandma Mary and Papa Johnny and was pleased to find that they could take John for the weekend. He looked online for a romantic getaway at a lake a few hours away where he found a lovely bed and breakfast with its own private Jacuzzi and a huge shower with two showerheads.

Ever since he found the site and booked the room, he had fantasized about the shower. The room looked romantic and feminine and he thought Maria would love it.

It was now the Friday of his surprise weekend. He had come home early to pack a small suitcase for each of them—jeans and t-shirts, shorts and bathing suits, extra underwear and socks. A nice shirt for him and a simple summer dress for Maria, and of course, shoes to go with it, in case they went somewhere fancy.

He packed the simple basics from the bathroom as well as one of Maria's favorite perfumes and his cologne. He decided that she would probably want a necklace and earrings if they went out somewhere special. *How did women decide which necklace and earrings to put with what dress*, he wondered. He chose a couple and hoped she would have chosen at least one of them.

He had done this once before, and forgot half the stuff she wanted. She had been so appreciative of what he had done for her, that she never complained or said anything. But he knew by the look on her face that it hadn't been what she would have chosen.

This time he wanted it to be perfect for her. He stood and looked around the ensuite, then the bedroom, then in their closet. Was there anything he had forgotten? He hoped not.

He went over the schedule with the girls. Jessie would be there for most of the weekend. Jasmine was really old enough to be on her own and certainly mature enough but he preferred to have them together, just in case something happened. Of course, everyone had everyone's cell number as well and the grandparents were downstairs. But everyone was cooperative and didn't mind him playing the "Daddy routine". He decided that they were probably just happy to have the parents gone for the weekend.

One by one, they had all found out what he had wanted to do for Maria, and they felt like co-conspirators. They had all been extra careful about glances, raised eyebrows, or hints.

Duncan had already taken John downstairs to spend the weekend with Maria's parents. When he gave John a hug goodbye, John had warned him, "Take good care of Mom and make sure she has a good time."

Duncan had to smile at his son's adult tone. "You bet, son. I'll do my very best," Duncan promised.

Duncan had told Maria he would pick her up at the office around 5:30. She was anxious to know what this was all about.

"Come on, give me a clue," she pleaded, laughing with him.

"Well, if I tell you, I'll have to shoot you," he teased back.

"Ooohhh, sounds serious, and here I thought we were going to have a fun time," Maria retorted.

"Well, we better have. I put a lot of work and effort into this. So just sit back and enjoy the mystery of it all."

He had put in some of their favourite CDs, the ones where they knew all the words to the songs, so they could sing on their way up into the mountains.

"Did you have a good day at work?" He knew she had a difficult client. She had shown the couple more places than she had ever shown anyone previously. They repeatedly changed their minds about what they wanted.

"I don't know how many times I have sat down with the Kelly's and gone over what they actually need. One time they focus on old architecture and remodelling, then the next time it is all about modern. Another time they want a basement suite to rent out and the next time they decide they want a townhouse. Each time they are sure they know what they want. But it never seems to last.

But regardless, I think we might have the found one that does the trick for them. I hope so. They decided that they would think it over on the weekend. I love the place myself. And they were certainly more excited about this one than any other one I have shown them.

The best part of the day was giving the Jones family the keys for their house. As usual, I had put a lovely bouquet of flowers on the kitchen island with a bottle of wine. You'd think I had bought the house for them they were so thrilled. I am so happy to be back to work again. You just have no idea."

She paused and thought about what she wanted to say. "I want to thank you so much for being supportive the whole time I went through my crap. You never complained once. I think I have bragged about what a wonderful husband you are to everyone in the office.

I'm sorry, hon, I've babbled on and on. I haven't even asked you how your day was. Tell me."

"When you are talking about your challenges and successes with your clients, I never think of it as babbling," Duncan said. "And when you are bragging about what a wonderful guy I am, I would certainly never call that babbling! It is so good to hear how good you feel being back on your feet and loving life again. I was so worried about you there for a spell.

Actually, my day was awesome. Twenty houses in the subdivision are now completed *and* all on time. So far no complaints—always a good sign."

Duncan continued, "With the other project, we had a small mishap but it ended up working to our advantage, so again no complaints. And," he paused, "that really big contract we were bidding on?" He paused to make sure she remembered what he was talking about.

"Yes…did you get it?"

"Yes, we got it, and that will take us through the next couple of years as a primary project. Damn, we did well. And not only that, Brian came in with another couple of good leads today. So, yes, I can definitely say that my work day went well."

"You have done so well, hon. I couldn't be more proud of you. I think I should take you out to dinner to celebrate!

"Okay, so really, where are we going?" She asked again.

They were only a half hour away now, so he thought he would let her in on what he had planned for the weekend. "Well first off, John is with your parents, set to play games with Papa Johnny all weekend. The girls are staying home together and it sounds like they have a good weekend planned. And we, my dear, are going to a romantic little bed and breakfast by a lake, just the two of us, for the whole weekend. It looked really dainty and pretty on the website, that part is for you, and it has a two headed shower and a Jacuzzi for me, where you can show me how much you appreciate all that I am doing for you and how proud you are of me." He let out a long low growl.

Maria laughed and responded in a sexy tone. "That sounds like you are planning on having your way with me, you dirty old man. Or maybe," she paused for effect, "you are planning on me having my way with you. Either way, I think I like the sound of it."

"I'm glad you are getting the picture." He raised his eyebrows in a devilish manner. "If, we choose to leave the 'den of delight', there happens to be a live play in town, although I can't remember what it was. The owners listed a couple of good restaurants we could go to before or after for dinner. This weekend is on me, both literally and financially." He laughed again at his own joke. "And I want to take full advantage of it and of you. This is to celebrate how much you have done to get your health back and how much you have done to get the whole family back into health. You deserve to be richly rewarded here, not just in heaven."

"Hey, you are doing good with the quips tonight," Maria acknowledged. "But even better, you are, as usual, the best husband anyone could ever ask for.

You were so supportive throughout the whole ordeal I could only get better. And thank you for this weekend. You are one in a million. I fully intend to take full advantage of the weekend and of your body." She drawled the last sentence out.

"Now we're talking," Duncan laughed. "Some people know how good "make up sex" is, we're going to show them how good "getting back into health sex is"."

"You're a hoot, but I sure hope we're not going to show anyone!" They were almost in tears they were laughing so hard. It was a good way to release the week's tension and prepare them for the weekend to come.

Thirty-Four

Returning the Favour had Never Been so Much Fun

*"We secure our friends not by accepting favors
But by doing them."*
Thucydides

They got to the Bed and Breakfast place easily as it was well marked and it was still light out when they arrived. Their hosts, Dave and Brenda, showed Maria and Duncan to their room and while Brenda showed them the little suite, Dave lit the fire for them.

There was a bottle of homemade red wine, a couple of wine glasses, and a platter of cheese and crackers for them, plus a bowl of fruit and the makings for tea and coffee in the morning.

The Jacuzzi had scented bubble bath and some pretty homemade soap. A couple of full-length dressing gowns hung on hooks by the shower.

"Oh my, it is just lovely," Maria cried. The color theme was a collection of blues and mauves and featured ornaments and paintings of dolphins and seagulls. The effect was gentle and romatic.

Dave explained where the hikes were and the paths around the lake and handed Duncan a map and pointed out the best swimming spots if they wanted to go for a swim privately. Duncan raised an eyebrow but didn't say anything.

Duncan saw the couple out, and Maria came back in and lay across the bed. "This is terrific and you are terrific and I love you so much."

"You better, but if I didn't organize this weekend for you, would you still love me?" Duncan countered.

"Oh, well, I don't know, maybe, perhaps, oh, probably," Maria teased.

"I'm not sure what I want to do first," Duncan looked around the room and then at Maria. "We could go on a walk around the lake and enjoy this beautiful scenery or we could sit here and get all cuddly in front of the fire and start in on the bottle of wine. Or we could start with a sexy shower in the wonderful two-headed shower and wash off the day's grime. Or we could relax in the Jacuzzi and drink some wine while we get our bodies turned on. There are so many options. What would my favourite lady like to do first?"

"Too many decisions for me to make after a long day's work. You created this wonderful weekend, I will do whatever your heart desires."

"Well, if that's the case, then we are headed for the shower. I have been having fantasies about playing in it ever since I saw it on the Internet." He put a hand out to help Maria off the bed and picked her up in his arms.

"This just keeps getting better and better," Maria whispered as she trailed kisses down his neck. "Exactly what did your fantasies entail, Romeo?"

Duncan set her down in front of the shower and found her lips with his, starting out with a gentle exploration but as she responded, he became more and more impassioned. He explored the inside of her mouth, dancing in and out as her tongue kept up with his. Then he traced kisses up her neck and around her ear. "Well, how about if I just guide you through them and you can just respond accordingly?"

He continued to kiss and nip at her neck, as he allowed his hands to stroke down her back, and back up her sides. When he reached the outer curves of her breasts, his hands sprayed open and cupped them. He gently stroked her breasts while his thumbs caressed her nipples. He loved that he could feel them respond to his touch under her blouse.

"I will do my best...ohhh...yeah, I'm here." She had already started to respond just like he had fantasized.

He moved his hands back down and around her buttocks and then moved one hand down in front of her and down, slowly across her belly, and further down, painstakingly slowly. Moving his fingers gently between her legs, he massaged her with one hand, and felt her arch in response he was looking for, the other hand moved to undo her pants.

Meanwhile, Maria had already unbuttoned his shirt and slid it over his shoulders as her hands glided across his tight chest. He felt so good to touch.

He removed his hands from her body so she could slide his shirt off then returned the favour by helping her glide out of hers. They danced their clothing removal as if in slow motion, as they enjoyed the sensual delight of not having to rush anything.

Out of the confines of her blouse, Maria started to undo his zipper and buckle. Duncan smiled approvingly and he reached over to get the showers going. But when she stroked his member, he had to come back to her fast. *Oh yeah*, he thought, *this is going to get good tonight.*

Maria slipped out of her pants, and as she moved to put them on the counter, Duncan's arms came around her. His hands moved up under her lacy bra and he cupped her breasts and his thumbs caressed her taut nipples as he dragged kisses down her neck. He loved it when she groaned in delight.

He turned her around in his arms and released her bra strap. She arched back so he could remove her lacy support and he greeted one of the out coming nipples with his tongue. "Well, hello, my sweet," he growled. "Welcome to our weekend of romantic delight." He left one nipple and moved to greet the other one that waited impatiently for his greeting. He sashayed his tongue around the tautness and them over it and then gently sucked its stiffness. "And welcome to you too, my dear friend. I am so glad you could come." And with that, he pulled her naked body up to his and walked them into the shower.

They both arched back from one another to allow the spray of water from both sides of the shower to waterfall over their bodies and soak them in a sensual wash. Duncan took two of the homemade bars of soap from the shower tray and handed one to Maria.

"Perhaps it is now my time to welcome your boys in a manner akin to how you welcomed my girls." She laughed in a sexy voice.

"Don't mind if you do."

Maria took the soap and created suds down his broad chest, making sure to acknowledge his nipples on the way down. She stroked and kissed her way down across his belly, and moved down along his hips to his thighs. Then teasingly she moved up and around his member and his boys.

She brought long, slow, soapy, sensual strokes to between his legs and gently cupped his boys in her hands.

"You teasing witch, you" he responded to her strokes.

"Welcome to the weekend, my favourite boys. This really ought to be interesting so make sure you stay tuned."

She worked with the soap in her hands to create more suds over his hips and around to his buttocks, pulling him toward her as she straddled him and loved how he groaned in response. She kept her eyes fixed on his while she brought her hands up from under his buttocks around his hips and down his length. "And you, are the star of the show. So don't get lost," she warned his hardened member.

She came back up and he kissed his appreciation of the welcoming package. They stroked each other with soapy suds in long sensual movements. Down her curves, around his boys, over his buttocks, cupping her breasts, they moved in a beautiful dance as if they had practiced for years. As their hands moved and glided over well-known territory, their mouths and tongues continued to meet and release and lick and suck and explore wherever they could. Their groans and growls created yet another level of sensory intoxication that enticed and excited them beyond belief.

His member was hard and ready and waiting. Her breasts were full and her nipples were reaching for his touch; her inner chamber was wet and ready, and yet they still caressed and soaped, stroked, and kissed until their bodies couldn't wait any longer.

She started to vibrate and then she arched and stretched, and then she released once, and then twice. He pulled her up with his hands under her buttocks, her legs wrapped around him and he slid her down on his member.

"Oh yes," he growled next to her ear. "Just keep moving." She braced her legs against the wall, and pushed against it to help him as he moved her up and down. "I don't know if I can hold on much longer..." He stopped to get his breath, to focus, to hold on longer, and then he began to move her up and down again.

At first they moved gently and then it became more intense, more passionate, as he moved her up and down, her sudsy taut nipples stroked his soapy chest. *Oh God, it's hard to hold on,* he thought.

The shower pounded down on her shoulders, his member pulsated against her insides, and her hard soapy nipples glided against his chest every time she went up and down. She tried to hold back but she started to come again, and as she looked up into his eyes, he exploded inside her.

He held her there for a moment longer and then slowly let her down as he tried to slow down his breathing. "God, we're good." The words came out with the first breath. "Man, I love you," he said with the second breath.

Maria started to laugh between gulps of air as her breathing started to slow down. "You love me because we're so good at this shower dance?" she teased. "Geez, and I thought," she panted, "we were good at the shower dance because we love," she panted again, "each other so much."

"How about, if I get the water running in the Jacuzzi, and we can discuss our options in there?" He laughed as his panting slowed down. Maria nodded and started to rinse herself off in the shower.

"No, don't do that," he admonished her, "that's my job, and I don't want to get fired. Just give me a moment."

She laughingly agreed to wait and let him do his job; she certainly wouldn't want him to get fired.

Duncan went and turned on the water in the Jacuzzi then came back to the shower. He washed her hair and then glided his hands down over every inch of her body to take off the suds they had created.

Recognizing his direction, she laughed. "Okay, so now that I know what to do, bend over and let me wash your hair and rinse you so I don't get fired."

He bent to let her wash his hair but she took her time to massage his scalp as well.

"Oh, now that feels good." He latched onto a nipple that had stood up as if to say 'thank you'.

"Hey you, stop that. It's my time to take care of you?"

"But you pulled my head down into your girls and I had no choice but to say hi," Duncan returned. As he brought his mouth up to capture hers one more time.

Laughingly they stood back and stretched up under their own showerhead for a final rinse. He couldn't believe how turned on he was, all over again. As if in a calculated dance step, they both reached out and spread their hands across each other's chest. Her hands slowly glided up his chest and around his neck, bringing her still wet taut nipples against his chest again. He moaned in delight and his hands followed a pathway down her back and over her buttocks. Their mouths locked.

She could feel his member getting hard all over again. "Ooohhh, again so soon?" she teased as she glided her wet hips back and forth against him.

"Do you think we should wait until we get into the Jacuzzi before we decide to dance again, or would you like to have a repeat performance here, my lord?"

"God, the decisions are just too hard to make. I would say we do the repeat performance here but I think we better get to the Jacuzzi before it overflows." He peaked out of the shower to see what the water level was in the Jacuzzi and shook his head. "Yup, we better move from this stage to the next, my lady, and you can have your way with me there."

"Oh you better be careful," Maria answered. "You may not make it till morning if I have my way with you."

"With you, my love, I am willing to take my chances." He scooped her up in his arms, gave her a moment to turn off both showerheads and then carried her to the Jacuzzi.

"Don't slip on the water," Maria cautioned. "Man, this must be our second honeymoon. I can't remember having so much fun. And what dance would you like to do in the Jacuzzi, my lord?"

He laughed as he turned off the water, "My lord, is it? Well, if I am your lord and master, then I can have whatever I want. And I want you." He growled.

"How about if I have my way with you, like you did that morning when you wouldn't let me touch you and I had to just lie back and receive. I think it is far past your time."

"My heart is pounding in anticipation."

"Well, let's just see what we can do here." She gave him a naughty look. She straddled his tummy with her legs, bent over his upper chest with her arms and intentionally allowed her nipples to stroke his face while she took each of his arms and placed them on the outer rim of the Jacuzzi. "Now you have to keep your arms and hands out of the tub, while I have my way with you."

He automatically went to take a taut nipple in his mouth when she squeezed her legs around him. "No, my lord, you are not allowed to engage. You have to lie back and simply receive. Remember when you serviced me? Same rules apply. Now you will find out just how difficult that can be."

Duncan laughed. "But again your girls were reaching out and I was simply obliging," he pretended to whine.

The tub was more than big enough for two, which gave her room to manoeuvre.

She gently stroked one finger around his lips and down his chin, his neck, his chest, right down to his member, and stopped.

She then leaned forward over him. She braced her hands on the tub on either side of his chest and gyrated her hips over his soapy member. She watched the expressions of pleasure move across his face. "Oh God, that is enticing. I can't believe I am up, again."

She manoeuvred further down his length until she was far enough that she could come down on him. He groaned with pleasure.

Her hard, taut nipples stroked his body as she teased him. Then she moved back up the tub once again. She left just enough space between her body and his that her nipples were all that stroked the length of him.

After several minutes of seductive enticement, she asked with an innocently demure look, "How am I doing so far, my lord?" and then started to laugh.

"You temptress, you. I love every minute of it. But I can't hold on much longer," he warned. "You are a witch, and know how to service a lord well."

She smiled seductively at him. She sat up and gave him a full view of her while she sat up on her knees and then lowered herself down on his member and began a dance of utter delight. She moved up and down slowly, then picked up the pace and gyrated her hips back and forth, then slowed down again. She pushed her torso back giving a different pressure and then moved forward.

"Oh, God," he groaned. "This is too much."

"Hold on, my lord." She commanded, "The longer we can make you hold on, the stronger it will be." And she continued to pulsate and gyrate on him.

"Am I allowed to use my hands, now that you have seduced me, my lady?"

"Well, I guess, being as it's you." She gave him her sexiest smile. He brought his hands back into the Jacuzzi and returned the delight that she had given him. But it didn't last long as he just couldn't hold back this time.

He struggled to hold off, but she couldn't hold it either, she grabbed the sides of the tub and arched her back and as soon as she started to come he was right there with her. He grabbed her buttocks and soapsuds flew everywhere.

She remained sitting on top of him after they both relaxed. Then she lay down in the Jacuzzi beside him.

"You are amazing. You have been up and down for an hour. Not bad for an old guy like you. I'm impressed."

"So am I," he agreed. "It must be because I am married to such an enticing witch."

Again they laughed. "Hey, I thought we were supposed to have a discussion in the Jacuzzi? I don't even remember what it was about, do you?"

He couldn't remember either but didn't really care. "I am more focused on how we just started this weekend off. I think we introduced this weekend beautifully."

"And I think I love you more than ever. This is like a second honeymoon and I didn't even have to do any of the planning."

"Just don't you forget it?" he warned. "I think we should snuggle for a bit here while the water is still warm then get up and get dressed. I should take you out for dinner, and feed that body of yours, never mind mine, so that we have enough energy to make it through the weekend."

"Sounds good to me." She snuggled down beside him in the water. "I am definitely feeling satiated on this level. Now I get to go and get satiated on another level. Do you want to have a nap first or just go for dinner?"

He hadn't thought of her tiring out. He didn't want her to start going backwards. "That's a great idea. Let's have a quick nap before we go out."

They stretched against one another and gently created soapy patterns until the water started to get cool. He got out first and gave her his hand to help her out. He wrapped a towel around her and brought her wet, naked body close to his. She felt to see if he was going to go for it again, but this time there was nothing hard pressing against her belly. *Good thing*, she thought, *I don't think I could go another round*. He gently dried her body and gave her a wink.

When he finished, she took her towel and wrapped it around him and dried him as he had done for her. She looked up at him and reached up for a kiss. He gave her exactly what she wanted, and they held each other there in a loving embrace for a long moment.

Then he let her go and they moved into the bedroom and slid between the sheets. He pulled her into his arms and she nestled her head against his shoulder as their legs moved into their usual place entwined with one another.

In moments, she was fast asleep with a gentle smile on her lips. He was thankful that she had suggested a nap. She had been such a great sport and had lived up to his best fantasies.

"Thank you Dr. Jim and Pappy, much appreciated," he whispered.

Thirty-Five

I'll Love You Until the End of Time

"The perfect guy is not the one who has the most money or the most handsome one you'll meet. He is the one who knows how to make you smile and will take care of you each and every day until the end of time..."
Melchor Lim

Next thing he knew, she was kissing him on the chest and calling his name softly. "Duncan. Are you going to sleep all night?"

"Hey there. I thought we were taking a nap for you. I didn't think I would doze off too." He stretched his arm around her and pulled her body close.

They rearranged their bodies, their arms and their legs until they were sufficiently entwined and then looked into each other in the eyes. It felt good to just lie there and be with one another.

After a few minutes, Maria asked, "Whatcha thinking?"

"What a sensuous, horny, sexy, fun, beautiful wife I have and wondering how I got so lucky?"

"I like those thoughts." She laughed. "Especially when you are too blind to see my body getting older and more wrinkled, and soon I will be turning grey on top of it. But if you don't see that, then I'm good."

"You do realize that sexiness has nothing to do with appearance, don't you?" Duncan asked.

"So what is sexy for you?" she asked, taking the bait.

"It is about how confident a woman is with herself and her body, not really so much what her body looks like. It's how she carries herself, her intelligence, her emotions, her attitude towards life and others. It's about her compassion for others and how aware she is of what is going on around her.

Sexiness is really more about who you are as a person, not what you look like. Now don't get me wrong. Any guy enjoys seeing a sexy babe on TV or on the street or on the beach. But that's different because you don't know her, you simply admire what God gave her.

The sexy babe you want to wake up with every day for the rest of your life, is the one who developed her intelligence, her attitude, and her compassion. Good looks on top of that is just icing on the cake.

Any intelligent man knows that. Too often the sexy babe is about looks only, and nine times out of ten, there is no depth or personality or intelligence. I am sure there are the odd few, who didn't use their looks to get what they wanted in life. They're the ones who actually developed who they were but you know as well as I do that they are far and few between.

Now, if we were to take my lady, for instance, she has looks on the outside but she has all the other qualities on the inside. So when her looks start to mature and develop and her girls start to race for her waist; when her laugh lines start to deepen and spread and her hair betrays the wisdom she has collected over the years, you just know that she is always going to be a sexy babe for you."

"I'm speechless," she responded and stopped. After a few moments, she continued, "I think that is the most romantic, beautiful thing I have ever heard you say."

They continued to just lie and look into one another's eyes, so full of love and caring and compassion. After some ten minutes had passed, Duncan rolled over on his back and suggested that they needed to get up and replenish their bodies.

"Let's get the list of restaurants the landlords left us and see how we might pleasure the palate." They both laughed and climbed out of bed. They got dressed and went to find the list. They found a Greek restaurant on the list and decided that was what they both wanted and went to find it.

The night air was balmy with millions of stars in the sky. They took a moment to appreciate the heavens before they got into the car and then again at the restaurant when they got out. They could see both the big and small dippers and a billion other stars.

They got a table right away. The waitress was young, cute, and efficient. She explained the night's specials and brought them their drinks. They ordered a bottle of their favorite white chardonnay and decided to have the Greek platter for two.

The waitress left and they both sat back in their chairs and just relaxed. Within moments the waitress had returned with their wine and filled their wine glasses. Duncan smiled and brought his wine glass up in a toast.

"This wasn't meant to be our second honeymoon, despite the way it started out. I thought our trip to Hawaii might be our second honeymoon. But heck, who said we have to stop at two? Why can't we have three?

So here's to us and setting the Guinness Book of World Records for having as many second honeymoons as a couple can have."

"I'll toast to that," Maria agreed with a big smile and a clink of glasses. "Man, we could get really creative and have a different honeymoon on every continent. Wouldn't that be interesting?"

"Okay, so where would you want to start? We have already had one honeymoon in Europe. If this were to be our second honeymoon and then of course, Hawaii, we've got two in the US. Where would you like the next one to be?"

"Well, you know I've always wanted to go on an African safari, so that could be one but I don't know if you could turn that kind of holiday into a honeymoon. I know you would love to go to Thailand, so that would be another. We've both talked about doing the Napoli Trek, but that would be more of a spiritual experience than a honeymoon, I think. I don't know, what about you?"

"I think one year we need to do Australia and another the Fijian islands. I think those kinds of holidays would be easy to turn into a honeymoon. I don't know of any romantic places in South America, so we are going to have to research that one. We are going to have to sit down and figure out what our honeymoon bucket list is."

The dinner came. Everything was done to perfection. The Greek salad had a generous portion of an excellent house special dressing. Their platter contained chicken and prawn souvlaki, plus moussaka, calamari, a couple of spanakopita, rice, and roasted potatoes.

The waitress asked if they would like desert and explained that it was a special recipe homemade by the owner made. Maria said they would have to come back tomorrow and try some, because she just couldn't eat anymore tonight. But Duncan suggested that they take some back to the suite. They might want to indulge in it later when they had more stomach room.

They were going to finish off the dinner with a cup of tea but Maria suggested that it might be nicer to go back to the bed and breakfast and have their tea in front of the fire.

They paid the bill and returned to the romantic little suite. Duncan relit the fire while Maria made chai tea.

With the doors and windows open, the night air was soft and gentle. The fire danced as they cuddled on the couch. Neither said much; they just enjoyed the sounds of the fire and the crickets outdoors, until Duncan suggested that they better go to bed before they fell asleep in front of the fire.

Thirty-Six

"Everything Happens for a Reason"

"There is nothing that can happen TO you that can't also happen FOR you…if you'll let it."
Mandy Hale, The Single Woman: Life, Love, and a Dash of Sass

It was 8:30 when Duncan woke up with Maria watching him lovingly. "I love you," she whispered to him as he adjusted to morning light.

"What a perfect way to wake up, seeing those big brown eyes gazing at me from the pillow next to me. I love you, too."

"I can't believe I actually woke up before you. I must have really tired you out last night, in the shower and the Jacuzzi," Maria teased.

"And, I hope you tire me out for the rest of my life. What would you like to do today? We could start off with another dance, if you like, perhaps a bed dance this time, or perhaps even another shower dance. I really don't mind what kind of dancing you want to do. Maybe some breakfast, just to keep those energies going, and then perhaps a hike. Remember the picnic we had last spring, up in the mountains. Maybe Dave and Brenda will make us a picnic or tell us where we can get one and we can take a picnic up with us. Would you like that?"

"That sounds perfect. Too bad, we didn't bring the picnic packsack."

"Three steps ahead of you, my lady. It's in the trunk. When I read on the website about the different walks and hikes they had, I threw in the packsack just in case."

"Wow, what did I do to deserve a husband who thought of everything? Or did you. We haven't even opened the suitcases yet. I was too preoccupied with the dances of the evening, and we never even got into pajamas to go to bed. What did you pack?"

"Well, I brought you some bikini underwear, a sexy bra, and some socks. Didn't think you would need anything else," he teased.

"You are a tease. Okay, so what did you pack?"

"Well, I brought us both jeans and shorts, long-sleeved and short-sleeved t-shirts, bathing suits, and underwear. I brought a nice shirt for me, and your blue summer dress for you. I even brought you a couple pairs of earrings and necklaces because I didn't have a clue what you would chose to go with your dress. And, don't ask...I brought the shoes you wear with it. Not bad eh, especially for a guy? I really tried to think of everything this time. I wanted it to be perfect for you."

"You are perfect for me. I couldn't ask for anything else. How many times do I have to thank you for all of this and for just being you?"

"I think a few more times this weekend would do…for this weekend…and then maybe for the rest of my life." He pulled her close and kissed her deeply.

They got out of bed, went and did their morning routines and then walked into the dining room for breakfast.

There were two other couples there and the third couple was coming up behind them on the path to the breakfast room. Coffee and tea, hash browns, bacon and eggs, and pancakes had been arranged on a sideboard. The couples were all friendly and there was easy talk between them.

Brenda said that she would be more than happy to put together a picnic lunch for them and asked what they would like. Maria told her to surprise them and Brenda laughingly went off to the kitchen to prepare it.

After breakfast, Maria went back to their room to get the map while Duncan went to grab a couple of sweaters they always left in the trunk, and the picnic backpack. When they returned to the kitchen they showed Brenda the backpack. She was impressed so with it she wanted to know where Maria had purchased it so she could get a couple of them for the couples who came to stay.

With directions for the hiking trail in hand, they were ready to go. It didn't take them long to get to the parking lot where they parked the car. They started up the hill and could hear dogs barking and people laughing further up the path. They passed a small family on the way, walking with a six year old. Everyone said hello while Duncan and Maria moved past them and continued up the hill.

After hiking for about an hour, they came to the clearing that Brenda had mentioned and saw another family racing around with two dogs, having a blast. The dogs looked like Rottweiler-Shepherds and were running after balls and Frisbees.

Maria pointed to a place under a nice tree, off to the side of the clearing and they walked over to it and put down the backpack.

A Frisbee flew nearby and Duncan ran to catch it, nearly tripping over a root on the way but he caught himself and snatched the Frisbee out of the air. The others in the field applauded him.

An older boy, who appeared to be in his teens, called to Duncan to throw him the Frisbee. As Duncan returned the Frisbee he offered his name and asked the teen what his was. Randy called out his name as the dogs continued to chase around the field, after birds and then after squirrels and, of course, after the Frisbee.

"Let's go join them for a bit," he suggested to Maria. They had often played Frisbee with their kids and always enjoyed the playful exercise.

Maria agreed and jogged to a different point in the field. The mother of the group, sailed the Frisbee to Maria as introductions were called across the field.

Maria caught the Frisbee beautifully. Anne, the mother of the group, pointed to her other son, and called out that his name was Brad, and suggested that Maria throw the Frisbee to Brad.

"Hi Brad," Maria called to him. "Let's see if I can get the Frisbee to you."

Duncan laughed and thought, *she sure as hell can.* She always had a good strong throwing arm, whether it was baseball or Frisbee, or even bowling. Maria not only had a good strong arm but an accurate follow through.

One of the dogs went to chase after the Frisbee that Maria threw and jumped up in the air in an attempt to catch it with his mouth, but couldn't jump high enough.

Brad caught the Frisbee that came right to him and called back surprised, "Good throw," and added, "that's my Dad," as he threw the Frisbee to his dad.

"Hi Dad," Duncan and Maria called out in unison as one of the dogs bounded over to Maria.

"That's Mutt," Ann called. "They're both terrifically friendly. The other one is Jeff."

"Dad" threw the Frisbee to Duncan and yelled out that his name was Steve and that the dog running towards to Duncan was Jeff. They played Frisbee for a while, and intermittently one of the boys would throw a ball for the dogs. As they played they called out occasional conversational questions to one another. They found out that the boys were seventeen and fifteen. The dogs were from the same litter and about five years old. The family often came up here for the hike and family picnics.

It was good fun and a way to stretch out after the hike up the hill. There were fluffy little clouds that meandered across the sky but were always careful never to block the sun for them. It was another gorgeous summer day. A day to relax and play and just have fun.

Eventually, Duncan suggested that they break for lunch. Steve asked if they wanted to come over and join them as they had their picnic basket as well. Duncan looked to Maria and she nodded in agreement.

"Sounds great. I will go get our backpack," Duncan called back and went to get it. Maria wandered over to where Anne had set down their picnic basket. The boys continued to throw the Frisbee and the dogs continued their playful antics in the field.

Anne checked out the backpack that Duncan brought and couldn't believe how well packed it was with dishes and cutlery, wine and glasses, and all the lunch treats that Brenda had prepared for them. Together, they discovered that she had put in some beautiful deli ham and cheese sandwiches, a small container of homemade pickles, a container with potato salad, and another with a bean salad, and some sweets for desert. Duncan had added a bottle of wine. And voilà, their picnic was complete.

The others gathered around for lunch. They too had sandwiches and potato salad but potato chips and sodas to go with it.

Maria thought, *Oh boy, they are going to have troubles down the road, if they keep that diet up but maybe it was just a special treat for them, rather than a daily fair.*

The conversation flowed easily. Duncan and Maria shared that they had come away for a weekend to recuperate; they didn't divulge that it had turned into second honeymoon. They admitted that they had never been here before and that they had booked in at the Bed & Breakfast.

Anne told them that Brenda and Steve were good friends. They had had the Bed & Breakfast place for years, ever since Steve had had a heart attack and couldn't go back to work. Brenda had always wanted to own a Bed & Breakfast and so they decided it was their time to do so.

Duncan and Maria told them about their family and how old the kids were. How Jessie had a summer job in a laboratory between her first and second year at university. How Jasmine and Nick had come in second in their first dance competition together and how John was becoming a beautiful artist at such a young age. It was obvious they were proud of their children as they spoke lovingly of them.

Anne queried why they hadn't brought their kids with them and Steve gave her a look, telling her it was none of her business. But Maria caught the look and said it was okay, they didn't mind.

"This terrific husband of mine decided to give me a mysterious present this weekend. He organized the getaway and took care of the kids, although Jessie and Jasmine are old enough to take care of themselves. He packed our bags and picked me up from work yesterday. I didn't know anything until we were just about here last night."

"Oh, what a romantic thing to do," Anne cried giving her husband a directed look.

"Yes, I got the message loud and clear. Maybe one day, I will have to think about that one."

Conversation turned to health issues, and Maria mentioned that almost everyone in her family had had some type of ailment diagnosed or recognized in the past few years. She explained that they were fortunate to have a unique family across the street with various degrees or designations in different healing modalities. They had all worked together and now everyone was getting back into health again rather than just managing the symptoms with pharmaceutical drugs.

"And it works?" Anne asked hesitantly.

Duncan responded with an adamantly. "Wow, does it ever work. We eat better as well. I thought at first our food bills would go through the roof but these doctors taught us all kinds of things and our food bills are less and our health is better. Even Maria's parents got into the program and her sister's family as well.

They recognized that all my exercise was actually causing a heart issue, which the MD confirmed, and I had to cut back on running. I couldn't believe that there was such a thing as too much exercise and that it was actually doing me more harm than good. I guess too much of even a good thing can be bad for you. Thanks to Maria, the girls and Maria and I do yoga almost every day instead."

Steve looked at Anne with a knowing look and asked, "What kinds of things, besides your heart, have you dealt with?"

"Everything from arthritis and dementia with my parents, to allergies for our son, sports asthma for our younger daughter, and diabetes for our older daughter." Maria left out that she had adrenal fatigue because she didn't want to have to explain what it was. But Duncan filled in for her.

"And Maria had adrenal fatigue, which left her exhausted and with a variety of other symptoms and now she is back to health again and doing great. That is partly why we are taking a special weekend for ourselves, just to celebrate her good health again."

"Maybe we should get your information and check this out." Anne raised her eyebrow to Steve. "We could do with some help like that." She turned to look at Duncan and Maria. "We have a variety of health issues in our extended family. Would you mind giving us the information for the clinic?"

Maria had a thought. "We are having a big potluck dinner, next weekend. Our whole extended family—and all of their issues—are coming. The Gibsons are also coming, plus various other friends. Why don't the four of you come as well and you can talk with everyone and find out what they can offer you?"

"Oh, that is awfully kind of you but we wouldn't want to impose on you," Anne responded.

But Duncan countered, "Hey, it's no imposition. We already have twenty-five or so coming. A few more will just make it more fun. Besides its potluck so it's not like we are doing all the work. We just have to find another table. And more chairs."

"Okay, so what if I bring a folding table and four chairs, and Anne brings one of her famous chili dishes, and I'll bring a bottle of wine. I don't know if I want to talk health issues all night but I am always game for making new friends and we have certainly enjoyed meeting and having fun with you today." Steve looked at Anne for confirmation.

All the boys had really heard was that they had girls. The girls were around their ages, so they were okay with it and both shrugged their shoulders in agreement then jumped up to go play some more.

Nobody had pen or paper to jot down phone numbers or addresses. Maria pulled out her iPhone to send all the info right away through her phone. Maria put Anne's phone number into the iPhone and texted her the required info.

"This is great. I am glad we all decided to come up here today," Anne told Maria. "Everything happens for a reason, as they say."

"You'll enjoy everyone. I invited some friends from work and so did Duncan. You don't need to worry about the Gibsons imposing anything on you but if you ask questions be prepared for the answers. When we have family potlucks we usually play Rumoli afterwards but I am not sure what we are going to do this time with so many people. We will have to get some lawn games and different board games going. But not to worry, it always works out."

At that point, the men went to join the boys and the dogs and the two women sat and compared family notes. Anne's son Randy had diabetes, Brad had ADHD, and her husband was on anti-cholesterol pills. Anne herself went through bouts of depression, although summers were usually much better for her than winters. They tried to get out and do as much as a family during the summer and just prayed that the next winter would be easier for her. She hated what the anti-depressants did to her.

Maria was just itching to tell Anne all that she knew but thought it wiser to let her hear the family stories and talk with the Gibsons herself. It would be more meaningful and more powerful that way.

Now she couldn't wait for the next weekend. It couldn't come soon enough.

Thirty-Seven

It's a Small World

"The world only exists in your eyes.
You can make it as big or as small as you want."
F. Scott Fitzgerald

When Duncan and Maria returned to the Bed and Breakfast, they thanked Brenda for the lovely lunch and returned all the containers. When Dave walked in, Duncan and Maria shared how they had met their friends up on the mountain.

Dave laughed. "It's a small world. They are lovely people and the boys are really turning out fine."

Maria was about to suggest that Brenda and Dave come to the potluck as well, but thought better of it. Brenda and Dave had most of their summer weekends taken up with the Bed and Breakfast; Duncan and she already had almost thirty people coming to the potluck and maybe Dave and Brenda would come to another one they would have later in the year. For now, they had the McDonalds to add to her list and that was enough.

Thirty-Eight

Do You Like Salsa Dancing

"Dancing is a vertical Expression of a horizontal Desire"
Robert Frost

Back in their room, Duncan and Maria sat down on the couch in front of the fireplace. They talked about their day, the people they had met at breakfast and the new friends they had developed in the mountains. How much fun it was to play Frisbee and how excited Maria was that they were coming to the potluck. Duncan laughed. "You're on a mission to get the world back into health, one family at a time, aren't you?"

"Well," she responded, "somebody has to do it."

Duncan raised his eyebrows and smiled, "And it might as well be my favourite wife."

"And how many wives do you have, Prince Charming? And are these wives of yours tucked away in your past lives, your fantasies or in another city I don't know about?"

"Oh, I'll never tell," Duncan quipped mischievously. He put his arms around her and swooped in for a luscious kiss. "Will you have another dance with me?" He wiggled his eyebrows.

"Oh, I think if you turn on your charm, we could manage another shower dance before we go out tonight." She paused and then said, "Geez, I can't believe I actually agreed to this again."

"Well, my lady, I guess I will just have to charm you." He picked her up in his arms and waltzed into the bathroom, setting her down in front of the shower.

"Did you see the CD player they have in here," Maria asked looking around for a music CD.

"No, we've been too busy dancing in here to notice anything else. What do they have?"

"Ohhh, they have a Hector Lavoe—you up for salsa, baby?" Maria moved her hips provocatively as she turned on the CD and Duncan laughingly responded.

She began to move sensuously to the music as she started to undress for him, and then slowly, seductively she slid her t-shirt up over her lacy bra, winked at him, and stopped.

Duncan took up the motion from there and with a husky growl he began to remove his shirt for her while he swayed to the music.

"Ohhh, this ought to be fun, you sexy thing." She swung her hips back and forth as she slid her jeans down to reveal a lacy pair of panties that matched her bra.

"God, you better believe it," Duncan breathed heavily. He was already hard and they hadn't even touched one another.

With a seductiveness he didn't know she had, she continued to remove her lacy bra, slowly, while she rocked to the music. She teased him with glances as she turned and provided him with a view of her lace-covered bottom. She glided her arms up above her head and teased him with a view of one lovely breast, then moved to the other side to taunt him with the other. Then she seductively, gracefully turned to him while she moved her arms in and out, then finally presented him with a full frontal view of full breasts and taut nipples.

Moving seductively to the music, Maria sidled up to him and promised in a sultry voice, "Let me take care of the rest of your things, my lord."

She unhooked his buckle, slid down his zipper, and slowly removed his jeans. When they reached his ankles, he kicked them off.

As she moved back up, she rubbed her nipples up his belly, hooked her finger into his briefs and sashayed back down pulling his briefs down with her, finishing the job with her toe. He groaned as she trailed her fingers near and around, but didn't touch the hardened member.

"Oh God, you're good," he whispered to her.

In salsa style, she moved back up his body and turned her back to him. He took her hands and glided their arms above their heads and danced her into the warm shower. As he slid one hand down an arm, he grabbed a bar of soap with the other and handed it to her, then reached for the second.

They continued to dance erotically in the shower, to the salsa music, as they allowed the warm water and soapy suds to ignite even more passion than before. The song played out and the music moved from one sensuous rhythm to another.

"I can't believe this," Duncan murmured into her mouth as he bent to take her lips with his. Their mouths continued to move to the salsa rhythm, taking and giving, pleasuring and enticing. Their bodies continued to move to the rhythm as they danced in and out, they connected and then released but their mouths never left one another. It was the most seductive dance they had ever done. And it just kept going on and on.

Duncan couldn't remember ever lasting this long—the pressure was unbelievable. How long had he been married to this woman and he had no idea that they had this within them.

As they moved into their third song, Maria arched back allowing her breasts to reach up to him. She caught her breath as he stroked her breasts with the soapy water, lathering them with a minty scent that now seemed sensual in and of itself. This was better than any movie she had ever seen.

As they stretched their arms above their heads in salsa style and his fingers delicately trailed down her arms, she wrapped her arms around his neck. Turning, she pressed her back into him and with her hips moving in time to the music, she slid down the front of him, stroking his member with the silkiness of the soapy water, and back up again.

As she turned back to face him again and started to sway against him, he wrapped his arms around her, his hands reached down and moved inside her just long enough to tease. Then he stroked back upwards towards her breasts as she moved back down the front of him.

As she came back up again, he cupped her breasts and stroked her nipples with his thumbs. One of her legs came up and circled his as he arched her back and stroked his tongue over a taut nipple. He brought her back up against him and they slithered around each other as their bodies moved to the rhythm, wet and soapy. He pulled her hard against his chest and then arched her back again. This time, he dragged one hand up between her legs, allowing his fingers to stroke her inner wetness while he held her, the water streaming over her.

She gyrated back down his front, curving her tongue around his member, then slithered back up his front. He groaned with a deep intense hunger.

This erotic dance went way beyond his fantasies. He reached down and stroked between her legs. She was as wet inside as she was outside.

He had already felt her shudder a few times, and it was difficult for him to hold on. They barely moved now, as she stretched up against his body with her arms above his head. He stroked her insides. She started to feel the waves come and arched back as she strained to contain the tension. With his other hand, he stroked his fingers around a breast and gently massaged an aching nipple between his fingers, as she felt wave after wave flow through her.

He loved that sensation and grasped her other nipple with his mouth. He felt her come and then again. She looked up at him and groaned. Her eyes told him volumes. But he already knew.

As she straightened, he grabbed her close to him and pulled her up. Her feet knew exactly where to plant themselves against the wall; she didn't even have to think about it.

He slid her wet intoxicating body up along his and eased her down into place. She groaned again, deeper and longer, as her body vibrated and released again. She had barely started to move up and down on him, before he started to come with her. He caught her mouth with his and penetrated her lips as his member penetrated her. He couldn't get enough of her, nor she of him.

And finally, it was over, their breathing heavy and full. He pulled her up and off of him. But his mouth didn't leave hers as they continued to hold onto one another. It was like their mouths took up where their bodies had left off, still dancing to the salsa. They held each other in their arms as the water poured down on their aching bodies and their breathing slowly returned to normal.

Finally, they let go of one another. "I don't think I will ever be the same after that," he said. "I think when you recovered from adrenal fatigue, it reset something inside of you to a different channel, my lady."

"I think you might have had a lot to do with it, my lord," Maria laughingly replied.

"I think we should turn on something a little more soothing and see if we can recover in the Jacuzzi. Although I am not sure I will ever recover from that."

Now, the tone had changed again. One from deep sensuality back to laughter, but a more a gentle laughter this time. Maria found another CD, one of popular love songs, and Duncan turned on the water to fill the Jacuzzi. She handed him the bottle of bath foam to put in the water while she lit some licorice-scented candles. He went to fetch the remainder of the bottle of wine from lunch and a couple of glasses and found a plate of cheeses and apples in the fridge as well.

"Well, well, aren't we being spoiled?" Maria acknowledged the food and wine, as Duncan placed it next to the Jacuzzi. "I don't know if I am ever going to want to go home."

"If we keep that up, I am going to need to go home to rest up. Even my fantasies don't live up to what we just did in there."

"I would like to know more about these fantasies," Maria said. That's twice you have spoken about them this weekend. Let me in on what is going on in that head of yours."

"Well, I don't know if I can let you into that chamber," Duncan teased, "but I can tell you, ever since I saw this suite on the Internet, my head was creating delicious scenes for us. But I think it is all your fault. Our Bathroom and Bedroom dancing sessions have developed a life of their own in the past several months."

He gave her a hand down into the Jacuzzi and followed her. Long and wide, it provided lots of room to manoeuver. Rather than lie alongside him as she had the previous night, Maria lay opposite him now.

He had poured them each a glass of wine and raised his in a toast to her. "To our dance, may it forever be a healthy, romantic part of our lives."

"Oh, I do like that," she agreed as they sat up to clink their glasses and then relaxed back into the tub. The music played gently in the background and they both laid back and allowed their bodies to recover.

"Why do you think we have never done that before?" Maria wondered out loud.

"You got me," Duncan responded. "It just seemed to come so naturally, as if we did it all the time. But you'd think we would have created something of the sort, way back when, when we took all those dance lessons. But it doesn't matter, now we know what we can do, we just better not forget what we can do."

"Well, if I get Alzheimer's and forget, I beg you to remind me."

"I promise," Duncan agreed.

They lay back and stroked each other with their toes, as they talked about the kids, and nibbled on the snacks that Brenda had left them. How lucky they were to have such cooperative, respectful children. They discussed different paths the children might take in their lives, for the hundredth time. As the children grew up, their focus changed and their dreams changed. It was always interesting to predict where they might go from the given place they were in.

Jessie was by far the analytical one, a leader in many ways, although not when it came to Steve. She allowed him the lead in a variety of ways.

Jasmine was the compassionate one and a good athlete. She used to be more of a follower but since the relationship with Nick had developed and since they had come in second in the competition, she had really come into her own. She seemed to be clearer about her boundaries and what she wanted from herself, her life, and even from her friends.

John was the artistic one, not too sure of himself yet, but he would get there. His artistic skills seemed to develop faster than he was, but he was holding his own.

"I have something to share with you, before I forget." Duncan lowered his eyes as if embarrassed.

"What? You have been taking sex lessons from some Greek god?"

"Well no, not exactly."

"Oh, my goodness, this is sounding good. Go on."

"Well, last year, before you got adrenal fatigue, I was getting worried that I wasn't getting as hard, or as fast, and I couldn't hold it for very long. We had always had a good sex life and I didn't want it to start dying. I started to get worried. We're not even fifty yet. Well, okay, we are almost fifty but I still didn't want to lose that part of our life. So I started to talk with Dr. Jim about it. And then you got adrenal fatigue and of course, you had no energy to do much. That let me off the hook for a bit but when you started to get your energy back, I went back in for another session.

It's because of him that we are eating watermelon and chocolate and almonds. They all have different amino acids and nutrients in them that help men get their mojo back. I also had to take a supplement to get my nitric oxide up, which worked quickly.

When I got my mojo back, I went in I had a talk with Pappy and basically asked him how his sex life was doing at his age. I wanted to know if what was happening was temporary, or all in my head, or if it would last. He explained different things that contribute to marriages losing their sex life and what I needed to do to attend to ours so that we kept going until our eighties or nineties or however long we last.

Anyways, I didn't want to tell you until I knew that it was a sure thing. But both Dr. Jim and Pappy say the same thing. If you have your health and you attend to your relationship then when you get to be our age, you can re-create your whole sex life in a variety of different ways. And so here we are. Reaping the rewards of our efforts."

"Wow, and you did all this without telling me? I am not sure if I should feel hurt that you hid it from me or feel thankful that you took the time to attend to it and follow through," Maria responded.

"Well, I would really appreciate it if you would do the latter."

"So that is why we are eating watermelon and chocolate." Maria started to laugh. "You have to admit that it is rather funny."

Duncan laughed with her. He had been concerned that she would feel hurt that he hadn't told her because they had always been so open with each other. But she had had so much to contend with, with her health never mind walking everyone else 'back into health', and he just hadn't wanted to put an extra load on her. But now it was all okay.

He breathed a sigh of relief and suggested that since the water was cooling, maybe it was time to get out and get ready for dinner.

"Before we get going," Maria said, "do you know where we are going for dinner?"

"Well, when I talked with Dave at breakfast he suggested that we go to the early performance at the theatre and then go for dinner at a Thai Restaurant, right around the corner."

"I think I should leave the planning of all weekends to you, you have done such a beautiful job this weekend and I really do appreciate it. It is so wonderful to just sit back and be taken care of. You have no idea what this all means to me."

"I would love to take full credit for it but at the last big potluck we had, Dr. Jim indicated that the reason you suffered with adrenal fatigue was because you had spent a lifetime taking care of the rest of us, on top of your business and maybe it was time you needed someone to nurture you the way you nurtured everyone else. I thanked him for the advice and asked if he had suggestions. He responded with, 'I will leave that to you.' So he provided the spark, I just had to figure out what to do with it. We have had such a busy summer there really hasn't been time to even think about it. But when we decided to have the potluck next weekend, I thought it might be a good time to take you away and give you some of that nurturing before you had to put out again."

She rubbed his feet that still lay at her sides and kissed the top of his big toe. "Well, thank you, Dr. Jim, for providing the spark and thank you, my lord, for listening and following through. You are the best." Maria stood up to get out of the tub and bubbles went everywhere. "And, considering all the work and time and effort you have put into learning about what we need to do with our relationship and our sex life, maybe I should leave you in charge of that too?" She winked at him. "Now, I think I will step into the shower and rinse off all these bubbles."

"Good idea, I'll come with you and wash mine too, but no funny stuff. I don't think I have the stamina to do it again... just yet." This time, they went into the shower laughing, quickly rinsed off and emerged to get ready for the evening.

"Maybe I should ask Brenda if she has any chocolate and watermelon?"

Thirty-Nine

There's Nothing like a Dame

"Reality really is theater.
There's no other way to describe it.
It's all so nonsensical, ridiculous and chaotic."
Joe Rogan

Considering that they bought tickets at the last minute, they got decent seats for the play. An acting group from the town presented their own rendition of *South Pacific*. It was a hoot.

Now, in the Thai Restaurant, they both ordered a Thai chai to drink along with Tom Yam Goong. It was always a good appetizer with herbs, mushrooms and jumbo shrimp. They decided on Gai Med Ma Moung, with roasted cashews and chicken, vegetables and a honey, chili, and garlic sauce, and Massaman Curry, a mixture of potatoes, peanuts, and chicken in coconut milk, bay leaves, cinnamon, sugar, and tamarind sauce. They added a small bowl of rice to soak up all the delicious sauces.

Once their order was out of the way and the drinks arrived, they started to talk about the play. Maria started to laugh.

"Man, I had to laugh when Nellie started to sing, "Gonna wash that man right out of my hair". She was a hoot and all I could think of was, I never want to wash my man out of my hair, especially after our recent escapades."

"Glad to hear that. And, yes, they did do a good job on that performance. I think I loved Bloody Mary the best. Mind you, they did a good job with Luther too and the song "There is Nothing like a Dame" was a great one as well. You may have had fun with "I'm Gonna Wash That Man Right Outta my Hair" but I think you might be able to imagine where my head went with, "There is Nothing like a Dame". Really, the whole play was done really well."

They continued to talk and critiqued the actors, the songs and the stage props.

Intermittently, they acknowledged what a good meal they had chosen. It was a little on the hot side and so they each ordered another Thai Chai to keep their mouths cool.

Later, they wandered back to the inn, entertained and well fed. Tonight, Duncan didn't light up the fireplace. They undressed and crawled into bed, rolled toward one another and manoeuvred their legs into their familiar places. They just lay and looked at one another for the longest time. Not a word was said between them—each with a smile of peaceful satisfaction on his and her faces and a gentle lovingness in their eyes. They didn't need to say anything. They just needed to be.

Eventually, Maria yawned and whispered a sleepy, "I love you."

Duncan watched as she closed her eyes and drifted out. He kissed her gently on the forehead and told her he loved her, too, then drifted off to sleep.

Forty

Sufficiently Serviced, My Lady?

"A hopeless romantic dreams of who they will spend the rest of their life with and what the two of them will do together. They want to be romanced with sweet simple things and thoughtful amazing surprises. They dream of being loved but also loving somebody. They don't just want somebody to hold them..."
From I Love My LSI

Maria woke up with Duncan blowing softly in her face. "Hey, sleepyhead. Are you going to wake up?"

Her eyes fluttered open and adjusted to the bright daylight. "What time is it?"

"It's only 9:00AM, you lazy witch." He laughed. "I got up and had a shower around seven. You were still in a deep sleep and I didn't want to disturb you, so I went for a walk around the lake and found a great spot to have a picnic today."

She lifted the sheets to see what he was wearing. He had taken off his runners and jeans to crawl back into bed with her.

"How long have I been sleeping?"

"Well, we got home around eleven last night and you went to sleep pretty fast, so I would say a good nine hours at least. I think it must be all that dancing we've been doing. You haven't slept like that for ages. Do you feel rested?"

"Yeah, actually, I feel like I overslept. I've got a bit of a headache." She rolled onto her back and stretched.

"That sucks. Would you like me to give you a scalp massage or do you just want to lay here till it goes away?"

"Let's just lay for a few minutes while it walks away," Maria said appreciatively. "I love to just snuggle."

They rolled into their favorite positions, with their legs entwined, while he explained what he had already organized for them. "I talked with Brenda and ordered us another picnic lunch. She wanted to know if we were enjoying our stay and I told her it had surpassed our expectations."

"I hope you didn't tell her how or why."

"No, of course not, but I could go and tell Dave?" he teased. Maria smacked him on the shoulder. "You had better not, you brat."

"Hey, watch it, girl, and what happened to, 'my lord'?"
She got out of bed and bowed down, before him. "What is your wish for the day, my lord?" She laughingly gave him what he was looking for and then raced for the bathroom, to sit on the throne.

He followed her into the ensuite, and leaned against the door frame. "Well, my lady, since the headache is apparently gone, there is no telling what I may want from you today," he said with a devilish twinkle in his eye.

He started to remove his t-shirt with obvious intentions and she looked at him, wide eyed, "You can't possibly want to dance again?"

In response, he sidled up behind her as she started to brush her teeth and reached down to slide his hands up under her lacy nightgown. He stroked his fingers up her legs and along her thighs, over her hips, and did not forget to tease around her sacred parts. He growled and she moaned in response as he continued to slide his hands around the front of her and up her breasts. He loved to cradle those breasts in his hands; they were always so responsive to him. He moved his thumbs across and around her nipples until they stood up for him.

"Oh, you are a sexy devil, my lord. I am not sure I could ever appease that appetite you have developed."

He then pulled her nightgown over her head and gazed at her in the mirror. "Ohhh, so good. My wanton witch."

"Oh, my lord, now that is not fair," she countered. "You still have clothes on, while I, my lord, I have nothing."

"Hymph," he responded. "And who might I ask, is to blame for that, my lady?"

"Well sir, I guess I have to take full responsibility." As she turned around and slid her hands down the front of him and reached into his briefs. "And oh, how I love to remove your briefs, my lord. There always seems to be some precious gift waiting for me underneath." She laughed as she hooked her finger into his briefs and pulled out his treasures. She then bent over his hardness, and kissed his length, sliding her tongue around it to tease it into fuller life.

She moved up against him, and teased their bodies with her taut nipples. She used her toe to slide the briefs farther down and glided her hands down and around his boys. "Oh, my lord, but there is so much here to revel in, I don't know if I can handle it."

"Oh I am sure you can," Duncan retorted with a wink.

He picked her up in his arms, this time carrying her back to their bed. As he lay her down on the sheets, he explained, "I thought we should try the bedroom dance before we forget how, my lady.

She reached for his boys. "I am thinking I would like to play with these this morning, my lord. Would you be so kind as to bring them over to me? Oh, and let's not forget this." She laughingly stroked his member. "I think I would like to have my way with this, too. Would you be so ever kind?" She made her way to the middle of the bed to make room for him, and didn't have to entice him any further.

They continued to laugh and have fun as they began their lovemaking, light, fun, and silly, acting out their medieval theme. They laughed and they played. They sounded like children but with the new found creativity in their adult sexuality.

She rolled on top of him and teased him with her nipples. She took him inside of her and went for a ride, but before he came, she released him and she moved to his side. She went down on him where she stroked and teased his member and his boys with her tongue and her fingers.

"I can't hold it anymore," Duncan warned. She mounted him again, straddling his hips with her legs and took him inside of her and pulsated until he came. She laughed, as she released him. "You don't think you are finished, yet, do you, my lord?"

"I guess not. Someone else needs to be dealt with and I think I know how to play her." He pulled her down beside him and rolled on top of her as she stretched out under the length of his body. He started at her ears, caressing them with his tongue, then moved his lips down her neck. He slowly teased and aroused her along the way. He moved his lips over hers and explored deep and long, until they needed to come up for air. He continued to explore her with his tongue as he moved down her front. He licked and sucked as if he couldn't get enough of her.

"Oh, my lord, you sure do know how to dance a lady," she groaned to him.

He moved slowly around her breasts and massaged them gently with his hands while loving her nipples with his tongue.

She groaned under him as he moved from her girls down and around her belly. He kissed and lovingly explored as if he would never get enough of her. He could feel her body tense as she struggled to contain the building tension. He then came down on her. He could feel the first explosion going off in her and he was hard all over again. God, he felt like he was twenty.

"I must admit, my lord," she said, "that does feel good, but please come back up to me."

"All in good time, my lady, all in good time." He reached up with one hand and gently massaged her inner wetness, as he kissed her behind her knees and then moved down to gently massage her ankles. They hadn't massaged each other's feet in a long time. *I need to make a note of that,* he thought.

When he reached the bottom of the bed, he stood up. "Well, I've done everything now. I guess we'd better get dressed."

"Oh, you beast, you. Get back here and finish the job you began," she laughingly demanded.

He kneeled back on the bed and crawled on his knees back up to her sacredness. "What, you call me a beast and then expect me to serve you?" he queried with a twinkle in his eye.

"Well, my lord, I promise you I will provide you with a feast if you continue to feed me," she said with a devilish tone.

He came back down on her and she groaned as her body arched and stretched against him. Nothing could be more sexually powerful than have his woman come as he provoked and teased her to her climax. Now it was time, and he glided back up along her belly. When he reached her nipples he captured one again in his mouth. He moved inside her and they started their dance, faster, harder, as she came again and again until he finally came with her and released all he had stored up into her. Then they both fell back to the bed.

"Oh, yes," was all she said. They lay on their backs and waited for their breathing to return to normal. He found her hand and took it in his. When his breathing slowed, he reached over to kiss her, stroke a breast and fell back on the bed, again. He was done. He needed time to recover.

"Well, my lady," he said after a while, "were you sufficiently serviced?"

"Oh yes, you done did a fine job. Bless you." She leaned over to reach his mouth and thank him properly with her lips and her tongue but she was too spent and couldn't finish what she had intended. She let out a chuckle as she fell back on the bed. "Sorry, my lord but you did me in. I am still in recovery mode."

He squeezed her hand. "So am I, my dear. So am I."

They both lay there for a while and allowed their bodies to recover, until eventually their hearts slowed down.

"Do you think you have recovered enough to go get cleaned up?" she asked with a chuckle. "That is one benefit of dancing in the shower."

"Can you believe, it? Within the span of twenty-four hours, we have made love in the shower three times, in the hot tub, and now in bed. You would think we were newlyweds or something."

"Well, you did call this one of our many second honeymoons," Maria pointed out. "What amazes me is our capacity to create new dance steps. I love it."

"Are you ready to get up yet? If we don't get up we will be late for breakfast."

"Okay, let's get a move on—quick shower, like last night, just to rinse off and then we go for breakfast. No funny stuff. Promise?" He nodded.

Forty-One

Stepping Out of the Box

"Humor helps us to think out of the box. The average child laughs about 400 times per day, the average adult laughs only fifteen times per day. What happened to the other 385 laughs?"
Anonymous

They arrived at breakfast within half an hour, and two couples were there before them. They greeted everyone and joined in the conversation. Everyone was talking about what they planned to do for the day. One couple wanted to get a last walk around the lake before they headed home. They had tried all but one of the trails so far and wanted to do the last one before they left. The other couple planned to do some shopping, to pick up some groceries before moving to the next stop on their holidays.

Duncan had left his picnic backpack with Brenda earlier so now he got it from the kitchen to show the other couples what they used to take their picnics. Everyone was impressed. Brenda had already filled it with today's picnic, so they could see how much it carried in it.

When breakfast was over, Maria asked Brenda if they had to be out by a particular time. She hoped it would be later, in case they needed a shower or change before they started for home again. Brenda was pleased to accommodate them, so there was no issue.

Maria thanked her for all of her hospitality and told her they would refer the place to all of their friends. It was just lovely. Brenda thanked her for that. Referrals were always the best form of advertising.

Duncan went to the front office and paid the balance they owed. He asked if they could take a couple of towels, in case they wanted to go for a dip, and if there was anywhere they needed to be careful of in the lake.

Brenda said, "No problem on any of those issues." Dave went to get a couple of beach towels.

Duncan went back to the car and pulled out one of his smaller gym bags. He came back into the suite and put the towels in the bag and asked Maria to get their bathing suits. "We're going for a swim, now?" She raised an eyebrow.

"Well, just in case. Brenda got a couple of beach towels for us and we might just find a place for a bit of a dip in the lake."

"You keep coming up with more and more surprises." She smiled with pleasure.

Duncan put the backpack on and got the bag. Maria locked the door and asked if she could carry the bag. Duncan claimed he was fine with it and showed her the way down to the path to start their walk. Today was more overcast than it was yesterday, but still a beautiful day with warm summer temperatures. They walked for a while without talking. They just enjoyed the immense beauty around them. Birds sang in the trees and a gentle breeze caressed the leaves and danced on the water. There was lavender everywhere along the paths that released beautiful scent, but there were also other scents drifting in and out. The sun was rising high in the sky and filtering through the branches in the trees.

They held hands as they walked along, neither wanting to spoil the sounds of nature with their voices. Then a squirrel jumped out of the trees and across the path. Maria broke the silence. "Oh, I wish we had something to feed him."

"Well, we could look in the backpack if you really want, but if there is one there will be more and we might find that they join us for lunch," Duncan cautioned.

"Well, we could issue an invitation, but I think I prefer to pass on it at this time," she chuckled.

Now that the silence had been broken, they began to talk— about what the kids might have done while they were gone, the potluck next weekend and the guest list. Before long they reached the spot Duncan had discovered on his morning walk.

There was a lovely little alcove off with a couple of picnic tables with attached benches. There was an old barbecue someone had built with bricks, a long time ago, but looked like it was still being used.

Someone had thrown wildflower seeds all around the alcove and while many of them had already finished their bloom there were still a few to add colour.

Maria took a bottle of fruit juice out of the backpack and Duncan filled each of their glasses, it was a cranberry, lemon and grapefruit mix that was both very healthy and quite refreshing.

Maria took off her runners, walked over to the lake, and put her toe in the water. "It's quite warm." She raised an eyebrow to Duncan. "What do you think?"

Duncan took on the tone and attitude of a weather reporter, "Well, the clouds have disappeared; the sun is high; the temperature has to be in the '80s." Then challenged, "If you're game, so am I."

Another thought occurred to her, "Did you happen to ask if there were any issues we needed to be careful of in the lake?"

"I did, my lady, and Brenda said it was safe all around."

"Well, the clouds have disappeared, the sun is high, and the temperature has to be in the eighties," she mimicked him laughingly. "If you're game, so am I."

"Let's do it then." Maria looked around to see if there was anybody in sight and took off her t-shirt. "There's really nowhere to change but if we're quick and stay back in this alcove, we should be all right."

"I did ask Brenda if she thought anybody would be on the trail today, and she said everyone was going to the fair in town. When was the last time, you went skinny dipping?"

"You have got to be kidding? Skinny dipping?"

"Well, why not? No one is around; we have been doing things outside of the box all weekend. Why stop now?"

"Well, my lord," Maria replied coyly, "if that is your command, I guess it is my bidding. But if we get caught, I will shoot you," she warned.

Duncan boldly went down to the water, put a towel at the side and stripped down. He turned his body to Maria, did a little jig, winked at her, then turned and walked into the lake.

Maria laughed at his little show. "What was that?"

She stepped into the alcove and quickly undressed and wrapped herself in a towel. She shook her head at the daringness of it all, and at their age. But she quickly ran to the water's edge, looked around again to make sure no one was in sight, and taking a deep breath, she dropped her towel and ran into the lake.

"I can't believe we are doing this," she said as she swam towards Duncan.

"We've have always had a thing for the water. We must be water signs…Are we? Do you know?"

"Haven't a clue but I agree, we have always had a thing for the water. This weekend a lot more than usual."

They gently swam and kicked around in the water, loving the feel of it against their naked bodies. Duncan turned over on his back and floated on the water presenting his boys and a rather shrunken member to the skies above.

"I dare you to float on your back and just revel in this, without a care in the world," he challenged Maria.

"I hate you," she threw back at him. "You know I can never turn down a dare."

"Well then, let's see what you have in you?"

Again, Maria looked around to see if there was any sign of anybody around then floated up on her back and gifted her naked self to the sky. She drifted over to Duncan. In case someone came by, she could hide behind him. He laughed at her; he knew exactly what her intent was.

As they floated along in the lake, Maria became less self-conscious and they both became more attuned to the environment around them. They reached out and held hands as they floated. This was really quite something, as much as she had been so hesitant, now they both lay naked on the lake and allowed the water to gently wash over them, without a care.

Maria felt twenty years old, young and alive, and ever so mischievous. She couldn't believe all that they had done this weekend. And now here she was, doing this.

Duncan rolled over and started to laugh.

"What's so funny?"

"When I rolled over, the sensation of my member and my boys floating down felt weird. Try it and see what happens to your girls."

Maria rolled over as directed. "It's a very freeing sensation, isn't it?"

He swam over to her, nose-to-nose, and reached for her breasts. She raised her head out of the water to touch her lips to his. "I don't know that I gave you permission to handle the merchandise."

Between kisses, he retorted, "And since what point in time, my lady, did I need to ask permission? In fact," he countered, "my impression is that they like to reach out to me and ask me to have my way with them."

"Oh dear, do they really?" She started to laugh with him and ended up with a mouthful of water. Her legs came down and wrapped around his waist. His member grew. She arched back and allowed her breasts to reach out to him, asking him to have his way with them, just as he had said they did.

"You don't mean like this, do you?"

"Now, that's my lady, giving me all that she has. What more could a man ask for?" He bent over and took a nipple into his mouth, circled it with his tongue and loved how it responded to him. He didn't want to leave the other breast out, so he caressed its curves and then circled his finger around the nipple as he asked it to respond to his touch, and of course, it did.

He moved closer into shore so he could stand against the ground, and have more support.

There was a rustle in the trees, and Maria shot straight up. With her breasts hidden in Duncan's face, she asked, "Did you hear that? Is there someone there?"

"It is rather hard to see with your girls blinding my vision, although I am really not complaining. But I did see a couple squirrels earlier and would bet that is what you heard."

Maria looked around, she couldn't see anyone, but she did see a squirrel scurry across the pathway and relaxed.

"Are we back here again?" Duncan asked as he lowered her onto his member. "Shall we try another dance?"

"Well, as I have been saying, all weekend, my lord. Your wish is my command." She pressed her feet against the back of his calves, while he moved her up and down.

She pushed up and off of him and threw her legs out behind her. "Surely we are going too fast. If we are going to do this new water dance, we need to do it properly."

Duncan grinned and said mischievously, "You are so right, my lady, but I guess I need some direction this time. What exactly are the steps to this dance?"

She swam around him and reached out for a kiss as she floated in front of him. "I really don't know, my lord. Let's see how many steps we can figure out."

Duncan never needed more encouragement than that. The water was clear and warm and sensuous. They dove down, under the surface, in and out of each other's reach, and back up to the surface as they allowed the front of their bodies to caress one another, while their hands stroked their backs.

This was an entirely different dance, they repeatedly grabbed each other's buttocks to pull them in towards each other and then twirled around and kicked away again.

One time, she dove down and as she came up, he reached for her breasts. They bobbled so freely in the water and were even more enticing than usual. He stroked around their curves and massaged her nipples as she arched them out to him.

Another time they dove down and as she surfaced she pulled him up with his member, then stroked it as they surfaced.

They dove between each other's legs and came back up again. They rolled and dove and stretched to the surface like dolphins frolicking in the ocean. It was so erotic.

She took a moment to float on top of the water and he slid his body along underneath hers, his hands moved along everywhere, gently, erotically, sensuously. He kicked faster than her as he moved along her full length and then beyond her. It was a very good dance.

He stretched his arms around her to stroke the front of her but couldn't do it and got a mouthful of water instead. He sputtered out the water laughing. "Well, that didn't quite work."

He was so aroused and so hard. He pulled her to him and down on his member and again she straddled her legs around him. She pushed against his calves with her feet to move up and down the length of member, stroking both them. He now groaned and strained.

Her breasts bounced against the surface of the lake. He moved to catch one in his mouth but couldn't hold onto it under the water. Instead he moved to her lips.

He strained to hold on until she started to come. Their tongues seduced and stroked and fancied one another. As soon as he felt her starting to release, he followed in step with her.

"Oh, my God," he groaned.

They held onto one another for what seemed like eons. Their mouths danced in and out in a rhythm similar to the dance of their bodies. His member retreated but she kept her legs wrapped around him for the longest time. Eventually, she let him go and they gently floated apart. Their bodies floated back and forth in the water with gentleness rather than with the previous intensity and passion.

Once their breathing had steadied, he found her mouth again. The meeting of their lips and tongues saying thank you and bless you and I love you and a huge amount more than either of them wanted to stop and say.

It was an entirely different dance than any of their other dances. And neither of them wanted to bring it to an end. Their hands continued to gently caress each other, as they calmed and steadied each other, both under water and above water. Until finally, they were both so satiated with one another, they mutually relaxed and let go.

"Really, my lord, I don't have a clue what to say."

"I hear you, my lady, I hear you."

They drifted with the water gazing at the sky and the forest around the lake and each other for a while longer, allowing their bodies to calm down. Both wore grins from ear to ear. Finally, they walked out of the lake. They both searched the paths for people, just in case, but found none. They picked up their beach towels and started to dry off.

Duncan wrapped his towel around his body and secured it at his waist and turned to Maria. He took her towel and ever so gently dried her hair and then her back and brought the towel around to gently dry her breasts. "Thank you for being you," was all he said. She just stood there looking at him with adoration and letting him do what he wanted as he tenderly dried her body.

He wrapped the towel around her; touched her lips tenderly with his; and then held out his hand for her to take, and they walked back to the alcove.

"That was good, my lord. So awfully good. Don't know if we will ever be able to top this weekend. Not to say I'm not willing to try. And thank you for enticing me into the water like that."

"Well, my lady, I can just see us sitting in our rocking chairs," Duncan said, "when we are ninety years old, saying, 'do you remember when....'."

They got dressed and unpacked the picnic that Brenda had prepared. Maria spread the tablecloth on the picnic table and placed the food on it. Duncan put the backpack and the bag on the seat closest to the water to weight it down and they both sat on the same side of the table so they could relish the view while they ate. . It was gorgeous, and so quiet and serene, now that the water mammals were gone.

"I obviously want to see our kids, but this weekend is going to be hard to leave behind," Maria said quietly while she ate her deli sandwich.

"But I am so glad we came," Duncan agreed. "We need to start taking more time away for ourselves to attend to us, rather than always looking after the rest of the world. And not just for all the dancing, all though, I must say, we certainly out did ourselves. We need to start taking more time away for ourselves— to just attend to us, rather than always looking after the rest of the world. As much as I enjoy making love to you, I also enjoy the playfulness and the laughter and the beingness when we just lie together."

"What most women wouldn't give to have a husband like mine? I am so blessed. I don't know what to say."

They were silent for a few minutes then Maria asked, "How long do you think it will take us to get home?"

"Well, it took us about one and half hours to get here on a Friday night, so if we leave when we get back to the room, it will probably take only an hour to get back, if we beat the rush."

"That sounds good. Don't forget we still have to pick up my car from work. How about if we take pizza home for dinner and surprise everyone with it. With all of the healthy eating we've done this past year, I can't remember the last time we had pizza. But I am far too spoilt this weekend to make dinner tonight."

"You deserve to be spoilt, my love, and pizza sounds like a great idea."

They stayed at the picnic table for about an hour before they cleaned up and headed back.

They had a quick shower, during which they managed to keep everything under control. Until the end when Duncan said, "It was this double headed shower that started it all. Don't you think we owe it to the shower to have one last quickie?"

Maria laughed. "You can't be serious. After all we have done just today?" But then she agreed. "All right, one last time, just for you. I don't know if I can get wet again but let's give it the ol' college try."

They laughed and soaped each other up, she soaped up his member and it quickly responded.

"Well no problem there," she acknowledged.

It was different this time, not erotic and sensual like the other times in the shower, or in the Jacuzzi, or in the lake. It was more like what they were used to at home—simple and gentle and sweet.

But now they knew what a broad range of dances they were capable of and might perhaps explore even more as they journeyed through life. They also knew the broad range of emotions and attitudes that they could share while making love.

But right now they needed to finish and get on the road. He planted a last kiss on her mouth, as if to say, "Okay that's enough. You're off the hook now. Let's go home."

Forty-Two

The Best Part of Going Away is Coming Home

"All travel is circular. I had been jerked through Asia, making a parabola on one of the planet's hemispheres. After all, the grand tour is just the inspired man's way of heading home."
Paul Theroux

It was a good homecoming. The house didn't look like any wild parties had occurred. John was downstairs with Papa Johnny but ran upstairs when he heard their car pull in. Everyone was happy to see everyone.

Duncan confirmed what they had always said. "Yup, the best part of going away is coming home."

Maria raised an eyebrow. "Well, that's usually what we say, but I might have to reconsider after this weekend," she responded with a mischievous smile. Duncan nodded and laughingly agreed.

Maria reached up and gave him a gentle kiss on the lips and said, "Thank you for that weekend, hon, that was the best present ever."

The kids asked if Duncan and Maria had had a good weekend and both grinned from ear to ear and nodded their heads, but didn't say anything.

The kids were happy to get pizza for dinner. They all went into the kitchen where they pulled out plates and napkins and sat down to eat.

"So tell us what you did all weekend," Duncan began. The kids took over from there. Duncan looked across the table to Maria and smiled. They wouldn't be sharing a lot about their weekend.

After dinner, Maria and Duncan went downstairs to thank her parents for agreeing to look after John and keep an eye on things while they were gone.

Pappy Johnny smiled. "It looks like the weekend achieved everything Duncan set out to accomplish," he said, winking at Duncan.

"They are sure good kids," Grandma Mary said. "Not what you see in the movies or hear about from others. They had a few friends over Saturday night but only a few—no loud music or drunken brawls, and everyone was gone by eleven. They also did housework and homework. Who could ask for more?"

"And this little brat, beat the pants off of me." Papa Johnny put an arm around his namesake who had followed his mom and dad downstairs. "We played every game in the book and he beat me every time."

"Well, you did win one game, Papa Johnny," John corrected and everybody laughed.

Later that night, when Duncan and Maria had unpacked, put John to bed, and prepared for bed themselves, they stood in the middle of their bedroom with their arms around one another.

"Thank you for that weekend," Maria said, kissing Duncan. "That was the best present ever."

"You know, the funny thing is, I did it for you, but I think I got more out of it. I need to thank you for being so willing to step out of the box and into my fantasies on so many occasions. Any man would give his eyeteeth to have a wife as willing to play as you are. I am so lucky and I love you so much." And he bent down to return the kiss.

They climbed into bed and rolled into one another as they always did, with their legs finding their familiar positions.

This time they both fell asleep in minutes.

Forty-Three

Please Put Me on Your Dance Card

"The only way to make sense out of change is to plunge into it, move with it, and join the dance."
Alan Watts

The week went fast, as usual. Maria's clients, the Kelly's, had finally put a bid on a house and it was accepted. Duncan followed up with his new leads, which looked promising. And suddenly, here it was Saturday again, the day of the big potluck. Duncan and Maria had told their kids about their new friends who had agreed to come.

John had gone to Carol's last night and Carol's family had taken him for dinner and to a movie for his birthday, and his cousins had even gone along. They had agreed that he would spend the day with them and teach Carol how to paint and then come back for his surprise birthday. His birthday wasn't until Monday and they had invited a number of his friends to a birthday party after school. So they didn't think he would expect anything was going on tonight.

The rest of family got up for breakfast and did their chores. Duncan mowed the lawn and set up the tables and chairs. He and Papa Johnny found a few lawn games and set them up. They brought out the board games and set them on the dining room table for later.

Maria had bought all the groceries needed for the lasagna the day before. Maria and both of the girls were each going to make their own lasagna. Maria's would be seafood, Jessie's vegetarian, and Jasmine's traditional. When they finished preparing their dishes, they put them into the fridge downstairs until they would be put in the oven at 4:45. There were no bee stings, no arguments or other emergencies to contend with, and no fights among the kids.

Duncan and Maria, the two girls, and Grandma Mary and Papa Johnny then set about fixing the whole yard up with decor for John's birthday surprise. They had helium balloons with funny sayings on them, ribbons around the trees, and banners down the patio posts that read "Happy Birthday". They had brought out an old artificial Christmas tree and decorated it with birthday streamers and placed his gifts under the tree.

Duncan and Papa Johnny had changed all the regular lights to coloured ones so that when the dusk came the yard would be full of colour.

Uncle Dave had come early to deliver an incredibly large birthday cake that had an image of an artist in front of his easel, drawing a picture. 'Happy Birthday, John' was written across the top and 'We all love you' written along the bottom. Uncle Dave had offered to get the cake. He had ordered it, designed it and picked it up for her, without even being asked. Maria loved it and thanked him with a hug. *Geez, he's a real gem,* Maria thought

When they finished, Maria still had a couple of hours to work on the computer and complete some real-estate research in the afternoon. Duncan and Papa Johnny went to look around the hardware stores to see if there were any sales on folding tables and chairs they could use in the back yard.

Jessie had taken Jasmine shopping, though they really didn't plan to buy anything. They just wanted to go and shop. Maria was thankful that they got along so well. Each had her own group of friends but still did many things together, just as sisters, which was so unlike her and Carol when they grew up. Duncan and the girls were back home by four o'clock.

Duncan came into Maria's office, announcing that the work hour was over. "How's it going, hon? Did you get done what you wanted today?"

"Well, almost. I think I am up to date on most things."

"Do you think you can retire for the day? How about you shut down the computer and have a quick shower with me?"

"Ok, that sounds like a plan." Ever since last weekend's escapades they were taking showers together, almost daily. Every shower was a sensual delight and she loved it. It was becoming a great habit. Some times with a Shower dance, sometimes not.

Duncan wanted to install another showerhead and extend the shower and put in a large shower seat. Maria only smiled.

Duncan went in to turn on the shower and started to strip down. Maria turned off the computer, closed the bedroom doors behind her, and went into the ensuite.

"So how much time do you think we have?" Duncan asked.

"I would say we have to be cleaned up and downstairs in about an hour. And what exactly do you have in mind, may I ask?"

"Well, if you move your body in here with mine, I will show you, my lady." That too had become a habit since last weekend. Whenever one or the other wanted to do any kind of dance, they started to refer to one another in the historical terms.

Maria turned on the CD they had now placed in the bathroom. Duncan had suggested that the music might cover up any sounds that they made, which was true, but Maria laughed and caught him on it. "It's really so we can dance in the shower, I bet." And he had grinned devilishly. She had read his mind.

She turned on a CD with jive dance music and started to perform a striptease in time with the music. As usual, whenever she tried to perform a sexy dance for him, she ended up laughing. He, on the other hand, was able to perform them for her with a devilish grin and without bursting into laughter. One day, she might be able to do the same, but not today.

He played along and soaped himself up dancing to the music. As she made her way to the shower laughing and stripping in time to the music, he wolfishly whistled and then laughed along with her. He entertained her with a little jiggy jig of his own while he stood under the spray, arms open, inviting her in.

When she got there, he moved so that she could stand under the shower and moisten her body. With the bar of soap he already had in his hand he gently soaped her up and then he pulled her into his arms claiming her mouth with his.

She had always loved kissing Duncan; he could speak volumes with his kissing. It wasn't just a sensuous connection of lips, and a roaming tongue but rather a conversation—an intimate communication that expressed love and desire and so much more. An energy exchange that merged their very beings into one. He always seemed to give more than he took and she melted right into him.

Finally, he released her. "Listen, my sexy lady. Do you know how much I love you, how much I love all this dancing we have been doing. Do you have any idea how much I love touching your body and how your body responds and how mine responds when you touch me? I think I will keep you around, how about for another...life time?"

"Oh my, my lord, whatever you say." She ran her hands down his chest, over his belly and around his gems, and down his already growing member.

"But how exactly do you plan on meeting up in another lifetime?" she asked as she chuckled.

"Well, I haven't got that quite figured out yet but keep doing the work you are doing now and I am sure my boys will figure out a way to find you." He laughed as he moved her around. "Now, this is why I need to build a bigger shower. There just isn't room in here to dance like we did last weekend. How can I twist and twirl your wet naked body in this tiny place?"

"You are just going to have to take smaller steps. If we focus more on the soaping and stroking and massaging as opposed to the twisting and the twirling, we might just be able to manage."

He twirled her around and pulled her in even closer. He knew how erotic it was for her when her nipples moved up and down his soapy chest and she knew how stimulating it was for him when she swirled her soapy hips against him. They were both good at recognizing what the other liked and acting accordingly.

He turned her around and pressed her back into him. She moved her buttocks back and forth across his member while he slid his hands over her shoulders and down towards her breasts. He caressed and lifted and stroked until her nipples reached out to him and she groaned as he gently massaged her erect nipples between his fingers.

As they continued their journey, he moved his hands down her sides to her belly. He sprayed his hands across her belly and again pressed her back into him, sliding his member between her legs. He trailed kisses around her neck and she reached her arms up and behind her and around his neck.

Oh, and how he loved it when she arched like that. His hands came around and cupped her breasts and stroked and glided around their curves. He massaged them and rubbed his thumbs around her nipples. She groaned in response.

He captured her mouth with his and his tongue found its dance partner again. They had created a beautiful rhythm, and as their tongues moved, so did their hands. She stroked him behind her while he stroked her in front of him until she began to vibrate.

When the waves started to come, she thought she was going to burst. His lips continued their journey and moved up her neck, up around her ears and then travelled back down another erotic pathway. While he enjoyed her soapy wet body, she continued to move her hips to the rhythm of the music.

Eventually, he twirled her around and she leaned back under the shower. Once again she provided him with full luscious soapy wet breasts and taut nipples that begged for his attention.

The music continued in the background as they moved to its beat. She groaned her pleasure as her own rhythm started to pulsate through her. She moaned deeper, her body tightened, and she arched back further. She struggled to hold onto the tension in her body as it continued to build but couldn't.

He covered her arched body with his and covered her mouth with his and she groaned out her pleasure, as their tongues expressed their inner tension.

She braced her hands against the shower walls. He pulled her up with his hands under her buttocks and she braced her hands against the wall. He slid her right over his member, housing it beautifully within her.

As he pumped her up and down, she started to come in waves, one after another. She vibrated against him with each release.

Again, he held on. How many times could she come before he released into her? She seemed to come more and more often the more they danced and played. It used to be once or twice but these days it was four, five, six, seven times. Then he couldn't hold back any longer and released into her.

"Ohhh, yes," they moaned together.

They held their position after they had both come and she stretched her arms up around his neck, turning her head and opening her mouth for his to come back in. He accepted the invitation and their tongues met between breaths. His arms were still holding her up under his buttocks. She laid her head against his shoulder as their breathing began to slow down and their bodies began to relax. They were finished but they continued to hold one another and gently massage their aching bodies.

When they finally released one another. "Yes, my lord, you did very well today." She curtsied before him. "I am forever at your service."

"Yes, my lady, and I at yours. We make fine dance partners. Please put me permanently on your dance card and please never let anyone else on your card," he said as he laughed.

"You keep performing like that, my dear lord, and there will never be room for anyone else on my dance card," she countered.

And with that, they lovingly washed each other and showered off. They dried each other's back and then themselves, quickly got dressed and went down to see what was going on downstairs.

Forty-Four

Let the Party Begin

"Laughing together is as close as you can get to a hug without touching."
Gina Barreca

It was 5:30, the lasagnas were in the oven, and the girls were at the kitchen table in conversation with Grandma Mary and Papa Johnny.

"Can I pour you a glance of wine?" Duncan asked Maria as he pulled out a couple of bottles from the fridge.

"Sounds good. Thanks."

"What about you Jessie?"

She answered no, and explained that she had made herself a cup of herbal tea.

Duncan poured Maria and himself each a glass of wine. The doorbell rang and Steve and Nick walked in. Steve still felt awkward with the open door policy but he knew everyone just walked in and announced themselves. There was no way anyone would do that in his house. But he loved the comfortableness he had always known with Jessie's family. They were always so welcoming. He had picked up Nick on the way over and they had bought a gallon of ice cream to contribute to the potluck. They both loved the kind of deserts that Auntie Carol usually brought and they knew there would be a birthday cake for John, so decided that vanilla would be best.

The family greeted them and the girls got hugs and kisses. Steve told Nick to put the gallon of ice cream in the outside freezer on the patio and he took his half pack of beer into the kitchen, to put in the fridge. He asked Jessie where to put the presents for John and she took him outside to see the tree that they had put up for him.

The whole Gibson clan came in next. Dr. Jim, Julie, Dr. Jane, and Dr. Daniel, Nanny Sarah and Pappy. They each carried something to contribute to the dinner plus a present for John. Again hugs all around.

Maria's widowed colleague, Jean, came after the Gibsons and brought chicken wings for an appetizer and a bottle of wine, and a present for John. She had met most of the Maria's family but needed introductions to the Gibsons. Maria asked if they could make the introductions outside as they hoped everyone would be out there before John got there.

Then Uncle Dan came in with a noodle salad, followed by Carol's group, with the usual deserts but different ingredients, and sourdough buns and a couple of bottles of wine and a bag that John had not noticed.

Maria told John to take his overnight bag up to his room and empty it and put his things away. She hoped everyone would be out on the patio before he finished and returned downstairs.

"Sorry," Carol whispered when he had gone. "He was adamant that we were going to be late. I texted you to let you know we were on our way."

"Don't worry about it, just go out back," Maria directed.

Next came the McDonalds. This time introductions needed to be done, so Maria guided them out back and asked Duncan to take care of all the introductions while she quickly went back to the front door.

Outside, Duncan explained to everyone how they had met the McDonalds. He explained to the McDonalds that this was also their son's surprise birthday party.

"Why didn't you tell us? I could have brought something," Anne asked.

"Don't worry," Duncan said. "He's going to have lots under the Birthday Tree."

Randy made a beeline for Sherry when he realized that Jasmine was taken with Nick. Brad wasn't quite sure what to do but Nick introduced himself.

Maria was back at the front greeting everyone and trying to shoo them out back quickly.

Duncan's colleague, Scot and his wife Bev, arrived next. Scott carried another appetizer. "That looks good. What is it?" Maria asked.

"That's spanakopita," Bev answered. "You said there were going to be about twenty-five people here, so I made lots. Have you room in the oven to keep them warm?" Maria showed her to the kitchen and told her to make herself at home but asked them to move outside quickly, indicating the tree where she could put John's gift.

Uncle Dave walked in the front door carrying a gift for John. "Does he know yet?" Dave whispered.

"No. Go out back quickly," Maria directed.

Harry arrived next and knocked at the front door and waited for Maria to come open it. "Hi Maria. Am I on time?"

"Of course you are. Come on in, Harry. How are you doing?"

"Not too bad for an old guy." He handed her a huge platter of sushi. "I hope that is okay. I never know what to bring to a potluck and my son suggested sushi. So I just went over to the restaurant and ordered it. Is that an okay thing to bring?"

"Harry, anything is okay to bring to a potluck. You did great. Now can you go out back quickly before John comes down?" She handed the platter back. "Take this and the bottle out to the back yard. Duncan is out there with everyone."

Just then, Diane came through the front door. "Hi Maria. Your place looks like a parking lot. You weren't kidding when you said you were having a yard full of people."

"Go out back and introduce yourselves. We're trying to get everyone out there before John comes down."

Diane and Harry said hello and moved out back quickly. When Diane got there, she saw the table for food and guided Harry to put his platter of sushi on the table as she did with her platter of veggies and dip. Harry noticed the tree with the presents and suggested to Diane that they put John's presents under the tree.

Maria went back in the house and closed and locked the front door. She let out a sigh. Everyone was here.

Duncan stood on the top stair of the deck and motioned for everyone to turn his way and whispered to them all to yell 'surprise' when John came through the door.

They waited silently then they heard John calling from the kitchen. "Hey Mom, do you know where my good black t-shirt is?"

"Can't hear you John, I'm out here." He opened the screen door and everyone yelled, "Surprise".

He just stood there, obviously surprised, as his face turned red. It was perfect. Duncan stepped up beside him to help guide him through the process. "You might want to just make it easy on yourself and simply 'Hi everyone,'" Duncan suggested.

"Hi everyone," John said, his mouth twitching into a grin.

He found his mom in the crowd and looked at her asking, "I thought my birthday party was on Monday?"

"Well, that's your other birthday party. This one is a surprise party and has a whole different group," Maria explained.

John had witnessed these adult surprise birthday parties before. Now that he knew what was going on, he said, "Well, thank you everyone for coming. You got me. I didn't have a clue. As my dad likes to say, 'Let the party begin.'"

He sounded so grown up. Duncan and Maria made eye contact indicating how surprised they were at John's composure and self-confidence. They had both thought that Duncan would have to guide him through a few things, but he managed just fine on his own.

Uncle Dave called to him. "Look John, we even have a special Birthday Tree for you with lots of presents underneath."

"Wow! All of those are for me? Thank you, everyone." Now he sounded more like a ten-year-old again.

Then his eye caught sight of all the helium balloons. "Wow, man, look at all those balloons."

The party had indeed begun. John had forgotten about his black t-shirt and moved down the stairs. He went about the crowd and said hello to everyone and thanked them for coming as if he did it all the time. Maria just beamed with pride as Duncan came over and took her hand.

"We certainly have a fine young man there, don't you think?" he asked Maria.

"I couldn't be more proud of him," she responded.

With that, Maria went into the kitchen and pulled out the dishes of lasagna. She pulled each foil cover back and stuck a fork into the middle of each to make sure that they were ready. Yup, they were hot and tasted great. The girls had done a good job.

Duncan and Papa Johnny had found a couple of extra tables earlier and put them up near the house—one for food and the other for drinks. Everyone had bought a drink of some sort—bottles of homemade wine, half packs of beer, and Dr. Jane's and Dr. Daniel's homemade drinks. Maria wasn't too sure what was in them.

Steve had brought a couple of folding tables and some chairs, and asked Duncan if he should bring them in. They went out together to get them. There was going to be lots of table room for everyone now. The men all dug in and the extra table and chairs were quickly set up.

Chicken wings, Spanakopita, and sushi had been set out on the food table. Maria caught Duncan's eye. He winked at her and gave her thumbs up. She put her hands together in a prayer motion, and he knew she meant that he should interrupt the flow of chatter to say grace. He nodded and called out for everyone's attention as Maria moved towards him.

"If I can have everyone's attention for a moment. We would like to thank everyone for coming to another Pot Luck dinner and this one to celebrate John's tenth birthday. Thank you for all the food and drink everyone has contributed, and thank you for all of your great personalities that are going to make this evening a huge success.

If we can take a moment to give thanks, we can start in on the appetizers and work our way through to the desserts."

He paused for a moment as everyone hushed.

"Mother, Father, God, Infinite Universe. Thank you for all that you have given us—family and friends, home and shelter, delicious food to nurture our bodies. We thank you for our children and in particular for our John as he turns ten years old. We ask that you bless this evening and gathering of family and friends and that you bless this food to our bodies and help our bodies to use it wisely. So be it."

"Amen and cheers as well," Papa Johnny called out and everybody laughed.

Maria called out to everyone to grab a plate and napkin and start in on the appetizers while they mingled. The kids all headed to the table first but everyone soon made their way there.

Maria watched to see that everyone got appetizers before she put out the rest of the food. As she did so, she attempted to listen to the different conversations. In her mind, this was a healing party-birthday party. The participants just didn't know it yet.

She and Duncan had discussed several times during the week, how they hoped someone would simply start to talk and it would weave around the table as it had last time.

Forty-Five

The Healthy Cover Up

"It's better to walk alone than with a crowd going in the wrong direction. Do what you feel is right."
Anonymous

After the appetizers had almost disappeared, Maria set all the rest of the food out on the table.

Again, she called to make an announcement and asked that everyone fill their dinner plates and find a seat around the long U shape of tables.

"Now that everyone is seated may I make the first toast?" Uncle Dan stood up and raised his glass. "Most of you may not know this, as I don't know many of you but at the last big potluck Maria threw, I learned some things about what goes on in the Gibson's Clinic. I used to have a cholesterol issue and I used to have hypertension but now thanks to the Gibsons, I got a clean bill of health from my MD last week." Uncle Dan paused for a moment as a chorus of cheers went up in response.

"I would like to toast all the different Gibsons and all their different healing modalities and say how lucky we all are that we have them in the world with us and across the street. To the Gibsons."

Again, a chorus went up as they all toasted the Gibson family and clinic.

Under the table, Duncan squeezed Maria's hand and the girls began to sing, "Another one makes the move, and another one and another one, and another one makes the move."

Dr. Jim started to laugh. "That's great you two. I love it. And way to go, Dan. We are all happy for you."

"Oh but that's not all that has gone on in this family," Carol piped up. "Because of the stories that went around at the last Pot Luck, we all made appointments with the clinic and we have some great news, too. Who wants to go first?"

Tim stood up. "Thanks to the Gibsons, we found that my paranoia was not due to mental craziness but rather an imbalance in the microbiota in my gut. I am still working on fixing it but doing so much better. Thank you."

The crowd broke into another round of applause.

George stood up next. "Many of you know that I have suffered depression on and off through most of my life. We found that I had a magnesium and glutathione deficiency. My levels are almost up to normal and I am doing great."

And another round of applause.

Papa Johnny followed George. "Well, I thought I had hit the end. I was losing my memory and the MDs said that there was nothing they could do about it. But the Gibsons thought differently. They put me on this funny diet where I had to eat a bunch of certain foods at once, in a certain period of time. After twenty-one days, my mind is back. You cannot imagine how much I give thanks to all of you every day."

And another round of applause.

There were tears in Granny Mary's eyes as she stood up. "Long before Papa Johnny went to see the Gibsons, I had started to go for my arthritis. It has taken awhile but I no longer have any swelling and I have no pain. Thank you, thank you, thank you."

Everyone was receiving applause as they shared their stories.

John stood up. He looked confident and pleased with himself. "And I no longer have any allergies, thank you."

And another round of applause.

Next came Sherry. "This is embarrassing to say but I had an obsessive-compulsive disorder and for a couple of years I had to go to a psychiatrist who put me on prescriptions that didn't help. At the clinic they found that I had heavy metal toxicities and it wasn't that I was crazy or needed a psychiatrist at all. Now the toxicities have gone and so has the obsessive-compulsive disorder. I have room in my head to think about a huge number of things."

Again, another round of applause.

Carol looked over at Maria and mouthed, "Thank you." Maria simply smiled and nodded.

"Well I had type II diabetes," Jessie said, standing to her feet, "and when I went to the Gibsons, they explained that it was a symptom and not a disease. I had the choice to manage it or eliminate it. First we had to find out the cause of the symptom profile and we found that I had too many free fatty acids in my system. They corrected it and now I have no diabetes."

And another round of applause.

Jasmine stood up after Jessie. "I had sports induced asthma and was afraid that I would have to give up dancing. But after going to the clinic, I not only got better but Nick and I came in second in our very first recital."

Everyone cheered, hooted, and clapped.

Dr. Jane, stood up next. "Is there anyone else who would like to say something?"

"Yes, I would, "Maria paused and then stood up. "I had adrenal fatigue and not only was exhausted but gaining weight, getting depressed and irritable, couldn't sleep properly, woke up exhausted, and a variety of other things. I had to take a break from work and get my health back. And thanks to my husband's support and the Gibsons', I am now back at work and enjoying life again."

And another round of applause.

"Anyone else?" Dr. Jane asked. She waited a few moments and then began.

"We would like to give our appreciation to the Smith family. They were open-minded; they listened, and they explored their options. They chose to take a healthy route back into health rather than simply manage their symptoms with prescription drugs and all of us at the clinic applaud them.

But they did more than that. People are so used to going to an MD and expecting that MDs have all the answers, when actually they have precious few. It is hard for us to get out there and publicize how many myths and misconceptions there are in western medicine. We work hard to bring truths and *real* medicine to everyone, and people like the Smiths make it all worthwhile. I don't know if what Uncle Dan did or what followed after him was intentional, but this was a grand gift to all of us at the clinic. To hear people publicly announce their path back into health is awesome. So thank you, all of you for what you have done."

A toast went up to the Smiths then everybody started to talk at once. Duncan leaned over and gave Maria a kiss. "You did it, hon. Who do you think is going to be next?"

"If we listen in, we might find out."

Forty-Six

How Many Causes are There of Weight Imbalance?

"We struggle with eating healthily, obesity, and access to good nutrition for everyone. But we have a great opportunity to get on the right side of this battle by beginning to think differently about the way that we eat and the way that we approach food."
Marcus Samuelsson

Carol started to talk with Dr. Daniel about her weight. Now that everyone else in her family was taken care of, she wanted to focus on her weight. She had talked with Nanny Sarah and Julie at the last potluck and both had suggested that she talk with Dr. Jane or Dr. Daniel. She wanted to, but like so many mothers, her family's health came first. But now that her family was doing so much better, she wanted to make an appointment.

Anne was on the other side of Carol. She listened to the conversation with more than idle curiosity. "Isn't weight really just about calories and exercise?" she asked.

Carol answered, "You would not believe how many different issues play into weight management. It is huge. And you can go to the clinic and they will help you figure out what is contributing to your specific weight issue. It's amazing."

"Well, like what?" Anne pushed.

Carol nodded to Dr. Daniel to take over the conversation. "Well, for one, the microbiota in your gut, or leaky gut syndrome, or adrenal fatigue, or low glutathione to the pH of your gut and/or the enzymes in your gut, or a host of other things from the psychological to the physiological."

"Wow, I never knew that," Anne responded.

Carol laughed. "You sound just like Maria. When she talks with the Gibsons, she forever uses that line."

"Well, I guess we are next in line then. Do you have a card, Dr. Daniel?"

"Of course." And he drew one out for her.

Forty-Seven

Addictions can be Driven by Pathogens?

"No one is immune from addictions;
It afflicts people of all ages, races, classes, and professions."
Patrick J. Kennedy

Maria glanced around the tables and watched to see who was engaged in conversations. She was curious when she saw Steve in a conversation with Dr. Jim and wondered if it was about his father and the alcoholism. She strained to hear as Dr. Jim explained something to him.

"You see Steve, they used to think that alcoholism, like other addictions had a psychological basis, which then altered chemistry in the brain and of course in the liver. Various theories were around about how it was a way of self-medicating their emotions like anger and/or depression. For others, it might be dealing with underlying life themes like not feeling good enough, or other beliefs such as feeling a failure, or believing that recovery isn't possible.

For some, alcoholism is a reflection of immaturity and not being able to align one's behaviours with one's beliefs. Consequently, these people react to every craving or impulse like a two-year-old child would. Think of the person who decides and commits to losing weight and five minutes later is eating a bowl of ice cream. A similar thing is going on. One becomes an alcoholic and the other becomes a diabetic.

Another type of immaturity that contributes to alcoholism is the person who lacks cognitive development of the executive functions like strategic thinking, problem-solving skills, self-monitoring, and such. Or one who hasn't developed the basic skills of looking at long-term consequences and therefore engages in impulsive behaviours.

Or what about the person who hasn't developed effective coping mechanisms to manage the need for connection and the need to manage pain?

If addictive behaviours begin younger in life before the brain has had a chance to develop, then the person has fewer resources to alter these addictions. There is also a correlation between alcohol and/or drug abuse among people who have rebellion issues, or thrive on adrenaline rushes to feel alive.

But we also know now that there are a variety of physiological and biological causes of alcoholism. When drinking alcohol, especially beer, wine, and vodka, you are setting up yourself up for yeast infections, whose by-product is alcohol, which in turn supports more yeast. Yeast infections can also be derived from anti-biotics, corticosteroids, birth control pills, and other medications, along with pesticides found in your food, the mercury in dental fillings, or swimming in chlorinated pools, and so much more. Unlike the common Internet belief, alcohol does not turn into sugar, which feeds bad bacteria and other pathogens in the gut. Rather, the yeast ferments the alcohol and turns it into sugar. What we do see is that the alcohol changes the microbiota composition in the gut. In addition, alcoholics tend to be low in nutrients that support good healthy microbiota.

The regular consumption of alcohol can cultivate a liver fungus and the imbalance of the microbiota in your gut both of which can lead to alcoholism. Actually we now know that imbalances in the microbiota of your gut can have a huge impact on your thinking, emotions, and behaviours.

Of course, once you have a balance of bad bacteria in your gut, all kinds of things can go wrong in both the body and brain. Further, moulds found in drinking water, food, or in the air of your home can set up residence in your body and also demand alcohol.

We like to think we are in control but when the parasites in the body are demanding nutrients for them to feed on, we can have a difficult time differentiating whether it is us or them, craving a food.

So, not only can alcoholism have many different psychological causes but it can also be a reflection of numerous different physiological issues. And unless the individual and his practitioner can identify the different contributing issues, it is more difficult to identify an effective protocol.

But regardless of whether your father ever alters his alcoholic pattern, you might be able to look at him with a greater level of compassion and understanding."

"Wow," Steve said softly. "I had no idea. I always thought he was just a loser. I wonder if I told him all of this if he would be willing to come to your clinic?"

"It is always a possibility. Perhaps if you explained that you were fascinated to learn how many physiological issues in the body can drive drinking behaviour, he might be more interested. Typically we find if we try to hold the person accountable psychologically, there is a greater resistance and denial.

When we explain that it could be that they are feeding a parasite in the body, they are more likely to come for help. Give it your best but always remember, you are not responsible for his behaviour. Whether it is psychologically driven or pathogen driven, it is still his choice as to whether he will do anything." Dr. Jim patted Steve on the back and got up from his chair.

Maria watched Steve as he sat there looking almost dazed. Maria was amazed at the information, having no idea of all the causes for alcoholism. She, too, had always just thought it was due to psychological immaturity.

She could only imagine what was going through Steve's mind. The possible potential of him being a key piece in his father's recovery was pretty big. She wondered if Steve would share all of that with Jessie.

Forty-Eight

And Another One, and Another One...

*"You gotta make a change. Its time for us as a people to start making some changes,
lets change the way we eat, lets change the way we live, and lets change the way we
treat each other. You see the old way wasn't working so its on us, to do what we gotta
do to survive."*
Tupac Shakur

Maria went over to where Duncan sat and whispered, "You have no idea what I just learned."

"Oh, I can only imagine, because of what I just heard."

Maria was intrigued. "Ok, I'm listening."

"Well, Anne was talking with Dr. Daniel and apparently she has low iron. The iron pills that the MD prescribes for her give her a lot of nausea and other problems and despite the fact that she has been on them for three years, her count has hardly moved.

Dr. Daniel, explained why the iron pills that the MD prescribe are hard on the gut, hard to absorb, and hard to eliminate if too high. Whereas the plant based iron that he provides has no gut reaction side effects, is easy to absorb, and the body can eliminate it if it gets too high. In addition, the iron count can come up within a couple of weeks. But, if there is copper toxicity, you can have high iron and the MDs won't know about it. So she is going to make an appointment to see him.

I didn't get to hear all of the conversation, but he also said that certain foods help in the absorption of iron, which hopefully she will start eating. What is it the girls sing? Another one makes the move?" And they both laughed.

"That is so good" Duncan confirmed.

Forty-Nine

Meridians, and Teeth, and Cancer?

"A traditional doctor gets paid to push pills, vaccinate, radiate, and basically
exterminate people. No different than a contract killer—except the hit man is more
honest, as he doesn't claim to be helping humanity. Holistic medicine is the only way
to go."
Jarod Kintz, Seriously delirious, but not at all serious

Jessie and Jean were in a discussion with Nanny Sarah about Traditional Chinese Medicine when Maria sat down beside her.

Jessie was all excited as she explained how Western science had now identified the material that the acupuncture meridians were made of. How the meridians run the through connective tissue in the body. "They have used nanoparticles to follow the acupuncture meridians and can follow the electro-magnetic energy that travels in the connective tubes faster than the speed of light. This is no longer 'flaky Eastern stuff'."

Jean had suffered from insomnia for years and was sick and tired of all the medications. They certainly didn't solve the problem and she had to keep taking stronger doses that caused other issues.

Nanny Sarah explained how acupuncture was used very effectively for things like pain, insomnia, headaches, and some forms of epilepsy; how they use acupuncture to work with root canals, which create energy roadblocks in the body which then short circuit the energy that flows through the corresponding organ and system.

"What?" Jean stopped Nanny Sarah and asked her to elaborate. "What do teeth have to do with organs and systems?"

"Oh, I love this part. Do you mind if I explain, Nanny Sarah?" Jessie asked.

Nanny Sarah chuckled. "I love it when young people, or anyone for that matter, start to learn all about the *real* sciences, rather than depending on the artificial synthetic myths and misconceptions of the western world. Now, don't get me wrong. If I were in a car accident or something, I would go to the hospital to get my bones set and the like. But to heal, I would leave the hospital as fast as I could. But go ahead, Jessie, tell your story."

"Well Jean, back in the early 1900s, a dentist-scientist called Dr. Weston Price worked with the Mayo clinic. He travelled around the world and studied teeth, gums, and jaw lines in different cultures along with their diets. They identified upwards of eighty channels for a given tooth, whereas dentists are taught there are around four channels for each tooth. Together with the Mayo clinic, they identified over 300 pathogens that could get into teeth, the gums, the channels etc. and cause everything from congestive heart failure to autoimmune diseases.

Recently, one of the big universities admitted that all the scientific data had been buried, although various naturopaths and other professions continued to work with the material. Can you believe it? Pathogens in your teeth can cause disintegration in your spine? Or, what about the high correlation between root canals and cancer? You should go to the Weston Price site and read all the stuff on it. It is so fascinating."

Maria loved the excitement she saw in her daughter, as Jessie tried to remember all the information that she had learned over the summer.

Jessie turned to Nanny Sarah, who smiled with obvious enjoyment of her enthusiasm. "Did I get it all right?"

"You did a good job, dear. Keep up the good work," Nanny Sarah encouraged Jessie.

Jean looked pretty impressed. "It sounds like I should give it a try. I have a bit of arthritis and I have been dealing with back pain for ages. Whether it is due to my teeth or the meridians or something else that is causing the problems, I would sure like to just get rid of it."

Jessie explained that she was in the middle of a research project. She wanted to understand enough of the different healing modalities so she could figure out what she really wanted to do with her life. The problem was, at this point, everything fascinated her as she moved from one field to another. Many meals throughout the summer had revolved around Jessie's current topic. It was fun for Maria and Duncan, although John was obviously bored with many of the topics. Jasmine, well, her interested ebbed and flowed.

Maria made a mental note to tell Duncan about how Jessie had carried the conversation with Jean and Nanny Sarah and how Jean had now decided to make an appointment.

Chapter Fifty
Gluta...What?

"Glutathione (GSH) is one of the most critical molecules of the entire body."
Dr. Garry F. Gordon MD, DO, MD

Dinner was over and it was time for deserts, tea, and coffee. When Maria started to clear the food table, Duncan went to start the coffee and put on the kettle for tea. Jessie went to get the deserts and Jasmine helped Maria clear the main course foods.

"Mom, guess what just happened?" Jasmine said conspiratorially. "I was talking with your friend Diane and she asked if the dinner routine had been planned. I told her if it had been, I sure didn't know about it. It just all seemed to flow from Papa Johnny who has been talking of nothing else in the last few weeks.

She told me she had Hep C. She got it from a blood transfusion years ago when she had surgery. When we were talking, Dr. Jane walked past and I asked her if I could ask a question. I didn't tell Dr. Jane that Diane had Hep C; I just asked her if she could help anyone with Hepatitis C.

She sat down and we started talking and she explained all about this compound, gluta' something."

"You mean glutathione?"

"Yeah, that's it. Anyways she explained all the different functions it has in the body and how most of it is in the liver. And how people who have Hep C or HIV or AIDS have really low levels. They can take a formula that actually turns on the DNA that makes...hmm." She paused looking for the words. "I remember. It turns on the DNA that makes the mRNA tools that make glutathione in every cell of the body."

She explained that that was one of the starting steps in helping people with those diseases and that they have had tremendous success. You also have to make sure that the...let me see, the methylation cycles and the mitochondria are working in order to make glutathione. She told us that glutathione was the body's secret healing agent. It was so cool. Diane got really interested. She started asking Dr. Jane a bunch of questions and then she agreed to make an appointment with her!"

Jasmine then started a little victory dance began to sing, "Another one makes the move, and another one, and another one, and another ones makes the move."

Maria started to laugh; she was so pleased. Not only was her daughter thrilled to be able to help someone heal but was so energetically happy about it. And even, more important, Diane had decided to make an appointment.

Diane never said much about her Hep C, but as one of her best friends, Maria knew that it caused a lot of problems for her. Maria had wanted to say something for ages but it just never seemed like the right time. Now here, at the potluck, Diane got the information that she needed.

Maria sent up another prayer of thanks.

Fifty-One

Being Patient has its Rewards

"Patience, persistence and perspiration make an unbeatable combination for success."
Napoleon Hill

"How long have we known Scott and Bev?" Duncan asked Maria when she brought an armload of food into the kitchen.

"Oh, I don't know, maybe fifteen years, maybe longer. Why?"

"Did you know they have a nephew with autism?"

Maria thought for a moment. "Yeah, I remember Bev saying something years ago, something about a niece or nephew that seemed fine until he got a shot or an injection or something and then all hell broke loose. Why, did she bring it up tonight?"

"Well yeah, Bev and Dr. Jane and Uncle Dan were talking about all the people who had stood up and said something tonight—wasn't that just awesome? We couldn't have planned it better! Anyway, we were talking and I was explaining that I got an enlarged left ventricle simply doing something that I thought was healthy, my running. And Bev chimed in explaining that her sister was doing what she thought was healthy and got her son the required vaccinations and after one of the shots, overnight, he became autistic.

She looked up to Dr. Jane to say something and Dr. Jane started to explain how and why and what the government and the courts and the pharmaceutical companies were hiding and how many people have actually been paid out and on and on.

Then...she got to the really good part, and started to explain what she does to help these children. Well, you should have seen the reaction in Bev's face. It was great. This whole party was worth doing just for that one facial expression. Anyways she said that she would pay for everything, if her sister would agree to see Dr. Jane and the group."

"Oh, that's fantastic!" Maria exclaimed and the girls behind her started to do their victory and dance and began the song again. "Another one makes the move and another one and another one and another one and another one makes the move." Duncan and Maria had laughingly joined in with them, when Uncle Dave walked in.

"You guys have put on quite the deal out there. Everybody's talking and asking questions. It's fantastic. But what was that little dance you were doing girls?"

Jasmine couldn't stop laughing but between breaths she explained to Uncle Dave that they were doing the victory dance and singing "and another makes the move and another one and another one" to the tune of on old 80's song, every time they heard about someone who decided to move over to *real* medicine.

Uncle Dave looked from Maria to Duncan. "You've got quite the girls here, and I think they might just change the world."

Duncan nodded. "Yeah, I sure do, and guess who taught them?" He nodded and looked over to Maria. "We have a whole team."

"Well, it's a winning team, so I guess I'd better join you." Uncle Dave picked up the huge cake he had brought and walked outside. "Someone bring the candles and a lighter," he called over his shoulder. And they all went outside.

The four inside all looked at each other in puzzlement. "Do you know what he meant by that?" Maria asked. "I wonder if he has something that he's not sharing, or if he is trying to get Judy into the clinic, or if he just means he will tell others about the Gibsons and their clinic?"

"Let's see if we can squeeze it out of him, but don't let on," Jasmine suggested to Jessie. Jessie nodded and they each picked up a platter with cups and different types of milk and different types of sugar and walked outside. Duncan picked up a platter with dessert dishes, spoons, and forks. Maria grabbed the box of candles and a barbecue lighter.

Fifty-Two

A Day to Celebrate

"Mature love is composed and sustaining;
A celebration of commitment, companionship, and trust."
H. Jackson Brown, Jr.

They put down their things on the food and drink tables. Duncan went back in to get the tub for the cutlery and a pail for the garbage. He brought it out to the end of one of the tables and got everyone's attention.

"Now some of you are new to our Pot Luck routines, so I will just explain what we are going to do. We have a tub here," and he pointed to it, "for everyone to put their cutlery in. Please put all your left overs and garbage in the garbage pail here." And again he pointed. "Then make a pile of your dishes here." He pointed a third time.

While Duncan explained the routine, the girls put the candles in the cake and lit them and Maria motioned to Duncan to introduce the cake.

"We have a table at the back and my girls have loaded it with coffee, teas, creams, and sugars and we have put out Carol's desserts—which are a new rendition of an old theme because they are now healthier. There are also some other desserts. You can make your choice or you can be like Uncle Dan and just say yes to everything."

He got a round of laughter in response.

"Before you get up and clean your plates and get your desserts, we want to honour our son, John. Girls, will you come forward now."

Jessie carried the huge cake, now with lit candles, while Jasmine danced behind her with flares. The two of them started to sing *Happy Birthday* to John. Duncan gestured with his hands for everyone to join in.

Jessie brought the cake around and placed it in front of John as they all finished the song. Maria held hands with Duncan and told John to make a wish and blow out his candles. Which he did, and in one breath.

And another round of applause.

John started to laugh when he looked at the cake. "Hey everyone, it's me standing in front of an art easel, painting."

Grandma Mary, who had brought up her camera for the occasion, took a picture of John and the cake...and then went around and took pictures of everyone.

Maria suggested that John take the cake to the food table, where there was a knife and a server, and he could cut it and serve everyone. When he got up to move to the food table, Duncan announced, "Okay, let's get dinner off the table and move on to desert, everyone."

Fifty-Three

Sickness Hides Behind Closed Doors

"When one door closes, another opens; but we often look so long and so regretfully upon the closed door that we do not see the one which has opened for us."
Graham Bell

Different coffees and a basket full of herbal and regular teas lined the table along with a selection of milks and cream, and an even bigger selections of sugars, including the toxic white kind, toxic artificial stuff, jiggery, coconut, beet, and turbinado. The desserts and ice cream stood next to plates, spoons, and forks.

Duncan directed people to the food table. "Steve, do you want to come over and dish out your ice cream? Carol, why don't you come and serve your desserts, and our birthday boy will give you a slice of his birthday cake that Uncle Dan was up all last night making."

Everyone laughed. John called, "Thanks Uncle Dan, for baking my birthday cake."

"An even bigger laugh from everyone this time, hon. You're on a roll," Maria whispered from behind him.

There were several different conversations going on, and while there was one about politics or economics, the vast majority focused on health. It seemed like everybody had a health issue. *How could everyone be so unhealthy?* Maria wondered.

After everyone had enjoyed dessert, Nick picked up the tub of cutlery to help move things into the kitchen. Duncan and Maria each took a stack of dishes.

Once inside the kitchen door, Nick exclaimed, "Wow, Mrs. Smith, you wouldn't believe how many sick people there are out there. I thought it was just my family that were so sick. Nobody talks about it; it's like it's all a family secret."

"You're right, Nick. There are lots more sick people out there than the general public knows about. What is going on in your family? Perhaps we need to invite your parents one time?"

"Well, my mom takes anti-depressants and my dad is on medications for his heart, but when I listen to all the people who stood up today, I think they should go to the clinic as well. And they are always complaining about how much money they put out on pills. So if the Gibsons could get them to stop buying the prescription pills that don't solve the problem and get them healthy instead, that would be great."

"If there is anything you think we can do to help, Nick, let us know. And thanks for helping. We always appreciate it when you dig in and help," Duncan added and put an arm around Nick's shoulders.

Nick smiled and nodded as he went back outside. This time Duncan started the victory dance and song, and Maria howled.

Pappy peaked in the door to see what was going on. "Hey you two. What's so funny?"

Maria waved Pappy to come in. She told him how the girls had started to sing "Another makes the move, and another one, and another one" to the tune of an 80's song and then added a victory dance to it.

"You are great. Best advertising tool we have is referral and you guys get first prize. What your family did at the dinner table tonight was awesome. We have to share this with everyone at the clinic." He paused for a moment. "I think the clinic is all here. We had better wait until everyone is gone, so others don't think this was a set up."

"Actually, Pappy, it really was a set up. We brought everyone together hoping the good news would come out. We didn't plan on Papa Johnny giving that speech or everyone falling in behind him. That was authentic. But the intent was there. We were just keeping our fingers crossed that with all the people in our family that have been helped, with everyone from the clinic being here, and with all the others being here, something would spark. Tonight Papa Johnny provided the spark we were looking for."

Pappy came over and gave them both a big hug. "What can I say? You guys are terrific, thank you." He respectfully folded his hands across his chest, bowed, and then left the kitchen.

Fifty-Four

Tricky Separations. Hidden Challenges

"Your big opportunity may be right where you are now."
Napoleon Hill

The group finished desserts and started to move to the yard to play Bocce at one end and Croquet in the middle and of course, their Horseshoe pit at the far end.

Some refilled coffee and tea, and some moved out to the yard. Some remained at the table engrossed in conversation.

Duncan and Maria took piles of plates into the kitchen. "This is turning out better than I had anticipated," Maria confided in Duncan. She put the plates down and turned around to put on another pot of coffee.

"Yup, I was thinking we are going to have to make some kind of annual tradition out of this." She could see the wheels turning as he made the suggestion. "You know," he continued, "Maybe that is too far apart. Maybe we should do this on a quarterly basis. Down the road, maybe a monthly basis. When the crowd gets big enough, we can start renting a hall. Now this has potential."

Yup, Maria thought, *the wheels are definitely turning.*

Dave walked into the kitchen with a cup of Earl Grey tea in his hand. "I need to talk with you a minute, Maria. Do you have time before the games begin or would you like me to stop over another day?"

She wasn't going to miss this opportunity. "No, now would be fine. Can we talk here or do you want to talk in private?"

"Here would be fine. Perhaps I should get Duncan's opinion as well."

"Ok, what's up?"

"Well, I have been thinking, actually since our last dinner, but it really hit home tonight. Do you think the Gibsons could help Joan?"

"I have no idea, Dave. You would have to talk with them and they would probably have to do an assessment of Joan before they could tell you anything. You would need Joan to agree to it for herself, not just because she wanted to get back with you.

Knowing Dr. Jim, he would probably suggest that you continue on separately and not think of getting back together, if that's what you're thinking, until she is well. But I am just guessing. Perhaps you should make an appointment with Dr. Jim and Dr. Jane and ask their opinions on whether or not they could help and how to proceed."

Maria wanted Joan to get better, and she knew Dave still loved her. But she could see Joan using this as a hook for Dave to stop the divorce proceedings, and she might not have what it would take to follow through. At least he wanted to help her.

Dave looked up at Duncan to see what his thoughts were. Duncan nodded. "I think Maria hit it on the nail, Dave. I wouldn't change anything you are doing at this point, but talk to the clinic and see what they suggest. We are here for you, whatever happens. You know that?"

"Thanks, guys. This has been a tough process already and I don't want to make it tougher. Should I wait until after the proceedings are over or try to help her now?"

"That's a question you should ask at the clinic," Duncan said.

"Ok, I guess I'll make an appointment for myself Monday morning. I just needed to run it by someone. I love how you are out there helping everyone. You really are doing a great job. Do you want me to take that coffee pot out with me?"

Duncan handed him the pot and waited until he was out of earshot then laughingly did the victory dance and started to sing, "Another one makes the move...."

"This one makes me apprehensive," Maria said. "I am not sure why except that Joan could try to manipulate Dave with it. I wonder what they will tell him at the clinic." Maria asked Duncan the rhetorical question they were both pondering.

Duncan shrugged. "Let's go outside and see what everyone is doing."

Chapter Fifty-Five

So the Right Food Gives you the Tools for Good Sex?

"One cannot think well, love well, sleep well,
if one has not dined well."
Virginia Woolf

Nanny Sarah came into the kitchen later, while Maria filled the dishwasher.

"I noticed you have been putting out watermelon with your desserts. You're getting good at carving it."

"Thanks," Maria answered.

"Do you know why watermelon is good for you?"

"Yes Nanny Sarah. I looked it up on the Internet and it said it was good for the heart and the immune system."

"What does it do for the heart?" she pushed.

"It helps your body make nitric oxide, which allows your arteries to expand and contract. If you eat enough of it, you will find it can have an impact on your sex life. Because the arteries in the penis can stay expanded longer, he can hold on longer. It is interesting to see how this alone can have an impact on your sex life." Maria then went on to explain. "I just found that out last weekend, from Duncan. I don't know if that is what did it but our sex life has gone through a phenomenal shift this summer. You would not believe it."

Nanny Sarah just smiled and patted Maria on the shoulder. "It can be amazing, my dear. I am happy for you." And with that she walked back outside, leaving Maria to wonder.

Fifty-Six

It's All about Choices

"In this life, we have to make many choices. Some are very important choices. Some are not. Many of our choices are between good and evil. The choices we make, however, determine to a large extent our happiness or our unhappiness, because we have to live with the consequences of our choices."
James E. Faust

Maria finished filling up the dishwasher again and turned it on. They might have to fill it again later but enough for now.

When she moved outside, there were people at the table deep in conversation and groups out on the lawn engaged in games of croquet, Bocce, and horseshoes.

"Let's get out the Rumoli game and put it on one of the tables and see if anyone wants to play," Duncan suggested.

Julie and Harry played horseshoes against Scott and Carol.

Pappy Johnny and Nanny Sara played Bocce against Pappy and Grandma Mary.

John, Nick, Tim, Steve, Randy and Brad were all engaged in a game of croquet.

At the table, Jasmine talked with Dr. Jane and Anne and Steve; Jessie talked with Sherry, Bev, George and Dr. Jim; Dr. Daniel talked with Steve, Uncle Dan and Uncle Dave, Diane and Jean.

339

Duncan and Maria laid out the Rumoli board and jars of pennies, and shuffled two decks of cards. Duncan called out to see if anyone wanted to play. Twelve wanted to play, so Duncan added in another deck of cards. He gave them a brief rundown of the game and left it to those who already knew how to play to help the others.

"We should set up another game, don't you think?" Maria suggested. "What game do you think would be the most appealing? We've got Pictionary, Scrabble, Clue, Monopoly, Rummy tiles, Hearts. You know what, why don't we just bring them all out and see who takes what."

Together they walked back into the house and into the dining room. Duncan stretched his arms out and Maria started to load him up with the different games. "You might as well add the cribbage board in there too. Papa Johnny might be able to find someone to play crib with him."

Maria reached up to give Duncan kiss and told him how much she loved him.

Duncan laughed. "And I love you too, but these games are heavy, so get moving, my lady."

Maria started to laugh. "Surely not here in the dining room, my lord," she said, and quickly moved outside.

They put the games on one of the tables in plain view and Duncan announced that there were more board games and card games if anyone was interested.

Everyone had shifted positions in the few minutes they had been gone. It appeared that people were mixing well. Duncan and Maria kept the coffee and tea going, and all the wine was gone by the end of the evening. It was a very good night.

Eventually people started to leave around eleven o'clock. Anne and Steve and their two teens left first as they had the farthest to drive. Maria's three kids and Carol's two teens had welcomed the two new boys and all had got along well. In fact, it looked like Sherry and Randy had got along particularly well.

After they left, Maria's parents decided it was past their bedtime and went downstairs, followed quickly by Pappy and Nanny Sarah who walked across the street.

Others left as their board games finished. Steve was the last to leave and agreed to drop Nick off on his way home.

John struggled to stay awake at 1:00 AM but when everyone had left, he needed no encouragement to go to bed. The girls followed him. Duncan and Maria sat down in the kitchen to finish their tea.

They reflected on the evening and who had done what, and funny things people had joked about. They tried to identify how many people had decided to make appointments at the clinic this week. They were happy that they could help build the clinic clientele but even happier that so many people were going to get help rather than just use medications. They had done a good job.

It would be interesting to see how many followed through with making appointments and then with their protocols.

Both of them tried to remember that they could put out the information to people, but it was not their responsibility to make the choice for anyone or how each person wanted to deal with it.

Each soul had his or her own journey and had the choice to learn and grow on umpteen levels of life, or not.

They talked about how they had grown and changed. Duncan had had to make big alterations in how he exercised, which was difficult because running had been a big part of his life for so long but he easily adapted to the yoga that he could now do with all of his girls.

He had also learned some valuable information about his father and about the number of possibilities that could lead to alcoholism. Even though his father had passed away, he thought of him now with compassion rather than as a loser.

Maria had gone through major changes as well with her adrenal fatigue. She still loved to nurture and help everyone but she did it from a different perspective now. She saw herself as being the catalyst of change and awareness, not responsible for what anyone did with it.

Their sex life had also changed dramatically. Maria chose not to tell him what Nanny Sarah had said. She was still working on what she thought had contributed to their new sex life.

"Isn't it interesting how life is so entwined?" Maria paused before continuing. "Our beliefs and our emotions are so entwined with the gut and the adrenals, which are so entwined with the liver and the immune system, which are so entwined with the cardio and the kidneys.

The same goes for people. The individual is so entwined with the family, the family with friends, and the friends with the larger community.

When we start to engage in a healing process, we can't just focus on the symptoms, or a given organ or a system, we have to engage the whole person. Nothing happens in isolation."

"Umhmmm," Duncan responded. "Remember our discussion up on the mountain…about energy? You could probably go further and discover how we are so entwined psychologically, energetically, universally. Everything is all so entwined. Life, happiness, health, love. Good topic for our next Sunday morning philosophy group. But you know, right now, my body would like to fall asleep entwined with yours. How about if we head up?"

They stood up and moved up the stairs. Duncan put his arm around her and kissed her on the head as they walked into the bedroom. They were so tired they didn't even bother to brush their teeth. It was still warm out and so they just stripped down, climbed into bed, and rolled into their familiar positions.

Duncan kissed her gently. "I love you."

She squeezed his hand. "And I love you more."

They closed their eyes and went to sleep.

Entwined.

NAMES AND FAMILIES

Smiths – 23 yrs. married at 24 and 25, October 25
Maria 47 (adrenal fatigue) realtor
Duncan 48 (enlarged left ventricle) contractor
      Jessie 20 (diabetes, biological sciences) (boyfriend: Steve)
      Jasmine 15 (sport related asthma; dance) (boyfriend: Nick)
      John 9 (allergies; Martial arts and art)
Maria's parents
      Grandma Mary (arthritis)
      Papa Johnny (dementia)
Maria's sister
      Carol (weight)
      Husband George (depression)
      Son Tim 19 (paranoid)
      Daughter Sherry 16 (obsessive-compulsive)
Maria's brother
      Dave (divorce)
      His bipolar wife Joan
Grandma Mary's older brother
      Dan (cholesterol, hypertension)
      Lost his wife Judy years ago
Duncan's parents
      Granny Vi (stroke)
      Papa Joe (alcoholic)

Across the street—Gibsons
Jim – Psychotherapist
      His wife Julie (physiotherapist)
      Daughter Dr. Jane (Doctor of Natural Medicine)
      Son Daniel (PhD in Nutrition)
Jim's parents
      Nanny Sarah (Acupuncturist)
      Pappy (Herbalist)
Julie's parents died in the war

Getaway—Wallace

Bed & Breakfast owners: Dave and Brenda owners
Couples at the Bed & Breakfast:
> First couple–Jim and Denise
> Second couple–Dave and Diane
> Third couple–Jeff and Leanne

Family playing Frisbee—McDonalds
> Mother–Anne, low iron, depression
> Father–Steve, anti-cholesterol
> Randy, 17 diabetes
> Brad, 15—ADHD
> Rottie Shepherd Dogs–Mutt and Jeff

Maria's frustrating clients, the Kellys
Maria's friend, Jen, for real estate office was widowed (arthritis and insomnia)
Maria's friend Diane who had gone through a divorce (Hepatitis C)
Duncan's colleague, Scott—wife Bev, no children (nephew with autism)
Duncan's colleague, Harry—divorced

ABOUT THE AUTHOR

Dr. Holly presents each of the individual modalities with a different practitioner in the book. But she has chosen to take training in all the various different modalities herself.

She has a PhD in Psychology, a PhD in Nutrition, a Doctor of Natural Medicine, a MA in Herbal Medicine, an Advanced Ayurvedic Practitioner, homeopathy, reflexology, hypnotherapy and all of the energetic healing modalities. Consequently, as a practitioner, she can bring all the different healing modalities to the client both from an assessment perspective and from a treatment perspective.

She teaches and encourages practitioners in all the different healing modalities to learn diverse methods in order to broaden their perspective and understanding of the human system as well as expand their capacity to help it engage in its own healing. The more perspectives one has to draw from, the better the understanding and capacity.

OTHER BOOKS BY DR. HOLLY FOURCHALK

Managing Your Weight
Why your body may be working against you and what you can do about it.

Depression
The real cause may be your body.

So What's the Point
If you have ever asked.

Your Vital Liver
How to protect your liver from life's toxins

Glutathione
Your body's secret healing agent

Your Immune System
Is yours protecting you?

Are You What You Eat?
Why your intestines are the foundation of good health.

Inflammation
The Silent Killer

Your Heart
Are you taking care of it?

Adrenal Fatigue
Why am I so tired all the time?

The Chocolate Controversy
The Bad, the Mediocre and the Awesome

Cancer
Why what you don't know about your treatment could harm you.

Diabetes
What your physician doesn't know

Entwined
A Romantic Journey back into Health

All Books Available on Amazon.com, Smashwords.com, and Dr.HollyBooks.com and other fine book and e-book retailers.